TAKE ME HIGHER

A Colorado High Country Novel

PAMELA CLARE

www.pamelaclare.com

TAKE ME
HIGHER

PAMELA
CLARE

Take Me Higher
A Colorado High Country Novel

Published by Pamela Clare, 2021

Cover Design by © Jaycee DeLorenzo/Sweet 'N Spicy Designs
Images: PeriodImages and @Jackbespalov

Content from Kahlil Gibran's *The Prophet* are part of the public domain.

Copyright © 2021 by Pamela Clare

This book is dedicated to the memory of Reginald A. Saner, my professor and mentor from my college days. Reg passed on in April 2021 after a long and successful career writing poetry and nature essays. He was a brilliant writer, but he was also a kind and sensitive man who truly gave of himself to his students.

Toward the end of my senior year, he told me that I was one of two students he'd met during his entire career at the University of Colorado in Boulder who had the ability to succeed as a fiction writer. Those words gave me the courage to try. Now, I'm a USA Today bestselling author of 36 books.

Reg, I cannot thank you enough. I'm not sure where I'd be today without your kindness and encouragement. Rest in peace.

Acknlowledgements

Many thanks to Michelle White, Benjamin Alexander, Jackie Turner, and Shell Ryan for their support during the writing of this book. You've stuck by me throughout this crazy journey, and I am forever grateful.

Special thanks to my brother, Robert White, Jr., who helped with some of the climbing scenes, and to my mother Mary White, a retired RN who once ran her hospital's ICU, for her insights into the medical scenes.

Chapter 1

September 25
Black Canyon of the Gunnison

MEGS HILL HIKED her way down the steep, rocky chute called SOB Draw, Mitch Ahearn, her partner of forty-eight years, a few feet ahead of her. Their climbing gear jangled as they hiked, the familiar weight of backpack and climbing rope comfortable on her shoulders, her helmet clipped to her pack. Though the first rays of sunlight had hit the rim of the Black Canyon of the Gunnison, the draw was still in shadow.

Mitch pointed. "Poison ivy."

"I see it." Megs had read somewhere that the canyon was full of that shit.

Every serious climber had a poison ivy horror story, and Megs had no intention of giving hers a sequel.

They'd gotten an early start, leaving the campground at six, an hour before sunrise. This was the fifth day of a two-week climbing vacation, a chance to get away from the day-to-day hassles and do what they loved. Today, they hoped to send Journey Through Mirkwood, a 5.11b route on Painted Wall, a beautiful but brutal granite cliff that rose 2,250 feet above the Gunnison River. The third largest rock wall in the Lower 48, Painted Wall was infamous for its tricky moves and loose rock. Many a good climber had been benighted—or bullied into giving up and going home.

There was a lot of loose stone in this gully, forcing Megs to step carefully so as not to twist an ankle or dislodge a rock that might injure someone in the canyon below. The Black Canyon was accessible to climbing only in late summer and early fall because of closures that protected nesting raptors, so, naturally, the park was now crawling with rock jocks eager to test themselves.

Megs couldn't care less about adding another ascent to her list of conquests. She and Mitch had been climbing for the better part of fifty years. They'd been part of the free-climbing revolution in Yosemite Valley in the early 1970s and had climbed professionally for much of their adult lives. Neither of them had anything to prove.

Once, climbing had felt like survival for Megs. Now, she climbed for the pure joy of it—or to save lives. She and Mitch were the founders of the Rocky Mountain Search & Rescue Team, a nonprofit organization headquartered in Scarlet Springs. She served as the Team's director. With the busiest months of the year now behind them, they could take some time for themselves.

By the time they reached the bottom of the canyon, the sun had risen. They stopped and hydrated. Warm from exertion, Mitch removed his outer layers, giving Megs a momentary glance of his rock-hard abs.

They were both in their sixties now—Megs was sixty-four and Mitch sixty-nine—but the fire was still there. Hell, yes, it was.

They hiked downriver toward the approaches to Painted Wall in companionable silence, the green waters of the Gunnison River splashing over rocks beside them. A *plop* brought their heads around in time to see three otters swimming close to the opposite riverbank. Megs shared a smile with Mitch, and they kept moving.

They needed to get on the wall soon if they wanted to top out before sundown. They'd come prepared to bivouac if necessary, but staying awake and roped in all night on a cold, hard ledge was no longer their idea of fun.

At the base of the wall, they found two young men putting on their climbing shoes and getting ready for their ascent. The men saw them—and stared.

Sweating beneath her layers, Megs set down the rope, her pack, and her rack of climbing gear and stripped down to a long-sleeved T-shirt that had the words *Climb Like A Girl* printed across the front—a birthday gift from Sasha Dillon, her protégé and the reigning world champion for women's sports climbing.

One of the young men turned to his buddy and whispered, "That's Megs Hill and Mitch Ahearn. They're fucking legends."

"Are you sure it's them?" the other whispered back.

"He's sure." Megs did her best to be polite, though the celebrity thing had gotten old thirty years ago. "Nice to meet you."

"Do you boys want to head up first?" Mitch drew his water bottle out of his pack.

The one who had recognized them shook his head. "No, uh, you go. You'll climb faster. We, um, wouldn't want to slow you down."

Mitch nodded, took a deep drink.

Megs packed away her jacket and flannel shirt and drew out her harness, her gaze moving over the Precambrian gneiss and schist, following the veins of much lighter pegmatite that shot upward like bolts of lightning frozen in stone. They'd researched the beta available for this route before leaving Scarlet Springs. They knew about the dangerous chopper flake and the loose block near the crux.

Both would come crashing down one day, but hopefully not today.

She followed Mitch, scrambling over loose rock toward the base of the wall, where they stepped into their harnesses. "You want to lead the first pitch?"

"Sure."

They roped in, strapped on their helmets, and adjusted the weight of their gear, both of them opting to use a GriGri as their belay device. GriGris braked automatically when someone fell, giving them an extra level of protection. When they were ready, Mitch reached back, shoved his fingers into his chalk bag, and stepped up to the rock, his gaze focused upward.

"Climbing!"

"Climb on!"

MITCH CRUISED his way up the first pitch, moving from one crimp hold to another, flagging with his right leg to maintain balance, the toes of his left foot tucked into a tiny pocket. He reached for a pinch, tested it, then grasped it firmly with his left hand, moving his right foot up to catch the edge of a thin flake.

He was in the flow now, his mind blank, his attention focused solely on meeting the challenge of the rock, Megs feeding him slack from below. This was what life was about —fresh air, vertical exertion, and being with the woman he loved.

Megs led the second pitch, a long crack system that angled to the left and ran up to a ledge. They took a short water break there, turning to look out at the rugged beauty of the canyon, the river a green ribbon 500 feet below them.

Megs pointed. "Mountain goats."

White shapes moved down a gully across from them in defiance of gravity, handling the vertical terrain with a grace no climber would ever master.

Mitch glanced over at Megs, the top of her helmet barely reaching his shoulder. "Did you think we'd still be doing this forty-eight years later?"

She smiled. "What—spending time together or climbing?"

"Smartass." He loved that about her.

"Back then, I didn't think about much beyond the next climb."

Neither had Mitch. Climbing was life. Life was climbing.

And then Megs had arrived.

He could still remember the first moment he saw her. She'd pulled up to Camp 4, stepped out of her battered, red VW Bug, and stood staring up at El Capitan. She hadn't seemed to notice them—the dirtbag climbers who'd made Camp 4 their home—not even when some of the guys catcalled her. With the dignity of a woman who didn't give a shit, she'd gotten her gear out of her vehicle, found a camping spot, and set up her tent without glancing their way.

He hadn't known it at the time, but his life had just changed for the better.

Mitch led the next pitch over good rock on a solid 5.10. It ended in a stretch of third-class scramble they could hike up. They could have untied from the rope, but they didn't.

They'd rescued enough climbers to know better than to take chances eight hundred feet above the ground. One slip could be fatal.

Megs led the next pitch—a 5.7 crack that unfortunately included an overgrown thorn bush that had somehow made its home there. "Ouch! Fucking bush."

That's one reason they wore long sleeves.

"Can you work around it?"

"Don't think I'm not trying." She ducked below one of the bigger branches and inched upward. "It's better than being bitten by a damned bat."

"Yeah. No shit."

Megs had been bitten several years ago when they'd been climbing in Utah. She'd had to get a series of rabies shots. She wasn't the first climber to end up in the ER with bat bites. Bats roosted in these cracks.

They pushed on through a chossy 5.9 section into the first 5.11 pitch. Mitch took the lead here, transitioning into a complicated layback as they edged upward toward the infamous chopper flake—a large flake of stone so loose that it creaked and moved.

"Watch out below!" Mitch didn't want it crashing down on Megs or other climbers if it chose this moment in history to break from the rock.

He made it past the flake, mantling onto a small ledge, where he switched to a belay stance. A short time later, Megs stood beside him. The sun was high in the sky now, so they slammed down some calories and hydrated.

Megs looked down at the section of wall beneath them. "That flake is a funeral waiting to happen."

She led the crux pitch, climbing toward an impressive overhang called The Roofs of Mordor, Mitch belaying and watching her progress as she moved cleanly upward. She climbed like no one he'd ever known, part athlete, part artist. She—

Crack!

From above came the ominous sound of stone breaking from stone.

"Rock!" Megs shouted.

"Rock!" Mitch repeated the warning just as something enormous hit the roof above Megs and broke into smaller pieces. "Rock!"

Unable to do anything, Mitch watched as Megs hugged the rockface, stone hurtling past her, hitting the wall, and heading straight for him.

He flattened himself against the cliff. A fragment struck his shoulder, but he barely had time to register the pain when a much larger piece struck his helmet.

An explosion of light. Pain. Darkness.

———

MEGS LET OUT a surprised shriek as she was jerked off the rockface and fell. The cam she'd inserted held, the GriGri braking as it was designed to do. The two devices stopped her fall, left her hanging.

She glanced down, saw Mitch slumped over, motionless in midair, a crack in his helmet. Her mouth went dry, adrenaline hitting her bloodstream. "Mitch!"

No reply. No movement.

"Ahearn!"

Fuck! Son of a bitch!

Fear snaked through her, turned her blood to ice. "Ahearn, can you hear me?"

Was he dead?

Please, no!

7

Then five decades of climbing and rescue experience kicked in.

Don't panic!

She drew one deep breath after another until the adrenaline rush had ebbed. She'd be no good to herself or to Mitch if she let her emotions get the better of her. Isn't that what she told Team members?

With Mitch's dead weight acting as her belay, she reestablished her holds and rappelled another twenty feet or so down to him. His head hung to one side, blood trickling down from beneath his cracked helmet, his shirt torn and bloody on one shoulder. "Mitch, can you hear me? Ahearn, talk to me!"

He was unresponsive.

"Shit!" She checked for respiration and a pulse, her own heart pounding as relief washed through her.

He was alive and breathing—for now.

"*Thank God.*"

But Megs had been involved in search and rescue for more than twenty years. She knew that an unresponsive victim and a cracked helmet were never good news.

Think! Pull it together!

She needed to build an anchor, fix her harness to his, and use his part of the rope, which was longer, to rappel them both to a safer position. Then she could call for help and at least try to render first aid.

She studied the wall below them, saw a ledge some thirty feet down. It was wide enough for both of them—if they could reach it.

"I'm going to get us out of this. Hang on, Ahearn. Just keep breathing."

Please keep breathing!

Pulse racing, she took a cordelette and three quickdraws off her rack and crafted a strong anchor, checking it three times just to be sure she hadn't made any mistakes. Then she clipped into his harness, telling him what she was doing, just like she would for any other victim in need of rescue. She was pretty sure he couldn't hear her, but it helped her stay focused. "I'm attached to your harness now. We'll rappel down to that ledge."

Before she untied herself from her half of the rope, she made one last safety check. If she had missed something or screwed up, she might shock-load the rope and exceed the strength of her anchor. There was no margin for error. If his harness broke or her anchor failed, they would both die.

When she was certain she hadn't missed anything, she began the rappel to the ledge below, using the braking mechanism in his GriGri to let them down slowly.

"It's going great. We're almost there."

Down, down, down they went, the anchor holding fast.

After what seemed like a brief eternity, Megs' feet touched the ledge. She lowered herself into a sitting position, drawing Mitch carefully onto the ledge beside her, resting his head on her lap. He needed a backboard to stabilize his spine, but she couldn't do anything about that now. "We're going to hang out here until help comes."

She created another anchor, fixing it to the wall behind them to keep them from falling and putting more strain on the rope should Mitch come around and start thrashing. Then she retrieved her satellite phone from the side pocket of her pack. The damned thing was finally going to pay for itself.

She called Forest County Dispatch. "It's Megs Hill. There's been an accident at the Black Canyon of the Gunnison, and Mitch Ahearn is badly injured and unresponsive. We're going to need a high-angle rescue at Painted Wall. Tone out the Team emergent, and contact the Black Canyon climbing rangers. They'll get here faster."

It wasn't unprecedented for the Team to conduct search and rescue operations far from Scarlet Springs. As a nationally acclaimed and respected rescue organization, they'd even been called out of state a time or two.

As she shared details, Megs felt like she was an observer, watching herself from the outside. She sounded calm, completely in control. But that wasn't how she felt.

She waited while the dispatcher called the Black Canyon ranger HQ, panic sliding into her veins again. It would take the rangers hours to set up the rescue. It would take even longer for the Team to reach them. Meanwhile, the man she'd loved since she was sixteen was fighting for his life.

"Megs, I reached the head ranger. He says they're on their way and asked me to tell you to expect a wait of several hours. I gave him your number so he can reach you directly."

"Thank you." Megs ended the call. "They're coming, Mitch. Stay alive. Do you hear me? Stay alive!"

Chapter 2

MEGS WAS AFRAID TO MOVE, worried that she'd make Mitch's injuries worse. If he had a skull fracture, if his neck was broken…

Blood trickled from beneath his helmet, but she didn't dare remove it. His eyes hadn't opened once, his dark lashes resting against his cheeks, his lips parted.

God, she loved him. He'd been the only man in her life, the only man she'd ever trusted with her heart, the only man she'd taken to her bed.

They both knew that climbing came with risks. They'd both lost friends to this sport. They'd participated in literally hundreds of rescues, not all of which had resulted in lives saved. Still, Megs had never imagined their life together ending like this.

Don't think that way.

She rested a hand against his sternum, felt his heartbeat, the rise and fall of his chest. "The climbing ranger just called. He said they're mobilizing, but it will be a few hours before they're set up."

She didn't know if Mitch could hear her, but she kept

talking to him anyway, trying to wake him, hoping he'd answer or open his eyes. He needed immediate care at a level-one trauma center, but the ranger hadn't exaggerated. They were still hours away from a rescue.

Megs was an expert at high-risk rescues and had run it all through her mind a dozen times. A high-angle rescue was a tricky job that required specialized equipment. First, they would have to anchor an AHD—an artificial high-directional tripod—at the top of Painted Wall. Then they would lower a couple of rescuers, who would transfer Mitch to a litter, lift him up to the canyon's rim, and fly him to a hospital.

If no more rocks fell, if the equipment didn't fail, if they made it in time, Mitch had a chance. He'd been wearing a helmet, after all. That had to make a difference.

Far below in the canyon, someone waved. It was one of the two young men they'd encountered earlier. Apparently, they'd heard or seen the rock fall and had decided against climbing today.

"We're going for help!" he shouted.

Megs just managed to make out his words. She waved, watching as he and his buddy jogged back toward SOB Draw.

The sat phone beeped.

Megs had clipped it to her harness with a quickdraw. "Megs here."

"Megs, it's Hawke."

Megs squeezed her eyes shut, a hard lump in her throat.

What the hell is wrong with you?

She saw Eric Hawke every damned day, for God's sake. He was the fire chief for Scarlet Springs and one of the Team's most dedicated members. Why should the sound of his voice make her emotional?

Get a grip!

She swallowed. "Hey, Hawke. It's good to hear from you."

"How is he?"

"He's still unresponsive, but he's breathing."

"We're doing our best to get to you."

"I know you are. I don't expect miracles."

It was a six-hour drive from Scarlet Springs to the Black Canyon. Flight time was about an hour, but the Team didn't own any rescue choppers. If they had, it would still have taken an hour to get the bird ready and airborne.

"I've got a miracle for you anyway. I'm on the way to the Forest County Airport with Conrad, Taylor, O'Brien, Belcourt, and Moretti. Joe moved heaven and earth to have a helicopter meet us there and fly us to the Black Canyon. We'll meet the Black Canyon ranger team in about ninety minutes."

The breath left Megs' lungs in a rush. "Joe did that?"

She shouldn't be surprised. Joe Moffat, called Caribou Joe by Scarlet Springs residents, was a billionaire whose family had struck it rich at the Caribou Mine in the mountains above town. He wasn't in the mining business these days, but owned a brewpub—Knockers—and acted as the town's primary philanthropist. He donated tens of thousands to the Team each year.

"We didn't even have to ask. The moment Joe heard what had happened, he picked up his phone and started making calls."

Megs swallowed again. "He's good people."

"Our ETA is roughly fifty minutes once we get airborne. I'll keep in touch. You two mean everything to this town. We won't let you down, Megs."

"I know you won't."

Hawke ended the call.

"Did you hear that? Joe arranged for a helicopter, and some of the boys are on their way to help."

All of them were skilled climbers with years of rescue experience. Hawke and Austin Taylor were both paramedics. Taylor was also a park ranger. Harrison Conrad was a well-known alpine climber who had summited all the big Himalayan peaks, including Everest. Malachi O'Brien was a climber and an ER doctor. Chaska Belcourt was an engineer and one of the most brilliant climbers Megs had ever known. Jesse Moretti was a former Army Ranger who'd recovered from the scars of war through climbing.

"Hang on, Mitch. The boys will be here in a little more than an hour, and then we'll get you to a hospital."

A golden eagle soared through the air below them, taking advantage of the afternoon thermals, sun glinting off its dark feathers. It was the sort of thing Mitch loved—the unique view of nature that one had to earn.

She described it to him. "I wish you could open your eyes and see it."

But he didn't budge.

"You have to wake up, Mitch. I'm not sure I know how to live without you."

———

A KNOT IN HER CHEST, Megs watched as the rescuers lifted Mitch out of the canyon using a complex system of tripod, ropes, and pulleys. O'Brien and Moretti rode on both ends of the litter to keep it steady and prevent it from striking the rockface.

Hang on, Mitch!

"He's in good hands." Taylor had rappelled down with Hawke.

The two hung on their ropes on either side of her, both of them stone-faced. They knew, as she did, how grave the situation was. More than two hours had gone by since the accident, and Mitch was still unresponsive.

He couldn't die. He couldn't.

Another helicopter flew overhead.

Taylor glanced up. "That's Life Flight."

Thank God.

"When we get to the top, remember to give us your car keys," Hawke said. "We've talked it through. O'Brien will fly back with you and Ahearn. The rest of us will work with the rangers to clean your gear from the route, pack up your camp, and load your vehicle. Then we'll drive everything back to Scarlet and leave it at your place."

Megs hadn't thought about any of that. It hadn't even crossed her mind. "Right. Thanks. You're good guys."

Hawke rested a hand on her shoulder. "We've got your back."

It felt surreal to be in this position, to be rescued instead of the rescuer. She had no radio and no idea what was happening up top. She wasn't in charge. She wasn't involved at all. Instead, she was waiting for a litter. Although she was uninjured and able to climb, there was no way she could reach the canyon rim before the Life Flight helicopter lifted off, and she wanted to stay with Mitch.

"Rock!" Moretti shouted from far above.

"Rock!" Hawke and Taylor repeated the warning, pulling themselves close to the rockface and shielding Megs with their bodies.

Stone struck stone as another rock crashed its way to the canyon below.

"Shit!" Hawke looked up. "This really is a vertical choss heap."

"The whole damned wall is just waiting to come down." Taylor adjusted his position on the ledge, stood a little closer to Megs.

"You've both got wives and kids back home." Megs had known both men since they were little boys. She knew their wives—Lexi and Vicki—and their young children, too. "Please don't get yourselves killed trying to rescue me."

"Hey, that's our job." Hawke glanced at Taylor, then reached for his handset. "Copy that."

Taylor explained. "They've got Ahearn and are sending the litter back down."

It seemed to take an eternity for the litter to reach them. While Hawke and Taylor held it steady, Megs climbed in, instinctively reaching to unclip herself from the protection she'd set and attach herself to the litter instead.

Hawke stopped her. "You need to sit this one out and let us do the work."

"You're right." She was too shaken to think clearly. Any mistake she might make would endanger Taylor, Hawke, and the other rescuers.

But doing nothing came at a price, leaving her mind free to fill with fears. What if Mitch was left badly disabled? What if he never regained consciousness? What if he died on the way to the hospital?

No. No, she couldn't let herself go there.

Mitch was strong. He'd been wearing a helmet. He would recover.

The ascent to the canyon rim was slow and steady, Hawke and Taylor keeping the litter from swinging into the cliff wall. Megs let out a relieved breath when they topped out, hands reaching to pull the litter to safety and secure it.

While hanging out on the wall had been quiet, the rim of the canyon was swarming with people. Belcourt had constructed the anchor and was now breaking things down with the help of several rangers. O'Brien, Conrad, Moretti, and Life Flight paramedics carried Mitch's litter toward the waiting helicopter.

Hawke and Taylor unclipped Megs from the litter and helped her out just as the head ranger, probably the Incident Commander, approached.

"Do you need medical attention, Ms. Hill?" He couldn't have been much older than thirty, mirrored sunglasses hiding his eyes.

"No. I'm fine. Thank you for your quick action."

"Your SAR team did most of the hard work. We're all admirers of you and Mitch, ma'am, and we're sorry that this happened here at the Black Canyon."

"Thank you." She fished her keys out of her backpack, handed them to Hawke. "Thanks, Eric. Thank everyone for me."

She hurried after the litter.

A sheriff's deputy stepped into her path. "Ma'am, I need to get a statement."

"A rock broke loose from the wall above us, missed me, but struck Mitch Ahearn on his helmet. That's the whole story." She side-stepped the deputy, jogged toward the waiting helicopter.

"I need your contact information!" the deputy called after her.

"Ask one of the Rocky Mountain Search and Rescue Team members!" She ducked down, accepted Conrad's help climbing into the chopper.

"Godspeed, Megs. We're all thinking of you two."

"Thanks, Conrad. I'm putting you in charge while I'm out. I know that's a lot to ask when you and Kenzie have a three-month-old at home. Please don't let the Team collapse while I'm away." Megs took her seat, put on her earphones.

"It's not a problem. I've got it. We'll be fine."

"Thank the boys for me. You've gone out of your way, and I know it."

"Who traveled all the way to the Himalayas to save my ass?" Conrad called to her as he backed away, a grin on his face. "*You* did."

The helicopter lifted up and flew out over the canyon, heading toward Denver.

MEGS SAT in the surgery waiting room, fear eating a hole in her chest. Sasha Dillon, Nicole Turner, Lexi Taylor, and Ellie Moretti waited with her. Ellie, Jesse Moretti's wife and an RN, did her best to explain to Megs what was happening, while Sasha, Nicole, and Lexi got her water and coffee and worried with her. O'Brien had asked to observe the surgery, and it gave Megs some comfort to know that he was with Mitch right now.

"Here you go." Sasha, the Team's youngest member, handed her another bottle of cold water. "I bet you got dehydrated waiting up there."

"Thanks." Megs twisted off the cap and drank.

"Have you had anything to eat?" Nicole, also a Team member and Sasha's best friend, sat on Megs' left. "I can get you something from the cafeteria."

Megs had no appetite. "Thanks, but I'm not hungry."

"Is it normal for this to take so long?" Lexi, Austin's better half, handled the Team's financials pro bono.

Ellie nodded. "The surgeon said it would probably take three hours."

"Oh, right."

As Megs understood it, they were cutting away part of Mitch's skull so that his brain could swell freely and so they could stop the bleeding and remove the hematoma and any clots that had formed. The bone they removed would be preserved by sewing it into a pouch they made in his abdominal wall.

It was a serious operation and not without risks.

"Who came up with that idea in the first place?" Megs didn't realize she'd spoken aloud until the others looked at her. "Who first said, 'Let's take this bit of skull and sew it into this guy's belly and see what happens'?"

Ellie smiled, took Megs' hand. "I have no idea. It sounds completely crazy, doesn't it? But it works."

Megs wasn't a touchy person—except where Mitch was concerned. Somehow, he'd broken through her armor to become the one person whose touch she needed. But right now, Ellie's grip on her fingers felt more reassuring than Megs could say.

The minutes crept by like hours, Mitch's status on the board unchanged.

Megs drew a deep breath, closed her eyes, trying to get the image of Mitch's bloody scalp out of her mind. She'd never balked at the sight of serious injuries, but when they'd taken off his helmet in the helicopter and she'd seen how badly hurt he was, she'd gotten dizzy. His scalp had been split to the bone, blood saturating his hair, a slight depression in his skull.

The doors to the OR wing opened, and O'Brien walked out, still wearing scrubs, surgical cap on his head, mask in one hand.

Megs steeled herself, got to her feet, Ellie beside her. "How is he?"

"They're finishing up now. I'll leave the details to the surgeon, given that neurosurgery isn't my specialty. Mitch made it through the surgery and is stable. When they did the scans, they found that one of his cervical vertebrae had cracked. There was no spinal impingement, which is excellent news. He also has a broken clavicle that they had to set through a second, quick surgery. They've got him in a collar."

Megs exhaled, then hugged O'Brien. "Thank you, Malachi. Thanks for coming and for being in there with him."

"Of course. He's strong and healthy, Megs. Hope for the best." He glanced at his watch. "Call if you need me, okay? I've got to get back to Scarlet for my shift."

Nicole stood. "I'll drive you."

"Thanks."

The two walked out together.

Thirty minutes later, the neurosurgeon came out and led them into a conference room for privacy. "I'm Dr. Schwartz. The surgery went well, and Mitch is stable. We managed to remove the hematoma and several small bone fragments and stop the bleeding. We'll move him to ICU and do our best to keep him comfortable. Right now, he's intubated and in a coma."

The doctor's words seemed to swirl through Megs' mind, left her struggling to put the pieces together. Hematoma. Bleeding. Bone.

She had to ask. "Do you expect him to survive?"

"With this kind of severe injury, he's got about a forty-percent chance of a favorable outcome. It's not just the injury. There are also potential complications. The next twenty-four to forty-eight hours are crucial."

A forty-percent chance?

Dear God.

Megs' heart sank. "Do you expect him to wake up?"

"It's hard to say right now, but I expect he will regain

consciousness in stages. Until he starts coming around, we won't know what kind of recovery he's facing. He'll probably need rehabilitation. Will he regain a hundred percent of the function he had before the accident? That's a question I can't answer. One thing I can tell you for certain. If he hadn't been wearing a helmet, he'd have died instantly."

Megs hated to bring this up, but she had a duty to Mitch.

"Mitch has a living will. It's his wish that…" She could barely bring herself to say it. "It's his wish that we withhold life-saving treatment if an accident or illness leaves him nonfunctional."

The doctor nodded. "The good news is that we're nowhere near making that determination—not yet, anyway. You might want to retrieve the document just to have it on hand, but there's a very good chance that he'll regain consciousness."

The doctor explained the different stages of recovery from coma and what she could do to help the process. Then he handed her several brochures about traumatic brain injury. "Do you have any questions?"

Megs had only one. "When can I see him?"

Chapter 3

MEGS WALKED UP to Mitch's bedside and took his hand, doing her best to process all that had happened. Six hours ago, she'd been afraid he would die before they reached a hospital. Now, he was stable in ICU after making it through surgery, and his doctors were hopeful.

Megs wanted to trust in their hope, but seeing Mitch like this took the heart out of her. He lay there, silent and still, a machine breathing for him. The head of his bed was elevated, electrodes on his chest, his body naked apart from the towel someone had placed over his privates. He had dressings on his collar bone and the incision in his abdomen, a subclavian line in his chest for IV meds and blood draws, and a pulse ox monitor on one finger. But what struck her hardest was the sight of his head. Wrapped in a white dressing, his skull was misshapen, the left side noticeably indented, an intracranial catheter rising from the bandages.

Jesus.

She fought a wave of dizziness, taking one deep breath after another, one hand gripping his bedrail.

When she'd come back to herself, she carefully kissed his cheek, afraid she might hurt him. "We always knew something terrible might happen, but I always thought it would happen to me."

Why wasn't it me?

She was the one who had always refused to accept limitations. Not that she'd been reckless—far from it. She knew the risks inherent to climbing, but she had always done her best to overcome them. Still, climbing at an elite level was inherently dangerous. There were so many variables—weather, conditions on the rock, gear, the actions of other climbers, wildlife. She and Mitch had been to enough funerals to know that even the most experienced rock jock could die.

A nurse stepped in. "Ms. Hill? There's someone here for you. She said she's a friend. Her name is Rain."

"Can you send her in? I don't want to leave him."

The nurse nodded and returned a moment later with Rain Moffat, Joe's wife and co-owner of Knockers.

Rain wheeled in a small suitcase, her long blond hair tied up in a messy bun, long sleeves hiding the tattoos of roses and skulls that covered her arms. She stopped when she saw Mitch, clearly doing her best to hide her shock. "How is he?"

Megs tried to act like her world hadn't just fallen apart. "He's not much of a conversationalist, I'm sad to say."

"Oh, Megs." Rain looked at her through eyes that saw everything. "You don't have to be tough—not now, not with me."

For the first time all day, Megs found herself blinking back tears. She couldn't cry. She couldn't. If she did, she'd shatter, and Mitch needed her in one piece.

She drew a deep breath, wiped her eyes. "The surgeon

said we should be hopeful. It's hard to see him like this and still feel hope."

Rain wheeled the suitcase to the side of the room, walked over to Megs, and hugged her. "Then let us do the hoping for you. The whole town is praying for him."

Megs wasn't sure she believed in a god, but that didn't mean she wasn't grateful. If there was any chance... "Thank you."

Rain stepped back, held up a paper sack Megs hadn't noticed before. "I brought your favorite entrée from the pub. Hopefully, there's a microwave you can use. I also brought you some clothes and personal stuff from home— toiletries, your laptop, power cables, chargers, reading glasses, the book on your nightstand. I figured you'd rather stay here than drive up and down the canyon."

"Thanks so much. Yes. I'm going to stay here. They say this chair folds out. It doesn't look particularly comfortable, but I've slept in worse places."

"When you get sick of that, Joe got you a room at the Marriott across the street. He thought you could use it for naps and showers. The room is under his name to keep the press off your back. You don't need to check in. I already did that. Here are your keycards. We don't want you to worry about anything besides Mitch."

Stunned, Megs took the keycards. She wasn't used to being the one in need. All of this generosity left her feeling uneasy. But these were her friends, people she'd known most of her life. "Thank you, Rain. Please thank Joe for me. I don't know what we would have done if he hadn't gotten that chopper in the air. Mitch might not have survived. I hope I can repay your kindness."

"Are you kidding? The two of you are kind of a big deal in Scarlet. You're on the Town Council, and you both run the Team, which is a source of pride for us all. After everything you've both done to save the lives of neighbors and strangers alike, you've paid it forward. This is just karma coming back around."

Megs swallowed—hard. "Thanks."

"Is there anything else I can do?"

Megs was about to shake her head when she remembered. "The surgeon said that hearing the voices of loved ones can help coma patients recover. He suggested I record myself talking about shared experiences and then replay those recordings over earphones for Mitch to keep him stimulated."

"What a great idea."

"Mitch kept journals dating back to before we first met. They're big, leather-bound volumes. You can find them in his office on shelves next to his desk. Could you bring me one of those, along with tapes and a cassette recorder or something?"

Rain bit back a smile. "I think technology has progressed beyond cassette recorders. I'll bring a digital recorder and earbuds and show you how to use it."

"You're a peach." It wasn't easy to say these next words. "There's one more thing. Mitch has a living will in a folder in his filing cabinet. The doctor said I should have it on hand just in case."

"I'll find it and bring it tomorrow morning, along with the journal and recorder." Rain hugged her again. "Please call if you need anything else."

Megs stepped back. "I can't lose him, Rain. I can't."

Rain took her hands, squeezed. "I know."

MEGS FOUND it almost impossible to sleep and spent most of the night sitting beside Mitch, talking to him, stroking his hand. She couldn't quiet her mind, couldn't turn off the gnawing worry. Medical staff came and went. The nurses checked the ventilator, the intracranial catheter, replaced IV fluids, and gave him antibiotics and other medications. Lab staff drew blood through the subclavian line to monitor his blood gasses. A radiologist brought a portable X-ray machine to his room to check the placement of the ventilator and the condition of his lungs.

She could have gone to the hotel, of course, but she couldn't bring herself to leave Mitch's side. It was almost a relief when the sun came up.

Dr. Schwartz, the neurosurgeon, arrived at seven o'clock on his morning rounds. He checked Mitch, read his chart, and repeated much of what he'd said yesterday. "He made it through the night. He's stable for now. This is what we'd expect from a traumatic brain injury of that severity. There is some evidence that people in comas can hear us, so keep talking to him."

"I will. Thanks."

After the doctor had gone, Megs made her way downstairs, used the restroom outside the cafeteria, and splashed cold water on her face. She glanced at her reflection, saw lines of fear and fatigue around her eyes. "You look like hell."

She ate a quick breakfast, got a large coffee with cream and some yogurt for later, and rode the elevator back upstairs. She found Rain waiting outside the ICU, a small duffel bag at her feet. "You're here early."

"I wanted to get these to you as quickly as possible." Rain held out Megs' car keys. "The guys got back with your vehicle last night and unpacked your gear. I drove your car down so you could have transportation. It's parked not far from the ER entrance. Joe is waiting for me downstairs, so I can't stay long."

Megs waved to the security guard, who buzzed them in, and the two walked back to Mitch's room.

Rain set the duffel at the foot of his bed. "How is he?"

"He's holding on." Megs set her coffee and yogurt on the small bedside table. "The doc said this is what he'd expect after this kind of injury."

"That's good news, right?"

"I suppose it is." Megs couldn't help but wish for more.

Rain knelt, unzipped the duffel, pulled out a file folder. "Here's a copy of his living will. I left the original at your place. I wasn't sure which journal you'd want, so I brought the first three."

"You are amazing. Thank you." Megs took the folder and the journals and set them on Mitch's overbed table. "This really helps."

Rain pulled a digital recorder, earbuds, and extra batteries out of her handbag and spent the next five minutes showing Megs how to record and play. "If you push the repeat button here, it will keep replaying until you stop it."

"Easy enough." Or so Megs hoped.

Rain set the recorder aside. "We're just up the canyon if you need us. Please keep us updated. Just shoot me a text message when you can."

"Will do."

When Rain had gone, Megs picked up one of the journals, ran her hand over the aged leather. She'd never read them, never even peeked. As far as she was concerned, Mitch's journals were his business.

"I don't want to invade your privacy, love, but if there's any chance this will help you, I need to try."

The first entry was from the fall of 1970. Mitch had

just started college and, like all eighteen-year-old boys, had been worried about the draft. He'd kept his grades up and had gotten deferments that carried him through to his senior year, when the US signed a peace accord and started bringing troops home.

"You got lucky, didn't you?"

She thumbed through the pages, his cursive neat and easy to read. She found herself skimming through passages, the pages bringing back the voice of the young man she'd met, the young man who had distracted her in the best possible way. She nodded as she read about his opposition to the war and laughed at his less-than-flattering description of his history professor's combover. When she read his entry about the death of his beloved grandfather, she got a lump in her throat.

I hope one day to be as good a man as he was.

Megs touched his hand, squeezed it. "You *are* a good man, Mitch. Your grandfather would be proud of you."

She continued skimming the pages, trying to find where she'd come into the narrative. It must have been the spring of 1973. She'd dropped out of high school on her sixteenth birthday and had spent the next month prepping for her GED. When her certificate had arrived, she'd packed up and had driven west.

At the time, it had seemed like a good idea. Looking back, Megs could see she'd been a scared kid running away. Well, no one could blame her for that.

Then she found it—the entry for May 28, 1973.

"You *did* write about me." She took another drink of coffee and got the recorder ready. If she could operate a radio, she could do this. "Damned electronic gadgets."

Then she pressed the button and began to read aloud.

28

Yosemite Valley
May 28, 1973

MITCH AHEARN SAT in his battered lawn chair in the shade of a ponderosa pine, reading Hunter S. Thompson's *Fear and Loathing in Las Vegas,* his shirt off to enjoy the warm spring breeze. The other guys sat shirtless around the picnic table smoking grass and shooting the shit, the Beatles' *Let It Be* playing on Jim Gridwall's cassette recorder.

"Too bad this was their last album, man."

"They might get back together. You never know."

"No way. It's over, man. Yoko messed with John's head."

"What do you know about it, Yoder? Were you there?"

Their conversation and the music drifted around him, Mitch's attention riveted to the page by Raoul's brilliant insanity. Had Hunter actually done all of this shit?

He glanced up as a rust-red VW Beetle with Colorado plates pulled up to the campground, Janis Joplin coming through its rolled-down windows. His gaze lingered as a young blonde climbed out. She was small, not much taller than the vehicle. She stood there, looking into the distance at El Capitan, a smile on her face.

Rick Accardo looked over his shoulder. "Who's that?"

"Fresh fish." Gridwall whistled.

Mitch couldn't understand why some of the guys treated women like this. "What's wrong with you? Don't you have a sister, man?"

"Yeah, but I don't want to screw my sister."

The others laughed, stoned off their asses.

Mitch glanced down at the page—or tried to. The woman shut her car door, walked around to the passenger side, and reached into her glove box to pop the trunk. She wore denim shorts and a yellow halter top, her long blond hair streaked by the sun, her body slim, her skin tanned, her legs slender.

"Check out that foxy mama."

"Hey, need some help?" Gridwall called out, the greasy tone in his voice revealing precisely the kind of *help* he was imagining.

"Hot chick, man."

She ignored them all, walked to the front of her car, and lifted the trunk lid, disappearing from view. When she closed the trunk, she had a large frame pack on her shoulders, climbing ropes hanging from one arm, a bag of climbing gear from the other.

"She's a climber?" Accardo sounded surprised.

"She's not a climber." Gridwall laughed. "Women can't be serious climbers."

"Why not?" Mitch truly wanted an answer.

But Gridwall ignored him, getting to his feet and heading toward the woman, who was now searching for a campsite on the other side of the campground, probably trying to get as far away from them as possible.

He couldn't blame her.

She found a site she liked and started putting up her tent—one of those new Nylon all-weather tents with a rainfly—just as Gridwall walked up to her.

"That's a slammin' tent, sugar. Let me help."

"Thanks for the offer, but I've got it. My name is Megs, not 'sugar.'"

That was an unusual name. Mitch bet it was short for Maggie or Margaret.

She worked quickly and confidently, clearly knowing what she was doing.

But Gridwall didn't get the message. "Lighten up, babe. I'm just being friendly."

"Your *friendliness* is noted, but, as I said, I don't need help."

Mitch found himself grinning.

"Fine." Gridwall raised his hands in mock surrender, a smirk on his face. "Are you some kind of women's libber?"

"I'm here to climb, just like you."

The woman—Megs—was a spitfire. Mitch liked her already.

"Is that right?" Gridwall was turned so Mitch couldn't see his face, but Mitch could hear the condescension in his voice. "Have you climbed before? Any first ascents?"

She almost had the tent up now. "What's your name?"

"Jim Gridwall."

"Dean Calder mentioned you. You're the draft dodger."

She knew Dean? That was news.

Gridwall sounded confused by this. "How did you meet Calder?"

"I bouldered with him in Joshua Tree last fall."

So, she had climbed with Dean.

"You went bouldering with Dean?" But the surprise in Gridwall's voice quickly became amusement. "I get it. You're one of those chicks who digs climbers."

"No, I dig climbing." She reached for a guy line.

Gridwall grabbed her wrist. "Hey, don't be so uptight. Come sit with us, smoke a joint, listen to some music, relax."

She jerked her hand away. "Not interested."

Mitch found himself on his feet. "Gridwall, leave her alone!"

"Mellow out, man." Gridwall glared at him. "I'm just making conversation."

But Megs could clearly stand up for herself. "It's been great chatting, but this conversation is over."

Then she stepped into her tent and zipped the entrance behind her, leaving Gridwall to stand there, looking stupid.

Chapter 4

MEGS STOPPED RECORDING and set the journal in her lap, smiling to herself at the memories. "I remember that day so well. It felt like coming home. I was so excited to be there, and then you and Gridwall had to complicate things. I was pissed at both of you—him for being a sexist jerk and you for assuming that I couldn't handle it myself. Don't worry. I forgave you."

She'd noticed him the moment she drove up. He'd been so damned handsome with his bare chest and short sandy-blond hair. But she hadn't come to Yosemite Valley to meet boys. She'd—

Beep, beep, beep!

The IV pump's alarm sounded, one of Mitch's IV bags empty.

Megs stood and moved her chair out of the way just as Debby, the RN, walked in, a new bag of fluids in hand.

"Let's get this changed." Debby removed the old bag and began to attach the new one. "How are you holding up?"

"I'll be fine when he's fine." Megs needed to ask. "You

must have cared for people with similar injuries before. Do most of them recover?"

Debby finished hanging the bag of fluids, then pressed some buttons on the IV pump to reset it. "Most do wake up eventually, but it's rare for someone with this level of trauma to return to their life without needing at least some rehabilitation—physical therapy, speech therapy, cognitive therapy."

It wasn't the answer Megs had hoped to hear. "Thanks for being honest."

Debby checked the other fluids, glanced at the monitors. "My husband was a climber when he was younger. He was nowhere near your level of skill. He mostly bouldered with buddies on the weekends. He's a couch potato now, but he's told me about you and Mitch and shared some of the things you've done. He's got your old Lords of Stone VHS tapes."

That was embarrassing.

"Just so you know, we didn't choose the title—or the music."

Debby laughed. "I won't hold it against you. I was really impressed, especially with you—a woman making it in a man's sport."

"That's kind of you. It's not a man's sport any longer." Megs thought of Sasha. "Women are leading the way."

Debby looked down at Mitch, compassion on her face. "We will do all we can to help the two of you get back to life and living."

"I can't ask for more. Thank you."

Megs got settled again and was about to start recording when a man in a suit knocked on the door. Megs closed the journal, stood.

He stepped inside, held out his hand. "I'm Tom

Gordon, the hospital administrator. I'm sorry to meet you under these circumstances, Ms. Hill."

Megs shook his hand. "What can I do for you?"

She thought she knew.

"We're getting press inquiries from around the world about Mr. Ahearn. We would like your permission to draft a statement. We'd like to hold a press conference this afternoon and get these folks off our backs. You don't need to attend or speak at the conference, but—"

"That's fine, provided I get to read the statement ahead of time."

The administrator nodded, handed her a clipboard and a pen. "This is what we'd like to say. Read through it, sign and date it, and we'll take care of the rest."

Megs read through it, saw that it was all very general information. She approved it, handed him the clipboard, and watched him walk away. She hadn't given much thought to the public impact of Mitch's accident. The two of them had retired from professional climbing to focus on their work with the Team. But she and Mitch had friends and followers out there, people who would be deeply upset by this.

"Where did I leave my fucking phone?" She searched through her backpack, found her smartphone, and turned it on. "Sixty-two messages."

There was no way on God's green and hilly earth that she could answer that many calls, but she had the time to listen. Some were from media outlets in the climbing community. The others were from friends, including their buddies from their days climbing in Yosemite Valley—Gridwall, Accardo, Cook.

Megs didn't have the energy or will to call them back, so she did the next best thing and posted a statement on all of her and Mitch's social media accounts.

"Mitch Ahearn was critically injured by
falling rock while climbing on Painted Wall
in the Black Canyon of the Gunnison.
Rangers joined with members of the Rocky
Mountain Search & Rescue Team to save his
life. He underwent surgery yesterday for a
skull fracture and a broken clavicle. He is
in stable but critical condition in the ICU
at Denver Medical Center. We appreciate
your support and concern and ask that you
respect our privacy during these difficult
days. I will update you as I am able. In
the meantime, remember to wear a helmet. If
Mitch hadn't been wearing his yesterday,
he'd be dead."

Within seconds, her posts began getting responses, but she didn't stick around to read them. Instead, she muted her phone, set it aside, and settled down once again with the recorder and Mitch's journal.

She glanced at the next entry and smiled. It had been a day that made climbing history, though no one had understood that at the time.

———

MITCH SPENT his morning bouldering with the boys at The Crystals. He, Gridwall, Accardo, John Baker, and Ron Cook took turns spotting each other on a few complex routes. Meanwhile, Ken Yoder, Gene Lewis, and Billy Ansel monkeyed around on the easier stuff for strength training.

Mitch battled a route someone had named Pride— probably because it stripped a man of his pride pretty quickly. He got a little closer to making it to the top each time, his body learning the moves. But it wasn't easy to focus with Gridwall there, tripping on acid and having conversations with birds.

"Fly, man! That's what you were *meant* to do. Fly and be free. The whole sky belongs to you, man. The whole fucking sky."

On the way back to camp, the guys decided to try their luck again with White Lightning, a route on Columbine Boulder. Close to Camp 4, this monster of a boulder was thirty feet tall with a nasty overhang that had defied everyone. Dean said it was unclimbable, and Mitch thought he was probably right.

One by one, they tried and failed, none of them clearing that damned overhang. There were no holds they could use to pull themselves over the top.

The sound of an engine turned his gaze toward the road. Megs drove up and parked, Janis Joplin's *Me and Bobby McGee* blasting out of her open windows.

Everyone looked her way, except for Accardo, who was climbing.

"She looks like a schoolgirl." Gridwall watched her as she crossed the campground, walking toward her tent.

Jim might be tripping, but he was also right. She *did* look like a schoolgirl—blouse, skirt, knee-high socks, real shoes. She glanced their way and then disappeared inside her tent. When she stepped out a few minutes later, she was wearing shorts and a T-shirt, her hair in a ponytail, climbing shoes in one hand.

Accardo struggled with the overhang, tried to reach a crimp to pull himself over the top, and fell, skinning his elbow on the way down. "Shit!"

"She's coming this way. Does she think she's going to climb?" Gridwall shook his head. "That would be a joke."

Gridwall went next, reaching the overhang just as Megs joined them. She watched, her gaze moving over the route as if she were studying it.

Mitch walked over to her, hoping she wouldn't get the wrong idea. He wasn't trying to hit on her. He just wanted to say hello. "I'm Mitch Ahearn. I'm a friend of Dean's, too. Good to meet you, Megs."

She looked up, her gaze meeting his, eye contact sending a jolt of awareness through him. "I'm … I'm Megs."

It was the first time he'd gotten a good look at her face and…

Damn.

Big gray eyes. Long lashes. High cheekbones. Clear, tanned skin. She was a foot shorter than he was, only an inch or two above five feet. Her body wasn't just slender but also strong, with well-defined muscles, her breasts small, her waist narrow. She looked so young, like a kid not even out of high school. But here she was, alone in Yosemite, driving a car. She couldn't be much older than eighteen.

She was so pretty that it took him a moment to realize that he'd left her flustered. He knew her name. He'd just used it. Still, she had repeated it.

That was interesting.

"You were all dressed up this morning." He spoke before he could stop himself.

"I got a job at the cafeteria."

"A job?" None of them had jobs.

"Yes, a job. You know—gainful employment. Don't you have to eat to climb?"

He did, but he got by on instant oatmeal, canned food from home, and expired items from the Village store. One time, he and the guys had brought back an expired case of canned dog food and fried that up. But he wouldn't admit that, not to her.

He lowered his voice. "Sorry about Gridwall. He isn't a bad guy. He's just—"

She shifted her gaze back to the boulder. "A chauvinist pig."

Mitch couldn't help but grin. "Yeah. A chauvinist pig."

Gridwall fell from the overhang, landed in the dirt with a grunt.

"Dean said he had a big mouth and a bigger ego."

"True." Mitch had to ask. "Did he say anything about me?"

"He said the two of you learned to climb together at…" She frowned, as if trying to remember. "Tahquitz Rock? He also said you're smart."

"That's true, too." His lack of humility brought a half-smile to her face. "You must be good if Dean climbed with you. He doesn't waste time with—"

"Ahearn!" Gridwall brushed the dirt off his hands. "Are you going to try, or are you too distracted by the blonde?"

Mitch saw fire in Megs' eyes, knew she was furious. "Her name is Megs. Why don't you let her try?"

He knew he was probably putting her on the spot, but the only way for her to earn their respect was to show them that she, too, could master stone.

Her gaze moved from him to the rock and back again, and he saw nervousness in her eyes—and defiance.

Gridwall laughed. "If we can't do it, there's no way a little girl can. She's too short. She doesn't have our reach or our strength. Asking her to try is just unfair to her."

"Sure, I'll give it a shot." Megs sat in the dirt, changed into her climbing shoes, got to her feet, and strapped on her chalk bag.

Determination on her face, she walked over to the boulder, studied the holds, clearly thinking through the moves in her mind. Then she chalked her fingers and stepped onto the route.

Her first several moves were like everyone else's. The opening crimp holds carried her up to that undercling crimp off to the right. From there, she shifted her left hand to the crimp high above, adjusted her feet, then used the muscles in her legs to surge upward to the next hold.

Mitch was impressed. She climbed with both athleticism and grace, making it look easy when they all knew it wasn't.

For a few seconds, she hung there by her fingers, the reach to the next hold far even for a six-foot-tall man. She searched with her feet, found a couple of small holds to support her—and lunged upward once again, her fingers closing on the thin lip of stone on the top edge of the overhang.

This is where they all fell. It was damned hard to hang on to that lip with one hand and reach over the top with the other. There was nothing to hold onto up there, no way to pull one's self over the top.

Then she did something completely unexpected.

Once again hanging on by her fingertips, she caught one heel on the edge of the overhang and used it to bring herself almost parallel to the ground. Then she shifted her left hand and used her arm as a lever, lifting herself up and over the edge. From there, it was just a bit of fifth-class scramble to the top.

She turned, looked down at them from the boulder, still out of breath, a bright smile on her pretty face. "Hell, boys, it's not that hard."

The guys stared up at her, some with open mouths.

Mitch found himself grinning like an idiot.

MEGS STOPPED RECORDING and set the journal aside, a smile on her face. She hadn't been familiar with Yosemite, so she hadn't realized that she was the first person ever to finish that route.

Not the first woman. The first *person*.

The climbing world took note of that first ascent at the exact moment when the sport began to take off. The Yosemite free-climbing revolution had begun, and she'd found herself at the heart of it—thanks to Mitch. Even before they'd gotten together, he'd been there, lifting her up every step of the way.

"Gridwall spent the next week trying to duplicate what I'd done, and when he failed, he started saying I'd succeeded only because I was lighter. I'd forgotten what a jerk he was in the beginning. You put him in his place, remember? 'Is she lighter, or are you stronger? Make up your mind.'"

It had been one of the most exciting times of her life—and Mitch was part of the reason for that. He was right. She *had* gotten flustered when he'd introduced himself. It had been pure hormones, a physical reaction. He'd been so damned good-looking, his T-shirt stretched across his pecs, a smile on those lips, his brown eyes warm.

"How like you to notice my reaction. You've always been able to read people. You knocked me off—"

His body jerked, and he went rigid.

Pulse spiking, Megs jumped to her feet, pressed the call button. "He's seizing!"

But they must have seen something on their monitors.

Debby and other nurses rushed into the room. "Please wait outside, Ms. Hill."

Megs managed to squeeze Mitch's hand and then got

the hell out of the way, medical staff speaking medicalese, their words clipped, their tone urgent. She left the ICU, stood in the hallway, her heart still racing.

Hadn't the doctor mentioned something about seizures?

She struggled to remember through her exhaustion and fear.

If she'd been the praying kind, a believer, she'd have said a prayer, but it felt hypocritical praying to a god she'd ignored all of her life. So she paced the hallway instead, stopping every so often to lean back against the wall or look at her watch or check her smartphone.

After about forty-five minutes, Debby opened the door, a smile on her face.

"You can come back in now." Debby walked with her to Mitch's bedside.

He lay still, just as he'd done before the seizure.

"Is he okay?"

"Seizures aren't uncommon after a craniotomy. They're especially common in the first twenty-four to forty-eight hours after surgery. The fact that he had a seizure doesn't mean his condition is declining or that he won't recover. We're taking him down for an MRI in about an hour."

"Another one?"

"It's routine after that kind of surgery." Debby rested a hand on her arm. "I know it's hard to leave, but you need to take care of yourself, too. You must be exhausted. Do you have a place you can stay nearby?"

Megs nodded. "The Marriott."

"You should go get some sleep. This is a long haul. You don't want to wear yourself out on Day One."

Some part of Megs wanted to rage at Debby. Mitch was the man she loved, the only man she'd ever loved. She didn't want to leave him, but she knew Debby was right. She was exhausted. She still had her climbing clothes on, Mitch's blood on her leggings.

"Can you please call me if anything changes?"

Debby nodded. "I promise. I'll keep the recorder playing, too, except for when he has the MRI. Then it has to come off."

Megs understood. "Thank you. I'll just take a minute with him."

"Of course. Stay as long as you like."

Megs set the recorder to play. "I'm just going to go take a shower and grab some sleep. I'll be back. Don't go anywhere while I'm gone, okay, bud? I love you."

She put the earbuds in his ears, pushed the PLAY button, took the handle of the suitcase Rain had brought, and reluctantly walked out of his room.

Chapter 5

MEGS WOKE WITH A START, glanced around, confused. She was at a hotel in the room that Joe had reserved for her. What time was it?

Disoriented from a deep sleep, she reached for her watch, only to find it still on her wrist. Seven PM already? Had she truly slept for five hours?

She scrambled out of bed, found her phone, saw that she'd gotten a message from the hospital. On a rush of adrenaline, she played it back.

"It's Dr. Schwartz. I just wanted to let you know we have the results of the MRI. There's no sign of clots or bleeding, and that's what we want to see at this stage. Have them page me when you get back to the hospital. I have something encouraging I think you'd like to see."

The doctor had probably gone home by now, so she didn't need to rush over in her underwear and sports bra. If it was good news—and it certainly sounded like good news—it could wait until she'd taken a shower and had something to eat.

She ordered supper from room service and hit the

shower while she waited for her meal to arrive. She couldn't help but sigh, the hot water helping her to feel human again. She shampooed, conditioned, washed her face and body, glad she'd taken the nurse's advice. The situation with Mitch still terrified her, but at least she was clean and able to think more clearly.

Thank you, Rain and Joe!

She'd just gotten dressed when her meal arrived— smoked salmon salad with French bread, fresh fruit, and green tea. She grabbed her laptop and took time to send a group email to the Team and to check in with Rain while she ate. Then she put a few things she might need into her daypack and walked back to the hospital.

She hadn't trusted herself to drive on no sleep.

Back in the ICU, she found a new shift of nurses hard at work. Mitch lay just as he had when she'd left—still and silent, earbuds in his ears, recorder in playback mode beside him.

She approached the nurse's station. "I'm Megs Hill, Mitch Ahearn's partner. I got a message from Dr. Schwartz about the results of today's MRI. I'd really like to talk with him. He said there was something he wanted to tell me."

Jackie, the evening RN, nodded. "I think he's gone home for the day, but I'll check. He's not usually here this late, as he has to be in the OR pretty early most days. If he's not here, the neurosurgeon on call can talk with you."

"Thanks." Megs walked back to Mitch's room, took his hand. "Hey, bud. I went to the hotel where Joe got me a room and slept for five hours. I didn't even dream."

Was Mitch dreaming? Did he have any perception of where he was? Did he have thoughts and images floating through his mind? Or was there only darkness?

A moment later, her phone buzzed.

Dr. Schwartz.

She answered. "Sorry I missed your call. I was asleep."

"Good. I'm glad you got some rest." He went over the MRI results, repeating what he'd said in the message. "The surgery accomplished what we hoped it would. The MRI showed no new bleeding and no clots. That's good news."

"I'm relieved to hear it. Thank you."

"I ordered a functional MRI, as well. That's one way we have to check brain function. He definitely has brain function. No doubt."

"Thank God."

Dr. Schwartz went on. "As a bit of an experiment, I decided to run the scan a second time, this time while he listened to the recording you'd made. The images of his brain showed a marked increase in activity in response to the sound of your voice."

Megs' throat went tight. "Really?"

"I'll show you the images on my rounds tomorrow. In the meantime, keep talking to him. I can't say for sure what the impact of hearing your voice will have in the final outcome, but anything that stimulates his brain is a good thing."

"I will. Thank you." She ended the call, looked down at the face of the man she loved. He was trapped inside this unconscious state, but he was there. "You really do hear me. I'll fight to get in, while you keep fighting to get out, okay?"

She sat down with the digital recorder and the journal and began skimming, looking for a new favorite memory.

She laughed. "This is when you knuckleheads asked me to be slow about clearing the tables so that you could breeze through the cafeteria and grab the leftovers off of people's dirty plates. You almost got me fired. Why couldn't you just get jobs?"

She turned the pages, came across an entry that made

her pause. "That's the day the rangers raided the camp. Do you remember?"

———

MITCH FLOATED in a deep and gaping darkness, unbearably alone. His mind empty of thoughts, he knew only dread—except when he heard her voice. Without a name to go along with it, he knew that voice. Somehow, the sound of it chased away the dread and kept him from sinking deeper.

———

MITCH WAS AWAKENED from a sound sleep by shouting.

"Rise and shine, boys! Come out with your hands up!"

What the hell?

Wearing only his boxer briefs, he crawled out of his sleeping bag and stuck his head outside his tent.

Rangers.

"Shit."

Another raid.

They came looking for illegal drugs and draft dodgers. Though the war was more or less over and the government had no plans to send anyone else to Vietnam, men who'd illegally avoided the draft could still be arrested.

"Come on out!"

Mitch grabbed his jeans, thrust his legs inside them, grabbed his draft card out of his wallet, and crawled out of his tent, hands raised.

A few rangers lined the guys up at the picnic table to check their IDs, draft cards, and frisk them, while others searched their tents. Mitch glanced around and saw that all of the crew were there now except Gridwall, who'd run into the forest to hide, and…

Megs.

She'd never been through one of these and might be afraid. Her tent was set apart from theirs, so maybe the rangers would leave her alone. One thing was certain. If he ran over to her tent to warn her, he would drag her into this.

"We know you guys have marijuana." The ranger in charge had a crew cut, his jaw square enough to cut glass, a nightstick in his hand. "Families come to Yosemite. They don't need you damned hippies hanging out, half-dressed, playing the devil's music, and doing drugs in sight of their children. Shame on you!"

The devil's music?

Accardo glared at him. "We're not hippies. We're *dirtbags.*"

Some of the guys laughed, but the rangers didn't find it funny.

"Tell that to the judge." A ranger checked Accardo's ID and his draft card. "You're nineteen. Have you been called up?"

"No, sir."

"Face the table and plant your feet wide apart." The ranger frisked him, found nothing, then moved on to Cook, whose long ponytail he disliked. "Is this how you want the world to see you, with long hair like a girl?"

"Do girls have razor stubble?" Cook asked, baiting him.

The ranger ignored him and moved on to Yoder. "I recognize you."

Yoder grinned. "I've got that kind of face."

Mitch doubted they would have cause to arrest anyone today. After Yoder got busted with a joint last summer, the potheads in the group had started burying their stashes in old tin cans before they turned in each night just to be safe. Still, they went through this ritual every so often.

The ranger finished with Yoder and stepped in front of Mitch.

Mitch handed him both his draft card and driver's license. "College deferments."

"You think you're smart?"

"Not particularly."

"I guess not, given that you're hanging with these jokers. Uncle Sam let you off the hook. Shouldn't you pay him back by doing something meaningful with your life?"

What was Mitch supposed to say to that? "I love climbing."

"Face the table."

Mitch laced his fingers behind his head and did as he was asked, his gaze on Megs' tent as the ranger patted him down. They hadn't yet noticed her tent, so...

Jesus!

This pat-down had just gotten personal.

"What's this in your jeans?" the ranger demanded.

"That's my dick."

The other dirtbags burst into laughter.

"That's your penis. Okay. Sorry."

Cook snorted. "Is that a foot-long in your pocket, Ahern, or are you just happy to see the rangers?"

More laughter.

By the time the lead ranger had finished checking their IDs and frisking them, the other rangers were done tossing their tents. Sleeping bags, clothes, and packaged food lay scattered on the ground, but, as Mitch had expected, they'd found no drugs. They also hadn't found Gridwall, who'd taken to climbing and living in national parks to avoid the San Diego draft board.

Then one of them pointed toward Megs' tent. "Anyone search that one yet?"

A ranger walked over to her tent, jerked down the zipper. "We told you to come out... Oh. I'm sorry, miss. I thought you were one of them."

Mitch turned to the ranger who'd just patted him down. "She's not with us."

The ranger in charge passed on that information. "They say she's not with them."

Megs crawled out of her tent wearing jeans and a T-shirt, her hair drawn back in a ponytail. "Is there a problem, sir?"

"I need to see your ID, miss."

Megs handed it to him, along with some documents.

The ranger studied both. "Come with me, please, miss."

Megs hesitated for a moment, her gaze seeking Mitch's as she walked by, worry in her eyes.

Something in Mitch snapped. "Wait! What did she do? Are you arresting her?"

"Stay where you are!" the ranger barked back. "Stanley, search her tent just to be thorough."

"What the—" Mitch took a step, about to follow her, but found himself restrained by a palm to the sternum.

"Hold on, Romeo. No one is going to mistreat her."

Megs climbed into the front seat of the ranger's vehicle, not the back. She and the ranger seemed to be having a conversation. It went on for ten or fifteen minutes before she climbed out, papers in hand.

"What was that about?" Accardo asked.

"No idea."

The lead ranger gave them a speech about following park rules and the evils of illicit drugs. Then the rangers climbed into their vehicles and drove away, leaving them to clean up the mess.

"Hey, why did they want to talk to you?" Yoder asked Megs.

She shrugged as if she had no idea.

Mitch didn't buy that. He fell in beside her, walked with her. "Are you okay?"

Her gaze met his, and she nodded, clearly relieved. "What were they doing here?"

"Looking for illegal drugs and draft dodgers."

"What are those papers?" Cook called to her.

She waved them. "My parole papers."

"You're on parole?" Accardo was apparently stupid enough to believe what was obviously a lie. "What did you do?"

"I killed some guy because he hit on me."

Mitch found himself biting back a grin.

Still, he couldn't help but wonder. Why had the ranger wanted to speak with her privately? And what were those papers?

———

MEGS STOPPED RECORDING and slipped the cafeteria receipt she'd been using as a bookmark between the pages, laughing to herself. "They all seemed afraid of me for a while after that. Not one of them ever tried to grab my butt."

As for those papers, Mitch had eventually learned the truth.

It touched her in a way she couldn't quite explain to read about Mitch's protectiveness toward her. He'd been there for her almost from the day she'd met him, watching out for her and supporting her as a climber. He'd always been good at reading people, but she'd had no idea how well he'd read her.

"You were right. I was terrified that you all would learn my secret—or that the rangers would kick me out of the park. He just wanted to warn me about all of you. He told me you weren't law-abiding young men and that you all would take advantage of me in ways I couldn't yet understand. I guess he thought I didn't know about sex."

She'd still been a virgin, but she hadn't been innocent. Her stepfather had stolen that from her. The bastard.

Megs let that thought go, slid her fingers between his, a smile on her face. "You know what else happened that day? I realized that you liked me, and that was the beginning of my crush on you. You were the first man to stand up for me."

It sounded a little pathetic when she put it like that. A girl falls for the first adult man to treat her with respect and dignity. But when she'd never experienced such kindness from a man before, how could she help but be drawn to him?

"I didn't know the ranger who'd frisked you had grabbed your meat." She laughed. "I wondered why the guys spent the next week or so joking about the size of your dick. I guess I can't really blame them. You were pissed—and probably a little embarrassed. I will admit that it *did* make me curious."

She learned that Gridwall was a draft dodger that day when he'd come down from his bolt-hole among the boulders, pumped up on adrenaline and proud of himself for once against sticking it to the man. When he heard all that had happened, he'd started calling Megs "our little murderer," which she much preferred to "the blonde."

"I always wondered how Dean became friends with Gridwall—the good-hearted Vietnam vet and the drug-using draft dodger. You told me that they represented for each other the road not taken, and—"

A knock.

"Lab." A young woman entered, a cart of phlebotomy gear with her.

Megs stood. "You're here for a blood draw."

"Yes, ma'am."

Megs understood now why they'd put in that subclavian line. Mitch's veins would be a mess with all these blood draws and all the IV meds.

She took advantage of the moment to go to the restroom and get a cup of coffee. When she returned, she found the hospital chaplain sitting at his bedside, praying in silence. Then he looked up, and she saw his nametag.

The Rev. Kurt Calder.

Oh, my God.

Dean's son.

He was grown up now and obviously some kind of pastor or priest. He was also the clear image of his father —same dark hair, same brown eyes, same mouth. The last time she'd seen him, he'd been a little boy, no more than five or six years old.

He saw her, stood, a smile on his face. "Hi, Megs. I hope you don't mind my coming. When I heard what had happened, I had to come see you, even if you didn't request me. I hope that's okay."

"Of course. I'm so glad you stopped by. You're tall, just like your father, and you look so much like him."

"I hear that a lot." Kurt stood, motioned toward the chair. "Please sit. I'll get another chair."

He returned a few minutes later with an extra chair and sat near the foot of Mitch's bed. "I'm really sorry to see you again under these circumstances. I've wanted to get in touch with you and Mitch for my entire adult life to thank you for keeping my father's memory alive. I wish I hadn't waited until now."

His words, so unexpected, made Megs' throat go tight.

She waited until she was confident she could speak without her voice breaking. "Your father was a good man —and a good friend."

Kurt seemed to take this in, then he met Megs' gaze. "How is Mitch?"

"You don't have to be a chaplain with me, Kurt. If you want to talk about your dad, that's fine. I've been thinking about the old days a lot."

Kurt was quiet for a moment, clearly a deep thinker like his father. "The hardest thing for me is that I barely remember him. He was away so often, and I was only six when he died."

In those words, Megs sensed a lifetime of loss. She recognized it because she shared it. Dean had been one of her best friends.

She thought about it for a moment, tried to imagine what Mitch would say. "Mitch kept journals dating back to when he was in college. Your father is in there from our early climbing days in Yosemite. I've been recording journal entries and playing them back for him, trying to stimulate his brain. I'm certain he wouldn't mind if I shared entries that include your father."

Kurt cleared his throat. "That would mean a lot to me."

Chapter 6

MITCH WAS STANDING on top of Columbine Boulder, pumped up on the adrenaline of having finally climbed White Lightning, when he spotted a familiar blue Chevy van heading their way. He pointed. "Hey, Calder's here."

"Dean?" The excitement on Megs' face made her look like a little girl—and left Mitch feeling strangely jealous.

Dean parked, climbed out, and headed in their direction. He was probably the best climber among them—excluding Megs, of course. He'd taken to climbing after getting back from a tour of duty in Vietnam and now lived out of his vehicle, traveling the country, always in search of new routes.

Megs waved to him, and Dean headed in their direction.

Mitch stayed where he was. It was his rock-solid proof that he'd climbed the route Dean had declared unclimbable.

Oh, yeah. This was going to be sweet.

Dean spotted him, grinned. "How the hell did you get up there—a ladder?"

"You wish! The unclimbable has been climbed." Mitch felt a moment of satisfaction at the astonishment on Dean's face, but it was quickly replaced by guilt. He hadn't been the first to get here. "Megs showed us how to do it."

"Why doesn't that surprise me?" Dean walked over to Megs and hugged her. "How's it going, kiddo? Are you putting these boys to shame?"

Mitch downclimbed and stood back while Megs demonstrated for Dean how she'd proven him wrong. Having climbed the boulder numerous times since her first ascent, she now had the route down, moving quickly and gracefully up the rock. Mitch could have watched her climb all day. He'd never seen anyone move the way she did, both athletic and graceful.

It went beyond skill. It was genius. It was … *art*.

When she topped out, Dean applauded. "Far out! Why didn't I think of that?"

"You guys climb using physical strength." Megs made her way back to the ground. "I have to use my brain, too."

Mitch couldn't help but laugh. She wasn't wrong.

They spent the rest of the afternoon at the boulder, until each of them had successfully climbed the route. Afterward, Megs pulled Dean aside, leaned close, said something that made Dean shake his head and rest his hand on her shoulder. When she walked to her tent to change for work, she looked pleased.

Mitch found himself watching her as she came out of her tent in her cafeteria uniform and climbed into her car. Did she and Dean have something going on? And why the hell did he care?

Dean walked up beside him. "You like her."

Mitch couldn't deny it. "She's one hell of a climber."

Dean chuckled. "No, I mean you *like* her."

"Yeah. There's something about her…"

"Tell me about it."

Mitch turned to look at his friend, needing to know. "Are the two of you…?"

"Lovers?" Dean laughed. "Oh, hell, no. I'm too old for her."

"Too old? You're only twenty-eight, man."

Dean laughed, shook his head. "Want to get away from camp and go for a hike?"

"Yeah." Mitch grabbed his daypack with its first aid kit, filled his water bottle, and met Dean near his vehicle.

"The Upper Falls?" Dean shoved a bag of trail mix into his backpack.

"Sounds good."

They walked in amicable silence to the Valley Loop Trail, following it until it intersected with the Falls trail, switchbacks passing through oak forest, their progress slowed by red-faced tourists who huffed and puffed their way uphill.

"Good grief." Dean apparently got sick of the human traffic jam because he picked up speed and began to thread his way through them, passing them quickly.

Mitch was right behind him. It felt good to get some motion, his heart thrumming in his chest, fresh air in his lungs. As they neared Columbia Point, the trail became sandy. Dean didn't stop to look at the view of Yosemite Valley but pressed on, pushing himself.

They passed Oh My Gosh Point with its incredible view of Half Dome, their progress slowed by tourists with cameras. They were roughly halfway to the top now, a pleasant burn in Mitch's quadriceps. More switchbacks led to chaparral and then manzanita scrub.

When they reached the top, Dean didn't take the stone steps to the overlook but instead headed over to the water —not the safest place to be. He knelt, splashed water on his face, then scrambled up a boulder, and sat looking out over the valley.

Mitch climbed up to sit beside him, pulled out his water bottle, and took a deep drink. Below them, Yosemite Valley stretched out like a climber's dream, Half Dome rising above the green forest. But Mitch's thoughts drifted to Megs.

When didn't he think about her?

Over these past few weeks, she'd become an obsession. He loved the sound of her laugh, loved her sharp tongue and her quick wit. And those gray eyes...

The sun was beginning to set, its rays turning the top of Half Dome a flaming shade of red-gold, turkey vultures soaring on the last of the thermals, jays squawking in the nearby trees.

Dean broke the silence. "Thanks for coming with me. There are days when I want to jump. If I did, I'd do it here at night when the tourists were gone. Long, fast drop, rock-hard stop. But don't worry. With you here, I wouldn't do that."

Mitch stared at him. He'd known that Dean carried memories of the war, but he hadn't realized the weight of those memories was so heavy. "Do you want to tell me about it?"

Dean laughed, a harsh sound. "It's the most fucked-up bullshit ever to kill some scared kid your own age just because your two governments decided to have a war. I can still see the shock in his eyes, the fear. He hesitated—and I pulled the trigger."

"I don't see what choice you had. It was kill or be killed."

Dean nodded. "That's what I tell myself, but his finger wasn't on the trigger. Maybe he would have just let me pass by."

"Maybe—or maybe he'd have gotten over his surprise and killed you."

Dean said nothing, and Mitch realized he was shaking, his face screwed up in anguish, tears on his cheeks. Mitch wanted to tell him that it would be okay, but how could he say that? He hadn't fought in Vietnam. He didn't know how it felt to kill.

"Thanks for trusting me with that." He put his arm around Dean's shoulder. "I can't begin to know what you're going through, but I'm here. I won't leave you."

<hr>

MEGS WAITED until the lump in her throat loosened enough to let her speak. "Mitch is so good about keeping people's confidences. I knew that Vietnam haunted your father, but I never knew he'd thought of ending his life. Mitch never told me."

Kurt wiped his eyes. "My mother said he'd found peace before he died."

The sharp edge of regret pressed in on Megs, Dean's death a tragedy she'd never put behind her. "That's true. He found peace with your mom, with climbing, with you and your little sister. He talked about you often. He told us he thought you were a good little hiker and might climb one day, too."

Kurt smiled. "I'm sorry to say he was wrong about that. I love the mountains. I hike and camp, but climbing…"

His words trailed off, but he didn't have to finish. Why would any child take up the sport that had killed their father?

"I guess I understand now why he didn't hold a grudge against Gridwall."

Kurt nodded. "My mother told me that he never judged draft dodgers. He believed Vietnam was a mistake and understood why a man might choose self-preservation over country. He never spoke of the war in front of us kids, but killing that young soldier stayed with him for the rest of his life."

"Is all of this why you became a minister?" Megs had learned a few things from Mitch about reading people. "Is it your calling to help people cope with their pain?"

Kurt seemed to consider this. "That could be. I believe God suffers with us, shares in our grief and pain. Losing my father was the worst thing that has happened to me. Easing the pain of others, giving them solace, isn't a poor way to spend one's life."

"No, it certainly isn't." Megs was about to find another entry that featured Dean when Kurt's phone beeped.

He slipped it out of his pocket. "I have to go. There's been a serious accident, and there are folks in the ER who are getting bad news."

Megs' stomach knotted at the thought. "Damn, you're strong—just like Dean."

"Before I go, I'd like to say a prayer for Mitch—if that's okay."

"I'd appreciate that. Thank you."

He took her hand, his fingers warm. "Gracious God in Heaven, I ask you to pour out your Holy Spirit on your servant Mitch Ahearn. Bless and guide the doctors and nurses who are working tirelessly to save his life, and grant him the miracle of complete recovery. Be with his partner, Megs, and strengthen her for these challenging days ahead. I ask all this in the name of the one who suffered for us."

He paused, then went on. "And, Dad, if you see Mitch, please tell him it's not his time, and send him back. Amen."

Megs barely managed to croak out an "Amen."

"I'll check on you tomorrow, if that's okay."

"That would mean a lot to me—and to Mitch, I'm certain."

"Thanks for sharing the journal entry." Kurt glanced at Mitch one more time. "I'll see you later, Mitch."

Then he walked out of the room.

Megs moved closer to the head of the bed, took Mitch's hand. "Do you know who that was? That was Dean's son—Kurt. I had no idea he worked here. Hell, I still thought of him as a little boy."

A knock.

Jackie checked Mitch's IV fluids and went through the oral care routine. Then the lab tech stepped in to draw blood. A respiratory therapist came in a few minutes later to check the ventilator machine itself.

It was getting late, time for Megs to head back to the hotel for her first full night's sleep since the accident. She put fresh batteries into the recorder, then kissed Mitch's cheek. "I'm going to the hotel now, but I'll be back in the morning. In the meantime, you can listen to me drone on. Keep fighting."

She put the earbuds on him, hit play, then reluctantly left his room. She made sure Jackie had her room number at the hotel, then took the elevator to the ground floor and searched for her vehicle. The air was chilly, the wind blowing away the antiseptic odors of the hospital and reviving her.

She'd wandered around in front of the hospital for about five minutes when she remembered they'd parked her SUV near the ER entrance. She made her way around to that side of the building to find two ambulances parked outside the doors. A man and woman jumped out of a car and ran toward the building, panic on their faces.

She'd spoken with lots of grief-stricken families during

her years with the Team, but this was different, the couple's distress hitting her in the chest, empathy for them swamping her, filling her with impotent rage. If God suffered with humanity, then why the hell didn't God do something about the situation down here?

She found her vehicle, unlocked it with her fob, and climbed into the driver's seat, slamming the door. "Damn it!"

She sat there for a moment, pressed the heels of her hands against her eyes to keep herself from crying. When she was in control once more, she turned on the engine and drove down the street to the hotel. She showered, checked her email, then crawled into bed. The last thought in her mind before exhaustion caught up with her was of Mitch with his arm around Dean's shoulder.

MEGS ARRIVED in the ICU to find the place busier than usual. Then she remembered. Last night's accident.

She made her way to Mitch's room, passing a room where the couple she'd seen last night hovered over the bed of a teenage boy, their faces twisted with fear.

God almighty.

Empathy washed through her, followed by a rush of gratitude. Unlike the poor child in that bed, Mitch had lived a full life. He'd known a level of success and fame in his field that few men could claim. He'd stood on the summit of Mt. Everest, climbed in Patagonia, traveled the world. They'd had forty-eight wonderful years together and made a difference in the lives of others. If this was the end...

It better fucking *not* be the end.

She wasn't ready to say goodbye.

Debby, the daytime RN, was in Mitch's room, hooking up a small bag of meds to his subclavian line. She looked up when Megs entered. "Did you get some sleep?"

Megs nodded. "How is he?"

"He started running a fever late last night."

Megs' stomach knotted. "Shit."

"It's not unusual for patients to run a fever post-op, but we're doing a full range of tests to make sure he's not developing an infection or sepsis. We're continuing antibiotics. I wouldn't worry too much. Dr. Schwartz wanted to talk to you, so I'll page him and let him know you're here."

Megs walked to Mitch's bedside, touched her hand to his cheek, and found his skin hot. She stopped the recorder, removed his earbuds. "Good morning. What's going on with this fever? I wish you could open your eyes and tell me. I bet you've got one hell of a headache."

Could he feel pain? She had no idea.

During the half-hour it took Dr. Schwartz to appear, Megs had all but convinced herself that the news could only be bad. But when he walked into the room, he had a smile on his face.

"Good morning." He shook her hand.

"Is there bad news?"

"You already know the bad news. He's not out of the woods yet. He could still die. He could have significant impairments. We can't be certain he'll ever climb again or walk or talk, for that matter. But I'm here to share some good news."

Megs' spirits sank to hear him describe Mitch's situation in such stark terms. "I'm listening."

"We've been monitoring his intracranial pressure constantly, and the indications are that the swelling in his brain is beginning to go down." Dr. Schwartz smiled. "Why is this good news? Often, as the swelling goes down, we see patients begin to progress through different stages of recovery. It generally takes six to twenty weeks for the swelling to go down completely, but this is the start of recovery."

"Are you saying he might wake up soon?" Megs couldn't even bring herself to hope, not when so much still hung in the balance.

Dr. Schwartz shook his head. "With an injury as severe as this, we typically see patients move from a coma to a vegetative state and then into a minimally conscious state and then a confusional state before regaining full consciousness. The faster they move through these stages, the fewer impairments they typically have, though there are no guarantees. It's all in the brochures I gave you."

"Oh, right." What had Megs done with those? "I guess I haven't felt like reading."

"Did Debby tell you about the fever?"

"Yes. She said you're running tests."

"So far, there's no sign of infection. We'll keep up antibiotic therapy, but at this point, I'm pretty certain this is just part of the healing process. It's not unusual for a patient to have a fever in the first forty-eight hours or so after surgery."

She realized with a start that it hadn't yet been forty-eight hours since Mitch's surgery. How could that be when it felt like half a century?

Dr. Schwartz touched a hand to her shoulder. "Hang in there. You're at the beginning of a tough journey. Debby tells me you're still reading to him. Keep it up. Take good care of yourself, too. He's going to need you."

Megs thanked him and watched him walk away. She took Mitch's hand, allowed thoughts she'd been holding at bay to enter her mind.

Was she selfish to want so desperately for Mitch to

wake up? Would the life he had after this justify his suffering? He'd been so clear that he'd rather die than spend his life helpless or with severe impairments. But maybe that was all just ableist bullshit from an elite athlete who couldn't imagine living a happy life in any other way.

She took his hand, steeled herself. "I don't know if you can really hear me. I don't know if anything I say matters one way or another."

She hesitated, tried to find the right words. She wanted to tell him that she would be okay if he needed to move on, that he shouldn't cling to life if he was so badly hurt that his life wouldn't be worth living. But that's not what came out of her mouth.

"Don't die on me, you son of a bitch. I don't know how to let you go."

She retrieved the journal and the recorder and searched for a new passage to read.

Chapter 7

MITCH BELAYED Megs on the tenth and final pitch, letting out the slack, his mind focused on Megs as she neared the crux move. Even so, some part of him was still aware that they were doing it. The two of them were about to finish the first free ascent of a new route on El Capitan.

The whole thing had been Megs' idea. They'd been taking turns climbing the lower pitches of The Nose with the rest of the gang when Megs had wandered off, her gaze on the rock. When she'd returned, she'd told him that she'd found a new route near the Salathé Wall that she wanted to try.

He'd walked with her to get a look. The first pitch was identical to the Salathé Wall, but from there, it deviated to the left. The line she'd picked out was gutsy and ambitious, a solid 5.11. In just ten pitches, it had everything that made climbing El Cap an adrenaline rush—opposing crack systems, loose flakes, a wicked roof, considerable exposure, smooth-looking granite with thin holds.

And now here they were, *so* close to finishing.

Mitch watched as Megs shifted her feet and hips to

increase her reach, caught a pocket with two fingers, then swung one leg over the roof, catching an edge with her heel. It was a tricky sequence for any climber, but she made it look easy. Every action she took was smooth and well-planned. She moved more like a dancer or a gymnast than a climber. When at last she stood on the ledge at the end of the route, she turned to face the valley, arms raised in triumph, her hair blowing in the wind.

"Woohoo!" She cheered, the smile on her face putting a hitch in Mitch's chest.

God, she was amazing. He'd never met another woman like her. No one else could match her wit or her smart mouth or her grace on rock.

She switched to a belay stance. "Belay on!"

"Climbing."

"Climb on."

It wasn't an easy pitch, but Mitch threw everything he had into it, knowing she was watching. His performance anxiety cleared as he got into the flow, and he found himself transfixed by the challenge and amazed again at her skill. But he was a foot taller than she was, so he climbed it a bit differently, dynoing through the crux move to the roof, then catching his heel and pulling himself onto the ledge beside her.

"I knew we could do it!" She threw her arms around him.

He drew her close, the adrenaline of the climb mixed with pheromone in his blood. It was the first time he'd held her like this, and, oh, she felt sweet in his arms, the scents of sunshine and pine in her hair. And he knew that he'd remember this moment for the rest of his life.

They fixed protection then hydrated and shared trail mix, their legs dangling over the side, Yosemite Valley a thousand feet below them.

"Look." Mitch pointed to a peregrine falcon that soared below them. "We're higher than the birds. Watch it dive!"

She smiled, seeming more relaxed now than he'd ever seen her. "It would be nice to have wings."

He had to ask. "How did you get into climbing?"

"I'm from a small town not far from Pueblo, Colorado. God, I hate that place. But we did have a climbing wall in our gym at my high school. It wasn't much, and the routes never changed. But I learned the basics—how to tie into a harness, how to belay, how to rappel. My PE teacher had a hard time getting me to come down."

Mitch laughed, an image of a younger Megs refusing to climb down coming to his mind. "I bet he did."

She told him how her teacher had noticed her ability and talked to some friends who were part of the climbing scene in Boulder. They'd taken her out on weekends, reluctantly at first. Then, when they'd seen how much she loved it and how quickly she learned, she'd become a climbing partner and not just some kid who was tagging along.

"By the end of the year, I was climbing the hard stuff in Eldorado Canyon. That's where I met Dean. How about you?"

"I'm from Colorado, too."

"Really? That's crazy!"

"I was born in a little town called Scarlet Springs. It's barely a blip on the map, but I love it. My parents moved to Stanford the year I started high school. Growing up in the mountains, I saw climbers all the time. I guess it was just natural that I'd want to try it out. A friend taught me to rappel, and I was hooked."

After that, the conversation drifted from treating sunburns to favorite hiking snacks to the climbing gear they wished someone would invent. Through it all, Mitch could barely take his gaze off her face.

By the time they started their long descent, rappelling pitch by pitch, Mitch had fallen for her—hard. He'd never expected to meet a woman who loved climbing as much as he did, who lived to be in the mountains. Not only that, she was damned good.

When their feet were back on the ground, a cheer went up, and they found the dirtbags waiting for them, Gridwall looking envious, Dean with a big grin on his face.

"What are you naming it?" Dean asked.

Megs looked to Mitch. "I hadn't thought about that."

"That honor should go to you. You spotted the line."

Megs nibbled her lower lip, her brow bent as she pondered the possibilities. Then her face lit up. "How about 'Free Spirit.'"

Mitch couldn't think of any phrase that fit Megs more. God, he wanted to kiss her. "That's perfect."

━━

MEGS SAT for a moment in silence, savoring the memory of that day. She'd spent three years dreaming of putting up a first ascent on El Capitan. When she'd stood on the Mammoth Terraces, the valley stretched out below her, Mitch beside her, she'd felt triumphant. The high had been incredible—better than when she'd summitted Everest or free climbed The Nose.

And, oh, she remembered that first hug, too—the hard press of his body, the warm scent of his skin, strong arms surrounding her. For the first time in her life, she'd felt more than a teenage girl's crush. She'd felt desire.

That day had changed everything.

"Remember what happened when we got back?"

A photographer had been waiting for them in Camp 4. Sent by a newspaper to get photos of the new rock climbing fad, he'd had his lens focused on El Cap and had seen Megs standing on the Terraces, arms raised. He'd taken a few photos of her and then asked around to find out if anyone knew who she was.

"He asked so many stupid questions. 'Do you have a boyfriend? What's a pretty girl like you doing in such a rough sport? Is this your contribution to the Battle of the Sexes? Do you really think women can compete with men?'" Megs laughed. "My answer made you and the dirt-bags laugh—and shocked the hell out of him."

Since a penis doesn't work as climbing gear, yes, I do believe that women can compete with men and come out on top.

The photographer had watched her send White Lightning, heard the story about how she'd climbed it first, and had taken more photos before driving away.

"I thought that was it." She'd had no idea that the story had been published in a major paper and would start a feeding frenzy.

A trickle of reporters became a flood, all of them wanting to interview the girl climber. The attention had scared the hell out of Megs. She'd been afraid her stepfather would see the coverage, show up in that ugly green Dodge Charger of his, and try to drag her away as he'd once threatened to do outside her high school.

"You got all protective. You didn't know about my stepfather yet, but you saw that the reporters made me nervous. You took me hiking to get away from it all, and that was our first kiss. Remember?"

She turned the page to see if he'd written about it and found that his entry went on for three whole pages, all of it about her. "You're going to like this."

She reached for the recorder.

MITCH HIKED ALONGSIDE MEGS, leading her through the forest to one of the high mountain tarns he'd stumbled on last summer. Surrounded by glades of aspen and open meadow, it was the place he liked to come when he needed to be alone. He'd suggested the two of them hike up to the lake to ditch the reporters who'd been hanging around Camp 4 all week. In truth, he just wanted to be alone with her.

Lately, he'd been getting signals from her that she liked him the same way he liked her. There was something in the way she looked at him, a softness she didn't show the other guys. She sat by him in camp, shared food with him, and asked him to climb with her. But her attempts to flirt with him—if that's what she'd been doing—were shy and uncertain, lacking her usual confidence. Then again, she couldn't be much older than eighteen. She probably didn't have much experience with men.

She stepped over a tree root, her legs mostly bare, her denim cutoffs dangerously short, her shoulders and back bare apart from the ties of her halter top. She wasn't wearing a bra, either, though he supposed she was small enough that she didn't need one.

Stop thinking about her breasts.

"Those reporters act like seeing a woman rock climbing is like finding a giraffe on the moon."

Mitch chuckled, but he understood her frustration. "They think we're all crazy, but they sit at desks all day. Not a single one of them took us up on our offer to try climbing. They don't know a damned thing about it."

"Good point."

"Watch your step." He took her hand, drew her to the

side so she wouldn't step on a hornet nest in an old ground squirrel burrow.

"Those little bastards." She held onto his hand a little longer than was necessary. "Thanks."

It took them almost two hours of hiking off-trail to reach the tarn. Just as he'd hoped, there was no one else there. The lake sat in the middle of a wildflower meadow, its waters almost turquoise, pine and hemlock forest surrounding it, no sound but birds in the trees and the buzzing of insects. It was his special place.

"It's beautiful!" A look of wonder on her face, she walked slowly to the lake's edge, almost as if she were entering a church. "Look at all the flowers!"

Warmth blossomed in his chest at her reaction. By bringing her here, he was sharing a secret part of himself, offering her something that he loved. "This is where I come to read and be alone."

Megs sat on a nearby boulder, then took off her hiking boots and socks and set them aside. "You like to read?"

Was that so strange?

"I do. I always keep a book in my backpack." Mitch removed his boots and socks, too. "I get to travel the world and experience all sorts of things I wouldn't otherwise. How about you? Do you read?"

"I read when I had to in school." She walked into the water up to her ankles, moaned, the sound sending a jolt of lust through him. "Oh, that feels good."

Mitch rolled up his bellbottoms and followed her in, the cold water soothing to his feet, soft mud squishing between his toes. "Do you have any favorite authors?"

She shook her head. "I just have a GED."

Mitch bit back a smile at her assumption that being well-read meant being well-educated. "Hey, a GED is cool."

But he hadn't brought her here to talk about books.

She kept walking until the water reached her knees. "How deep is the lake?"

"I've gone in up to my chest before."

Her next question made his mind go blank.

"Have you ever gone skinny-dipping here?"

"Um…" It took him a moment. "Yes, but I was alone."

"Are you sure there are no leeches?"

He chuckled. "Yes."

"Then turn around."

His heart gave a hard knock. "Megs, I…"

She made a turning motion with her finger. "Turn around."

He did as she asked, heard her stepping through the water, blood rushing to his groin when he saw her halter top, shorts, and panties land on the rock beside her boots.

Splashing. A gasp. "This is cold!"

Thank God for that.

"Okay, now I'll turn around, and you can undress and come in."

Mitch glanced over his shoulder, saw that she was in the water up to her breasts, her back turned toward him, her hair floating behind her. He walked to the boulder, stripped down to his skin, his dick still half hard.

Naked, he turned to walk into the water—only to find her gaze raking over him. He couldn't help but grin. "That's cheating."

She stared at his cock for a moment, her cheeks flushed pink. Then she turned away. "Sorry. I couldn't resist."

Mitch wasn't ashamed of his body, and, judging from her reaction, she hadn't seen many naked men. He waded in and made his way over to her, sucking in a breath when the cold water reached his nuts, the shock of it stealing his wood. Well, that was probably a good thing. "I'm in now."

The words were out before he realized their double meaning.

He coughed.

But she hadn't picked up the double entendre, her gaze fixed on the scenery. "The view is incredible. That's the back of El Cap, isn't it?"

"Yes."

He was a foot taller than she was, and the water was almost crystal clear. He could see her breasts with their puckered, rosy tips. He ached to touch her, to run his hands all over her, to kiss her.

Damn.

She turned toward him, took a step in his direction, rested a wet palm on his chest. "What would you do if I told you to kiss me?"

He sucked in a breath. "I would—"

———

A KNOCK.

Startled, Megs jumped. "Oh, hey."

She stopped recording, tucked the receipt in the journal to hold her place.

Debby walked in, rolling a cart beside her. "His blood work for sepsis came back negative again, and his fever hasn't climbed."

Megs let out a breath. "I'm relieved."

"I've come to give Mitch a sponge bath. We do what we can to keep down pathogens. It helps reduce infection rates. Would you like to help?"

"Yes, I'd love that." Megs set the journal aside, put on a pair of gloves, and followed Debby's lead, washing Mitch's body with a warm washcloth dipped in an emesis basin full of soapy water. It felt strange to see another woman's hands on Mitch's body, but there was nothing sexual about this.

Debby worked with an efficiency born of experience. "We need to keep his incisions dry, so be careful on his abdomen."

"I'll leave that to you." Megs might be an EMT, but she'd never dealt with anything like this before.

She focused on his legs after that, working her way upward. When she came to the towel that covered his privates, she stopped, feeling strange about touching him in such an intimate place with another person present.

Debby noticed. "Would you like me to handle that?"

Megs shook her head. "No. I was hoping to have privacy. I know it probably seems silly to you, but—"

"I understand." Debby set her washcloth on the cart. "Let me know when you're finished, and I'll come get this stuff out of your way."

Megs drew the curtain, shielding Mitch from view, then removed the towel and began to wash his testicles with their dark curls and then his penis. She'd always loved this part of his body. He knew how to use it to make her scream. He'd always been an incredible lover—considerate, skilled, passionate. Not that she had any way to compare him to any other man…

She'd never been with anyone else.

It was strange and bittersweet to care for him like this just after reading about that day at the lake. It was the first time she'd seen him naked. She'd heard the dirtbags joking about his "meat" so often after the ranger raid that she'd had to see him for herself.

She remembered the sweet thrill of it so well. "I got belly flutters."

She'd only seen one other man's junk, and that hadn't been consensual. How freeing it had been to *choose* to be naked with him—and to see him nude. When she'd touched him, her heart had raced. It had been like stepping into a new world, one in which *she* had power. *She* decided who got to touch her—and where and when.

Megs couldn't help but smile, the memory so fresh in her mind now. "I had no idea you'd asked me to go with you just to be alone with me, but I did understand on some level that it was your special place. I was touched that you shared it with me."

After that day, it had become *their* special place.

Megs finished washing him, dried him, and covered him with a clean towel. Then she drew the sheet over him, thinking he might be cold from his bath. She took off her gloves, opened the curtain, and waved to Debby, who came for the cart.

"I'll be in to check the vent in a minute."

Megs thanked Debby, waited for her to finish, wanting to get back to the journal—and what she remembered came next.

Chapter 8

MEGS TURNED TOWARD MITCH, took a step in his direction, rested a wet palm on his chest. "What would you do if I said I wanted you to kiss me?"

He sucked in a breath. "I would say get closer."

He slid one arm around her, drew her against him, and watched her pupils dilate. Then he ducked down—and brushed her lips with his.

She sucked in a breath. "Do that again."

Far be it from Mitch to ignore a request like that.

This time, he cupped the back of her head with his hand and brushed his lips over hers again and again, teasing her with light kisses, until her eyes drifted shut and she stopped breathing. He drew back, chuckled. "Megs, inhale."

Her eyes flew open, and she sucked in a breath, both palms coming to rest on his chest, her touch scorching his skin even in the cool water. "Again?"

What an unusual mix of confident and unsure of herself she was—bold when she was climbing but shy about her body and sex. Mitch couldn't help but wonder if she'd never been kissed before.

"Now I'm really going to kiss you." He lowered his mouth to hers, caught her lower lip, then stroked it with his tongue.

She stiffened as if surprised, and he knew for certain that this was new to her. Then she parted her lips slightly, yielding to his tongue's exploration, her palms sliding up his chest, the contact making his pulse pound.

His tongue met hers, and she seemed to understand, her tongue now caressing his, returning stroke for stroke. He drew back for a moment, searched her face, saw only need. And that's when he lost it.

He crushed her against him and kissed her deep and hard.

She made a sound that was somewhere between a squeak and a sigh, her body melting against his, her breasts with their pebbled tips pressing against his ribs, her hands sliding behind his neck to draw him down to her. Either she had more experience than he'd imagined, or she was one hell of a fast learner.

Hunger for her surged through him, his blood going hot, his cock growing hard despite the chilly water. He wanted more of her, so much more.

He bent her head back, kissed and tasted the sensitive skin beneath her ear, inhaling her sunshine scent, nibbling his way along her throat, the fingers of his other hand slowly tracing the length of her spine. "*Megs.*"

He cupped one soft, firm buttock, instinctively rocked his hips against her, and she stiffened again. She'd felt it— his hard-on.

He took a step back. "Does that scare you?"

She didn't answer right away, seemed to consider her words.

"Not really," she said at last. "Can I touch you there?"

Hell, what was he supposed to say to that? "If you want to."

He took her hand to guide her, but she pulled it from his grasp. Okay, so she wanted to do this herself. "Go ahead. I trust you."

Her hand closed tentatively around him, moved the length of his erection, her thumb exploring the aching head.

He clenched his teeth, sucked in a breath, ragged darts of pleasure shooting through his belly.

She jerked her hand away. "Did I hurt you?"

He couldn't help but laugh, arousal hot in his veins. "No, it felt good."

She reached for him again, but this time he stopped her.

"We should stop before things go too far."

Disappointment flashed through her eyes, became defiance. "I'm not a little girl."

"Of course not, but I don't have a condom."

Her brow furrowed with confusion. "A ... what?"

Mitch couldn't believe she'd never heard the word before. Then again, he knew from some female friends he'd met at college that too many parents told their daughters next to nothing about sex. "A condom—a rubber."

Understanding dawned, her eyes going wide. "Oh. Right."

"Come." He walked back to the edge of the lake, then stepped naked onto the boulder and sat beside their clothes, the breeze raising goosebumps on his wet skin.

She stayed in the water, arms crossed over her breasts, her gaze exploring him with a sweet combination of curiosity and desire.

"Do you want me to turn around?"

She shook her head, then drew a breath as if gathering her courage. Then she lowered her arms—and walked out of the tarn.

Mitch wouldn't have been able to avert his gaze if he'd wanted to, the sight of her doing nothing to cool the heat in his blood. She was fit and slender like a dancer, her breasts tiny but firm, their taut nipples peeking through the wet ends of her hair where it clung to her skin. Her legs were long for her height, her waist narrow. The triangle of curls that covered her sex were wet, clinging to the sweet flesh beneath.

She shivered, scrambled up the boulder, and lay down on her belly beside him, her hair spilling over one shoulder. "Mmm. The rock is nice and warm."

They talked about everything except what had just happened. The weather. Megs' job. What they might climb together next. Whether God was real or a myth created by people to explain the universe when they didn't understand science.

Mitch took a chance. "I believe God is real."

"I don't. If God is there, why does He or She let so much awful shit happen? How can there be God and Nazis in the same universe?"

"I don't know. It doesn't make sense." Mitch found himself looking into her gray eyes and feeling completely lost. "I guess some things aren't meant to be understood."

Then clouds moved in, threatening rain. As they dressed and began the long hike back to Camp 4, Mitch knew he was in trouble.

He was head-over-heels in love with Megs.

MEGS CLOSED the journal and took a bathroom break. As she washed her hands, she stared at her reflection. "Damn, girl, you were clueless."

Mitch had always been so perceptive. She'd wanted to seem like an adult, a sophisticated woman who knew what she was doing, like one of those naked women in the *Playboy* magazines her stepfather had left in her room. But Mitch had seen through her façade to the confused teenager inside.

Megs had never been close to her mother. After her father's death when Megs was seven, her mother had become distant. All she'd taught Megs was that a man's penis went into a woman's vagina, and then a baby came out—as if a woman's body were a vending machine that took dicks instead of dimes.

Megs had been nine when her mother remarried. Wayne, her new husband, hadn't paid Megs much attention at first, though he hadn't been shy about using his belt when he thought she'd done something wrong. But then she'd gotten older, and Wayne's attitude had changed. By the time she was twelve, she was doing all she could to avoid him.

Rot in hell, Wayne.

The girl Mitch had met had been caught between unwelcome knowledge—and the complete lack of it. Megs had heard of rubbers at school, of course, but she didn't understand how they prevented pregnancy. She'd known what an erection was but not that it could serve her enjoyment. She'd known that men could be dangerous. But when it came to the emotional and physical nuances of sex —consent, foreplay, the many ways to give and receive pleasure—she'd known nothing.

Luckily for her, Mitch had been an excellent teacher.

Megs dried her hands, left the restroom, and made her way to the cafeteria for a late lunch. The sun was shining, so she decided to sit outside. She wasn't used to being cooped up indoors for so long.

The fresh air was invigorating, the grilled chicken salad not so much. She picked at it, trying to decide whether she could stand another bite of wilted lettuce or prefabricated grilled chicken strips when her phone buzzed.

Rain.

Megs took the call. "How's my favorite Deadhead?"

"I'm doing well. Thanks. We're all doing well. We're just worried about you and Mitch. I don't want to take too much of your time, but I thought you'd like an update."

"Sure."

"Everyone here wants to help somehow, so Joe has set up a kind of fundraiser."

Megs started to object, but Rain cut her off.

"I know you're about to tell me that the two of you have savings and you don't need the help. But you don't know where this will end—how long Mitch will be in the hospital and rehab or whether you'll need to modify your home."

Hell, Megs hadn't even thought of that. "Shit."

"I know. It's a lot to handle. But if you don't end up needing the money, you can donate it to the Team or St. Barbara's or go on a vacation to the Bahamas."

Megs was touched. "I guess I've just been focused on the moment. Thanks for thinking ahead for us."

"You bet. Everyone wants to get in on it. Frank put up a jar at his filling station. Father Ted at St. Barbara's passed the plate a second time at Mass, asking for donations. Sasha, Conrad, and Gabe Rossiter are giving climbing lessons at the rock gym in exchange for donations. I think Sasha's schedule filled up the first five minutes. The Timberline Mudbugs made a mixtape of Mitch's favorite tunes that I'll bring when I come to see you next. They're doing a special concert in Boulder next week. All of the proceeds will go to Mitch."

"Wow."

But there was more.

Rain told her how Kenzie, Conrad's wife, a professional search dog trainer, was doing a raffle for free puppy training. Jason Chiago, a former Shadow Wolf, was working with the US Marshals on their own fundraiser, offering tracking classes.

"He hasn't forgotten that the Team saved Winona's life last year," Rain said.

Naomi Belcourt, a Lakota artist and Chaska's wife, was running an auction for a few of her signature jewelry pieces. And Bear had put money someone had given him for a meal into the donation jar on the bar.

"We fed him anyway."

Of course, they had.

Megs was overwhelmed. She knew that the people of Scarlet Springs were big-hearted, but she hadn't grown up in Scarlet like Mitch had. She'd never experienced this kind of close community until they'd moved there in the early Nineties to start the Team.

She swallowed the lump in her throat. "That's incredibly generous."

She was especially touched by Bear's donation. He'd grown up by himself in the mountains after a fever had killed off his family. That same fever had left him with brain damage. He was big and had a bushy beard—hence the nickname. But he was as gentle as a child and as poor as a monk.

"Hey, we take care of our own. Oh, I almost forgot.

Rose is giving free tarot and aura readings in exchange for a donation of twenty dollars or more."

That last one made Megs laugh. Rose was the town's psychic, astrologer, tarot card reader, past-life therapist, sex toy consultant, and lead gossip. She dressed like a runner-up at a Stevie Nicks costume contest. Mitch had always described her as a flower child who didn't know that the Sixties were officially over. Still...

"Please let them know how grateful I am for everyone's generosity and support. This would be so much harder if it weren't for their kindness. And thanks to you and Joe for that hotel room. It's been a godsend."

"I'm so glad to hear that."

Megs shared what positive news she had. "The fever isn't sepsis or infection. Also, the doctor ran a special kind of scan that showed a big increase in Mitch's brain activity while he was listening to my voice. Even I could see the difference between the scans. When he hears my voice, his brain just lights up."

"Oh, Megs! That chokes me up. Even in a coma, he knows your voice."

"Thanks so much for that recorder and for bringing the journal. It's been an interesting trip down memory lane."

"You're welcome! Please let us know if you need anything else."

"Will do. Thanks." Megs ended the call, dumped her lunch into the compost bin, and rode the elevator back upstairs, eager to return to Mitch and his journal.

MITCH SAT in the passenger seat of Dean's van as they drove into the Village for supplies, *D'yer Maker* from Led Zeppelin's latest blasting on Dean's eight-track player, the two of them singing along. They parked outside the Village store and walked inside. Mitch took a small cart and began filling it with canned food, soap, dish soap, toilet paper, and other necessaries. But he hadn't seen the one thing he'd hoped to buy.

Condoms.

They weren't with the medicine. They weren't with the women's hygiene products. They weren't with the toothpaste.

He and Megs had spent the past few days making out every time they got the chance, sneaking away from camp to kiss and talk. He'd kissed her in every way he could, kissed her until he thought he might spontaneously combust, until she'd pleaded for more. But he'd made sure their clothes stayed on. It was hard to stay in control once the heavy petting started, and he didn't want to put their futures at risk by getting her pregnant. They wanted to climb, not change diapers.

He *had* to find condoms.

He walked up to the counter, glanced over his shoulder to make sure Dean wasn't listening. "Do you sell condoms?"

The man, a heavyset older guy with a gray crewcut, looked disapprovingly down at Mitch and pointed. "They're in the men's room."

Mitch turned to walk in that direction.

"Hey!" The man held out a meaty hand. "Leave the cart here. You're going to need change—fifty cents each."

Mitch put a five-dollar bill into the man's palm and got three dollar bills and eight quarters in change. "Thanks."

He walked into the men's room, saw the dispenser on the wall. It offered three types, each one accompanied by cartoon images of half-naked, big-breasted women with eyes closed and mouths open. Arouse. Sensation. Pandora's Box.

"Hell." The last time he'd bought condoms, he'd been at a pharmacy, and they'd come in packages with information on the box. He wasn't sure what he'd be getting today —or how good they would be. With no idea which was better, he bought one of each and was just picking them out of the dispenser when Dean walked in.

Mitch quickly slipped the packets into his pocket. "Hey."

"Hey." Dean headed to the urinal and unzipped his fly. If he'd noticed the condoms, he didn't say anything about it.

Mitch walked back to the register and paid for his supplies. He was waiting by Dean's van when Dean walked out.

They headed back toward Camp 4.

Dean glanced over. "You're spending a lot of time alone with Megs."

So, he *had* noticed the condoms.

Damn.

Mitch wasn't about to expose Megs to any shame. "She's a fantastic climber. She's also a lot prettier than the rest of you."

Dean grinned. "Just be careful. She's young, and she's been through a lot."

Mitch looked over at his friend. "How do you know so much about her?"

"We weren't involved, if that's what you're thinking."

That hadn't been what Mitch was thinking, but it was good to hear again anyway. "Then what's your interest?"

"She's just a friend. She and I spent about six weeks camped close to each other in Joshua Tree. The Rangers came through and asked to see our IDs. They asked Megs a lot of questions. I just happened to overhear. She made me promise not to say anything to anyone, so that's all you're getting from me."

Mitch wondered if she truly was on parole. But that made no sense. Megs was the responsible one in the group. She had the job, the steady paycheck. How would she be able to get a job if she'd been arrested or done time?

By the time they got back to Camp 4, Mitch had half convinced himself that Megs had done something stupid as a kid and been arrested, and now the police were keeping tabs on her. Maybe that's why she had a GED instead of a high school diploma. He didn't think they let kids take classes in juvie.

Should he feel differently about her now?

No. Everyone deserved a second chance. Hell, he'd done a few things as a teen that might have landed him in jail. Like the time he'd strung TP all over his science teacher's house and trees. Or the time he'd strapped a dead fish to the bottom of that same teacher's chair so that the classroom reeked of rotten fish. Or the time he'd checked out more library books than the rules allowed and returned them late.

He climbed out of Dean's vehicle, saw that Megs' car was gone. She must have already left for work. The guys were gathered around the table, their heads bent together as if they were studying a map or something,

He walked toward his tent, carrying two paper bags, his mind on Megs. He'd just stowed his canned goods away when Gridwall bounded over to him, clearly tripping on acid, a huge grin on his face.

"She's not on parole." He shook his head, repeated himself three or four times. "Little Meggie's not on parole."

"What the hell are you talking about?"

Gridwall burst into laughter, his pupils dilated, a broad grin on his face. "She's sixteen! She outclimbs us, and she's fucking sixteen!"

Adrenaline rushed to Mitch's head. "What are you talking about?"

"After she left, Accardo and I searched her tent, got out those papers."

"You did *what*?" Mitch was on his feet now, rage hot in his chest, pulse thrumming.

"We had to find out if we were dealing with a murderer, man." Gridwall shrugged, as if breaking into another person's belongings could be justified. "The papers say she's an emancipated minor. There's some kind of case number—charges against her stepfather for sexual abuse."

Mitch's fist struck Gridwall in the mouth, and the bastard hit the ground. Mitch bent over him, knuckles stinging. "You do *not* break into other people's tents, go through their shit, and share their secrets with everyone. What the hell is wrong with you? Have you forgotten that you have a secret, too?"

Mitch didn't wait for an answer but stomped over to the table, where the dirtbags sat in silence, eyes wide. "You're lucky I don't knock your teeth out, too, Accardo."

Dean ripped the papers out of Accardo's hand, gave them to Mitch. "Megs is going to be devastated when she learns that everyone here knows."

"I can't blame her." Mitch took the documents. "If any of you brings this up or throws this in her face, I'll beat the living shit out of you. Got it?"

Heads nodded.

Gridwall walked over, his lip bloody. "Are you going to call the cops on me?"

"I should, but unlike you, I'm not an asshole." He

carried the papers back toward Megs' tent, resolved not to look. But some part of him couldn't help it.

There, near the top of the page, were the words *Emancipated Minor*. And in the middle of the document he saw it —her full name and her birthday.

Margaret Anne Hill, October 24, 1956.

Chapter 9

MEGS TUCKED the receipt into place and closed the journal, moved by this private side of the man she loved—his thoughts about her, his reflections, his deep, dark secrets. "You borrowed more books than you were allowed—and you turned them in late? You bad, bad man."

God, what a rough night that had been. She'd gone to the Village early to do laundry at the employee lodge, take a shower, and shave her legs in hopes of finally having sex that night. Then she'd had a lousy evening at work because some jerk had grabbed her butt, and the manager had refused to do a damned thing about it.

"When I got back to camp, it was quiet. I should have known something was wrong, but all I could think about was you." Megs stroked his arm, his muscles firm beneath her palm. "I'd never felt closer to anyone in my life. I'd never felt as safe with anyone as I did with you."

She'd certainly never felt as horny. After that day at the lake, she'd lain awake fantasizing about Mitch every night, filling in the sexual blanks with nonsense. It seemed to her that she was on top of the world. Her life was finally coming together. All the pieces had seemed to fit—Mitch, climbing, escaping her past.

That night it had all come crashing down—at least for a time.

She had put her duffel bag of clean laundry in her tent, changed into shorts and a T-shirt, and had gone looking for Mitch. "I saw Gridwall with his split lip. I thought he was acting stranger than usual, but it was hard to tell. You know him. He's odd on a good day. He told me he'd fallen and hit his mouth on a rock, and I believed him."

Then Mitch had crawled out of his tent, and she'd known the moment she'd seen his face that something was wrong.

"You took my hand and told me we needed to talk. All I could think was that I'd done something to make you angry."

The truth had been much darker.

"You tried so hard to break the news gently." Megs hadn't taken it well. "I felt violated, completely humiliated, exposed, ashamed. Not only had they gotten into my tent, but everyone knew the truth about my age—and why I'd had to leave home."

Of course, no one had known *precisely* what her stepfather had done, but the sordid details didn't matter. The case number was on the court document alongside the phrase "sexual assault on a minor by a person in a position of trust."

Then Mitch had given her even worse news.

"When you told me we couldn't have sex until I turned eighteen, I couldn't believe it. I thought you didn't want me any longer and were making excuses. You had to explain statutory rape laws and 'age of consent.'"

God, she'd been naïve, ignorant—a child.

"When I reminded you that I was an emancipated minor and free to make my own decisions, you told me that didn't change anything, at least not when it came to California's consent laws."

Megs had tried to tell him that it didn't matter, that she wouldn't report him. But Mitch wouldn't hear it. "You told me that it didn't matter if no one found out. If the state deemed it a crime for you to have sex with someone under eighteen, you felt honor-bound to respect that."

Megs had been so hurt and enraged that she'd crawled out of his tent, broken down her tent, shoved everything into her frame pack, and hiked away from Camp 4, the flashlight in her hand her only source of light.

Mitch had come after her, tried to stop her. She could still hear his voice.

Megs, honey, it's not safe out there after dark! There are mountain lions!

But something about that night had stolen her sense of safety and the new self-image she'd wrapped around herself like a shield. She'd felt naked, betrayed, and utterly alone. Except that she hadn't been alone.

"You packed up your gear and followed me. You kept your distance, but you followed me. After I set up my tent, you said my name and stepped out from behind the trees, pack on your back. I was too damned tired to hike any longer. You walked over, took me into your arms, and held me while I lost it."

It was the first time she'd cried in front of anyone since she was little.

"That's when I saw your bloody knuckles. You told me you'd punched Gridwall." Megs raised Mitch's hand to her lips, kissed those knuckles. "That might be why I fell in love with you. No one had ever stood up for me like that."

He'd been her hero that night—and every night from

then on. What he'd gotten out of their relationship was still a mystery to her.

"You thought I was an adult woman, but I was still a kid. You thought I was hot, but I was just a hot mess. Most guys would have walked away, but you stayed and waited until…"

Megs stopped, studied Mitch. It took a moment for what she was seeing to sink in, and when it did, adrenaline hit her bloodstream in a rush. "Oh, God!"

His eyes were open.

"Mitch? Can you hear me? His eyes are open!" Megs ran out of his room, her gaze seeking Debby, her heart thudding. "Mitch opened his eyes!"

⸺

MEGS STOOD IN THE HALLWAY, hands shaking, while Mitch's medical team examined him. She fished her phone out of her pocket and texted Rain to let her know that Mitch had opened his eyes.

I don't know if he's out of the coma, but I will keep you posted.

Rain replied immediately.

That's great news! Please let us know.

After what seemed an eternity, Dr. Schwartz walked over to her, his expression giving nothing away. He gestured toward the private room at the end of the hall.

When the door was shut, he smiled. "Mitch has moved into a vegetative state."

Adrenaline made her head buzz. "He's a ... vegetable?"

"It's all in the brochures I gave you." Dr. Schwartz explained. "Generally, as a person with TBI begins to regain consciousness, they move from a coma into a vegetative state. It doesn't mean he's a 'vegetable' in the colloquial sense. It's a *good* sign. The majority of people in a vegetative state within a month of a brain injury regain consciousness within a year. Mitch got there in forty-eight hours. That doesn't mean he'll keep progressing at this rate. He could still face complications. He could still die. But I'd say this gives us another reason to hope."

Megs inhaled, refusing to cry. "Thank you."

"We're going to start physical therapy, working to keep his muscles from getting tight. We will also start turning him, changing his position every few hours to prevent pressure sores. Depending on how the next few days go, we might also put in a feeding tube and try weaning him off the ventilator."

"What can I do to help?"

"You can help with his stretching exercises. The most important thing is that you keep talking to him, touching him, letting him know you're there."

Megs nodded. "I can do that."

When Mitch was back from his CT scan, Riana, his physical therapist, arrived and taught Megs how to stretch major muscle groups without aggravating any of Mitch's injuries or incisions. Then Debby and a few other nurses carefully turned Mitch onto his side, using pillows to ensure that his head and neck remained safely positioned.

When they were gone, Megs moved her chair so that she could see his face. His eyes were still open, and he blinked at regular intervals. Even so, his gaze wasn't focused on anything.

Still, progress was progress.

She sent an update to Rain, then put her phone away.

"I haven't seen those brown eyes of yours in what feels like forever." She caressed his arm. "Thank you, Mitch, for fighting so hard. Please keep fighting."

She told him what everyone in Scarlet was doing to help. "Can you imagine being a newbie climber and getting lessons from Sasha, a five-time world champion? They have no idea how lucky they are. People love you, Mitch. I'm not the only one."

Debby left for the day, and Jackie began her shift.

Then Kurt came. He stopped first in the room with the parents whose young son was so badly injured. Then he came to check on Mitch.

Megs shared the good news. "He opened his eyes."

The smile that came to Kurt's face was genuine. "That's great news."

But no sooner had Kurt arrived than he was paged away. He offered another prayer, this time thanking God for Mitch's improvement.

"Does it bother you that I don't believe in your god?" Megs asked afterward.

Kurt shook his head, gave her a warm smile. "The most important thing is that God believes in you."

His words gave her goosebumps. She had no idea what the hell that even meant, but somehow it touched her.

"I need to go." He rested a hand on Megs' shoulder. "I'll check in again."

"Thank you, Kurt."

Afternoon became evening. Vent care. Oral care. X-rays. Changing IV bags. Stretches. Turning Mitch. What had seemed so foreign to Megs two days ago was now the new normal, the daily routine. She decided to eat at the hotel and not risk another meal at the cafeteria. Still, she didn't want to leave just yet.

"How about one more story?" She scanned through the next few entries, laughed, reached for the recorder. "Oh, yes. The great waiting game."

———

DARKNESS. Pain. Emptiness. Shadows.

But there was also light now.

Mitch drifted, rudderless, his mind empty, some part of him reaching in wordless desperation for the light, for the sound of her voice. It carried him like a warm current, lifted him up, filled the emptiness, chased the darkness away.

———

MITCH AND MEGS stayed at their private camping spot for several days. They climbed together, shared meals, and talked. Occasionally, they kissed, but Mitch did his best to ensure it was rated PG and not R.

God, it was hell keeping his hands off her.

When she was ready to face the others, they hiked back to Camp 4.

He did his best to encourage her. "Just remember that you didn't do anything wrong in any of this."

She walked into camp, chin up. "I might punch Gridwall, too."

"Let me know if you want me to hold him."

That made her smile.

But Gridwall and Accardo were gone, apparently too ashamed of themselves to hang around. The others did their best to act as if nothing had happened. But something *had* changed. The men had quit making sexual jokes about her or teasing her for being a girl—at least when Mitch was around.

Dean welcomed Megs back with a big hug. "Glad to have you back. Don't let these knuckleheads get to you, okay?"

Megs had regained her sharp tongue. "I make no promises in that regard."

Dean held up his keys. "I'm driving to my brother's place in SF to pick up a new tent I ordered. I'll see you two when I get back."

"Mind if I tag along?" Mitch had an idea.

"That would be cool."

Megs' expression fell. "I wish I could go, too. But I have to be at work at five-thirty, and there's no way you'll be back by then."

Mitch hugged her. "Don't worry about these guys. Just do your own thing. I'll be here when you get back from work—and I'll have a present for you."

Her face lit up. "A present?"

"You'll see." He kissed her cheek and walked with Dean to his van.

"Drive safe!" she called after them.

Dean popped in an eight-track. "This is Peter Frampton. The album just came out toward the end of last year. He's pretty good."

"I want to thank you."

"For what?"

"For keeping your promise to Megs. For not telling me when I asked about her. I hate that I found out the truth the way I did. She was hurt enough as it was, but it would have been much worse if that betrayal had come from you."

Dean grinned. "For a college boy, you're pretty smart."

Music blasting, they left Yosemite behind, heading almost due west. Three and a half hours later, they pulled up in front of Dean's brother's house. Three small children burst out of the front door and ran toward them.

"Uncle Dean!"

Dean climbed out of the van, scooped up his niece and nephews, and gave them hugs. "How are my favorite rug rats?"

He introduced Mitch to his brother, Chris, and his sister-in-law, Renee, then disappeared in the back with his brother to retrieve the tent.

"I hope the two of you will stay for dinner," Renee said when Dean returned, large box in hand. "I'm roasting a chicken."

"We probably ought to get back."

Mitch was about to object, his mind on that roast chicken, but Chris beat him to it.

"Are the rocks going to turn into pumpkins if you're not back before midnight?" Chris asked. "Take some time for family. The kids are happy to see you."

Dean caved. "Okay. You're right. Thanks. We'd love to stay."

Mitch reminded Dean that he had his own mission. "I need to buy something for Megs. Is there a cool bookstore nearby—someplace hip?"

Dean chuckled. "Hey, man, you're in San Francisco."

With promises to return with a bottle of Chardonnay, Mitch and Dean left to find a bookstore, ending up at a collective on 17th and Sanchez.

Dean dropped Mitch off. "I probably shouldn't go in. See you here in thirty."

Inside, Mitch found a hippie haven. The walls were covered with images of Che Guevara, Angela Davis, and

Karl Marx on its walls amid peace signs, posters with anti-war slogans, and blacklight posters.

He looked around, tried to orient himself.

"Hey, baby killer!"

He didn't realize the man was talking to him until someone walked up behind him and repeated the slur. "Hey, baby killer! What are you doing in our store?"

Baby killer?

His short hair. The guy thought he was military.

Mitch turned around to find a skinny guy with long, dark hair in a Kerouac T-shirt and faded bellbottom jeans. There was a faint whiff of grass around him—and a look of intense dislike on his face.

Now Mitch understood why Dean hadn't come inside.

Mitch could have told the guy that he'd never been in the military, that his short hair was just his preference because he lived in a tent all summer, but that would feel like a betrayal of the men, like Dean, who had served. "I'm here to buy books—something by Walt Whitman and that new book for women out of Boston. I think it's called 'Our Bodies, Ourselves.'"

A dark eyebrow rose.

Apparently, Mitch's literary choices had passed muster, even if his haircut hadn't.

The man pointed. "Poetry is over there. The women's section is in the back."

Mitch grabbed a used copy of *Leaves of Grass* and a brand new copy of *Our Bodies, Ourselves*. He'd learned about the book from one of his friends at school. She'd let him borrow it for a night, and he'd learned a lot from it.

Then he noticed a new release titled *My Secret Garden*, a collection of women's sexual fantasies. Hell, he might want to read this one. He grabbed it, too.

Mitch paid, thanked the man, and walked outside, just

as Dean pulled up in front. Mitch opened the passenger side door and climbed in.

"Did anyone hassle you?"

"No." Mitch didn't repeat what the asshole had called him. He knew it would hurt his friend. "I got what I came for."

"Good. I'm dying for that roast chicken."

Dinner aside, Mitch couldn't wait to get back to camp. It was time that Megs got the education about her body that every girl deserved.

Chapter 10

MEGS LEFT Mitch's side to head back to the hotel, unable to get the smile off her face—until a reporter rushed her in the parking lot.

"I'm from Chalk and Rock webzine. How is Mitch Ahearn doing?" The young woman held up a smartphone, clearly filming. "Do doctors expect him to survive? Do you think he'll live a normal life? Will he climb again?"

It took all of Megs' self-control not to tell the reporter to fuck herself. Instead, she ignored the questions and walked quickly to her vehicle, the reporter following her, camera still raised, heels clicking on asphalt.

"Is it true that he's going to be a vegetable now? The sheriff's report said you were lead climbing when Mitch was injured. Megs, were you the person who knocked off the piece of rock that hit him?"

That last question struck Megs square in the chest.

She whirled on the reporter. "Jesus tap-dancing Christ!"

She grabbed the phone, deleted the video file.

"Hey, you can't do that! That's mine! Give it back!"

The reporter was several inches taller than Megs and lunged for her.

Megs side-stepped her. "You can't harass me on hospital property."

A security guard had seen them and jogged toward them.

"To answer you, no, I didn't knock down the rock that struck Mitch. It came from somewhere above me, hit the Roofs of Mordor, and broke into pieces, one of which struck Mitch. I was protected by the roof. He was further down, more exposed. But none of that means anything to you, does it? You're not a climber. Those long, fake, glittery nails give that away."

The security guard reached them. "What's going on here?"

"She took my phone and deleted my interview!"

Megs handed the phone back. "My partner is a patient in the ICU, and I didn't consent to an interview. She's harassing me."

The security guard pointed toward the parking lot exit. "This is private property, miss, and you're trespassing. You need to leave, or I'll have you arrested."

"Thank you, Officer." While the woman spluttered and raged about the First Amendment, Megs climbed into her vehicle and drove the short distance to the hotel, pulse still racing, her face hot with anger. "Damn it!"

Back in her hotel room, she took a shower to cool down and wash the smell of the hospital off her skin. When she was calm, she ordered from room service and booted up her laptop. She'd spent the past two days ignoring a world that wanted answers. The hospital press conferences weren't enough. Unless the climbing community heard directly from her, reporters like this one would keep showing up.

But she wasn't going to do this their way.

She called the *Scarlet Springs Gazette* and left a message for Wendy, offering her an exclusive interview. Then she updated their social media accounts.

```
"Mitch is improving ahead of expectations.
We are grateful to the medical staff for
the excellent care he is receiving. We
have a long journey ahead of us, but we
have many reasons for hope. Thank you for
your good wishes. Also, I was accosted in
the hospital parking lot this evening by a
reporter from Chalk and Rock webzine, who
asked insensitive questions and was
removed by security. I understand that
people are curious about Mitch's accident,
but I will not answer questions just
because a stranger claiming to be a
reporter chases me with a smartphone.
Chalk and Rock should be ashamed. The
climbing community is better than this.
Meanwhile, we thank you for your continued
support, and we ask that you respect our
privacy."
```

Little good that would do.

She'd just put her empty supper dishes outside her door when her phone buzzed. "Hey, Wendy."

"I just got your message. First, I want to say how sorry I am—how sorry we all are—about Mitch's accident."

"Thanks. I appreciate that. Do you have a few minutes?" Megs told Wendy that the only way she would be able to counter speculation was to give someone the whole story. "I want that someone to be you and the

Gazette. You're our hometown paper, and you haven't been chasing me through parking lots."

"Good grief! Don't tell me someone did that."

"Yes, just a short time ago. That's why I'm going on the offensive."

"What can I do?"

Megs spent the next hour going over the climb and Mitch's accident in excruciating detail, including the gear they'd used and how she'd self-rescued to that ledge while awaiting the Team. She left the details about Mitch's condition vague for the sake of his dignity. "He's in a coma, but he is showing signs of regaining consciousness."

She thanked everyone in Scarlet for their donations and for all the ways they were contributing to Mitch's recovery. "I want to give a special shout-out to the Team for helping the rangers at the Black Canyon to rescue him, and to Rain and Joe, who stepped up immediately to help and have made this hard time so much easier."

Wendy asked a few clarifying questions. "Can I steal photos from your websites, or do you want me to drive down to take a photo of you?"

"Please steal. The Team website has some great photos of Mitch, too."

"I can't get this in tomorrow's paper. We've already put it to bed. This will be on the front page of the Gazette the day after. Thank you, Megs, for trusting me and for reaching out. I'm sorry other reporters have been assholes. It isn't part of the job description, despite what you must think."

"I know—and thanks." Megs ended the call and got ready for bed.

She was dog-tired as she crawled beneath the covers, but it was a long time before she fell asleep.

———

MITCH KISSED MEGS TO WAKEFULNESS, his lips doing amazing things to hers.

She opened her eyes, saw that he was young again. "But you're hurt. You're in ICU in a vegetative state."

He gave her a smile that made her melt. "This is an erotic dream."

Okay, then. "Bring it on."

He kissed her long and deep and slow. She relaxed into it, ran her hands up his chest and over his shoulders, savoring the hard feel of his muscles.

He was strong. He'd always been strong.

One callused hand found an aching nipple and teased her until she wanted more. Then he kissed his way down her throat and took that same nipple into his mouth, groaning as he began to suckle her.

Her hips jerked, pleasure building deep in her belly. Aching for him, she reached for his cock, found him hard and ready for her. "Fuck me."

"Glad to." He nudged her thighs apart, angling his hips and thrusting slowly forward as she guided him inside her.

God, it felt good.

They moaned in unison as he moved, his cock filling her, stretching her. But no matter how hard he drove into her and no matter how aroused she became, she couldn't seem to come.

Mitch's gaze met hers. "It's just an erotic dream. Remember?"

Just a dream.

Megs awoke with a jerk to find herself alone and incredibly horny, an unbearable ache in her heart—and between her thighs.

Mitch.

It had seemed so real, as if he'd truly been there, kissing her, touching her, making love to her. But he was still in the ICU, fighting to live.

She closed her eyes, reached down to touch herself, trying to bring the dream back. Mitch wouldn't mind. Of that, she was certain. He's the one who'd encouraged her to masturbate, after all.

She imagined him there, pounding into her, her climax coming hard and fast. But there was emptiness in its wake —no Mitch to laugh with or to hold her. Nothing but cold, harsh reality.

She glanced at the clock on the nightstand, saw that it was just after six. She got up, took another shower, and ordered breakfast—an egg white omelet, sliced fruit, and coffee. She ate, dressed, and headed back to the hospital, this time parking near the ER and not outside the main entrance.

When she reached the ICU, she found the room with the young boy empty, the bed made. Had he gotten better or… She remembered the anguish on his parents' faces and decided she didn't want to know.

Mitch was in a semi-sitting position, the head of his bed raised, his eyes closed, the earbuds in his ears, the recorder playing.

She removed the earbuds, turned off the recorder, and leaned close to avoid being overheard by nurses standing near his door. "I had the most erotic dream about you. I had to take matters into my own hands afterward. I got so turned on—"

A beautiful black nurse with long braids walked into the room. "I'm Fabiola, an RN here in ICU. I'll be Mitch's nurse today while Debby's off. I hear you've been helping Riana with his PT exercises and making recordings for him. That's great."

It didn't feel like much to Megs. "How's he doing?"

"He's still running that fever, but his intracranial pressure is slowly dropping. That's what we like to see."

"He opened his eyes yesterday, but they're closed now. Does that mean he's going backward?"

Fabiola shook her head. "It's normal for people in vegetative states to revert to a normal sleep schedule. He'll probably open his eyes again here soon. I'll be back to tend his vent shortly. There's fresh coffee if you'd like some."

"Hell, yes. Thanks." Megs made her way to the coffee pot, poured herself a cup, and walked back to Mitch's bedside.

She picked up the journal and recorder and sat in the chair beside him. "As I was saying, that dream turned me on so much that I had to handle things myself. I would much rather have been with you."

She skimmed through the next several entries, laughing to herself. "You poor thing! You could've just gone and gotten yourself laid, especially when you went back to college. But you waited for me to turn eighteen."

It dawned on her that perhaps he *had* gotten laid and hadn't told her.

How would she feel if she discovered in his journal that he'd had a few one-night stands while he was away?

It wasn't like Mitch to lie or omit something important.

Except that he *had* lied to Dean about the hostile hippie in the bookstore.

Megs didn't have to think hard. If it turned out that Mitch had hooked up with women while he was away for his senior year, she would forgive him. She wouldn't even mention it to him. He'd promised her that he wouldn't date or have sex with anyone else, but that would be a tough promise to keep at the age of twenty-one. Besides, she'd been the only woman in his life since her eighteenth birthday, the two of them spending virtually every moment together. *That* was what mattered.

She chose an entry, smiling to herself. "Thus begins the Education of Ms. Megs Hill."

———

MITCH SAT NEXT TO MEGS, who lay on her belly in her tent reading *Our Bodies, Ourselves* by lantern light. She had burned through the first several chapters, which touched on healthcare, exercise, drugs and alcohol, mental health, and healthy relationships.

"The health stuff isn't very interesting. I know I have to brush my teeth. But the relationship stuff—that's pretty deep. I hadn't thought of those things. I guess I only had my mother's fucked-up relationship with my stepfather as a model."

"What about your real father?"

"He died in a car accident when I was seven."

"I'm so sorry." Mitch waited for her to say more, but she didn't. "What's the next chapter about?"

"Chapter Eleven is about sexuality." She turned the page. "Sex with ourselves: Mastur… Mastur…"

"Masturbation."

She looked up at him, both amused and confused. "How can people have sex with themselves?"

He tapped the open book. "Read."

She shifted her gaze back to the page, read that section, and then moved on to the next one, which was titled *Orgasm*, the baffled look on her face telling him she had zero experience. "People touch themselves, and it gives them this orgasm thing."

He wouldn't laugh. He *wouldn't*. "Yes. It's more common to talk about men doing it. Haven't you ever heard someone use the term *jack off*?"

She nodded. "That's what that means?"

"Yes."

"Do you jack off?"

Mitch coughed. "Sometimes."

He did it a lot more often since meeting her, but he kept that to himself.

"Have you had sex with someone besides yourself?"

Mitch nodded. "I had a girlfriend my sophomore year of college."

"Did she jack off, too?"

Mitch tried hard not to laugh. "I never asked, but I bet she did."

Megs turned the page again and found a labeled anatomical drawing of women's genitalia and a chapter about the clitoris. Pink crept into her cheeks. "It's embarrassing to read this with you sitting there."

Mitch chuckled. "That's one sign that you're not yet ready for sex."

She looked indignant. "What does that mean?"

How could he explain this without feeling like a dirty old man? He wasn't grooming her for sex—though he could see how someone might think that. She wouldn't be eighteen for a while yet, and she needed to know this stuff regardless of whether she had sex with him in the end or not. He was giving her a chance to learn what no one had taught her from an authoritative source. He just also happened to be attracted to her—and in love with her.

Yeah, watch yourself, buddy.

He tried to explain in very mild and general terms. "For both people to find pleasure in sex, they have to be able to talk about stuff like this. If you can't talk about sex, you're not going to enjoy it."

"Really?" Clearly, this made no sense to her.

"You need to know what you like, and you have to be

able to tell your partner. Otherwise, he's just guessing. Every woman is different."

"Don't men just know what to do? I mean, isn't it obvious?"

"Sex isn't something I do *to* you, Megs. It's something we do together—and for each other." He tried to find an example. "It's like making someone dinner. If you don't like liver and onions and I keep making you liver and onions, you're not going to be happy. You need to tell me what you like so I can make that instead."

"I hate liver and onions."

He laughed. "Good to know."

She seemed to accept his explanation and went back to reading. She was focused on it now, her brow furrowed in concentration. Mitch read the subject headings upside down. Communicating About Sex. Exploring Lovemaking. Oral Sex. Anal Stimulation. Intercourse. After Lovemaking. Variations in Lovemaking.

"This is complicated." She turned the page—and froze.

Rape and Sexual Assault.

It was Mitch's first impulse to close the book and tell her that she'd read enough for one night, but he held himself back, waited.

"I'm not as innocent as you think. If you read those documents, then you know."

"I only glanced at them when I put them back in your tent. I saw that there was a case against your stepfather for hurting you."

"Wayne didn't hurt me—not really." She kept her gaze on the page, her voice neutral. "He used to touch me in places he shouldn't or walk in when I was in the shower and look me over. There were lots of times he touched me through my clothes—between my legs or on my butt or my chest—and then pretended it was an accident. I would push his hand away or tell him to stop. He acted like I was crazy."

Mitch tried to keep his voice calm. "What did your mother do?"

"When I told her, she slapped me and told me to stop dressing like a tramp."

"Jesus." That was despicable.

"Then Wayne came into my bedroom one night and pulled his … penis out of his pajama bottoms. He grabbed my wrist and forced me to touch him. Then he told me to lift my T-shirt and pull down my panties. I kicked and hit him and screamed for my mother. She found him half-naked on my bed—and threw me out of the house. She called me a slut and said the problems in her marriage were *my* fault."

Mitch struggled to take this in, rage hot in his veins. "Oh, Megs. None of that was your fault. He *did* hurt you. He was supposed to be a father to you, and instead, he abused you. So did your mother. She ought to have thrown *him* out."

Mitch stopped himself from saying more. Megs didn't need his anger. She needed him to listen. "Where did you go?"

"I went to my school and climbed up to an open window on the second floor."

Mitch grinned. "Of course you did."

She smiled, too. "I slept in the library. One of the teachers found me. She asked what had happened and called the police. She got me in touch with a friend of hers, a judge. The judge listened to me, told me about emancipation, and eventually granted my request to become an emancipated minor. That's how I was able to drop out of school and get my GED at sixteen. I wanted to spend my time climbing."

"I'm glad your teacher was there for you." Then it hit him. "How old were you when this happened?"

"I was fourteen when I was finally emancipated."

Fourteen?

Good God!

Mitch's heart broke.

She must have been thirteen or younger when the abuse had started. That wasn't long ago. She was only sixteen now. The sexual and emotional abuse were probably still fresh—an open wound that she tried to cover with steel and sharp edges.

"Thank you for trusting me with that." Mitch took her hand, realized she was trembling. "I'm so sorry this happened to you, Megs. You didn't do anything wrong. Your stepfather is entirely to blame. But nothing he or your mother did can change who you are. You *are* innocent—and incredibly brave."

When she looked up at him, there were tears in her eyes, her fingers now clinging tightly to his. "Do you mean that?"

"I know it must be hard to accept when your mother blamed you, but, yes, I mean it. What your stepfather did was a crime, and what your mother did… That's probably a crime, too. It's unforgivable. It wasn't your fault."

"I *hate* them." She spat the words, but fear quickly replaced fury. "What if Wayne reads those news stories and comes after me? He's out of prison now."

"You're safe with me, Megs. If he shows up, Dean and I will rip him apart."

Her lips curved in a wobbly smile. "Can I help?"

"You bet."

Chapter 11

MEGS STOPPED RECORDING and closed the journal, uncertain she wanted Mitch to listen to that particular memory over and over again. She would find something happier. "It's time for some stretches."

She stood, went to the foot of the bed, and flexed his right ankle, his eyes open now. "Do you know how lucky I was to meet you? That night was the night I began to heal. Your reaction and your reassurance meant more to me than you could know. I stopped feeling guilty—mostly."

She looked into his eyes. "Most guys your age would probably have taken advantage of the situation to get laid, but you truly *cared* about me. I've never really understood why. You could have had any woman—one with a college education who wanted children or who didn't cuss as much —but you chose me."

She'd learned so much from him and from those books, reading them all cover to cover more than once, discussing them with him at night.

Our Bodies, Ourselves had changed the way she'd thought about herself and what Wayne and her mother had done. It had given her language to describe what had happened to her, ways of expressing her emotions and sexual feelings. It had given her confidence that she'd lacked, strength that was based on something more than her determination not to break.

Walt Whitman's poetry had opened her eyes to the beauty of language and the ability of words to describe the wonder she felt in the natural world. That book had been the start of a tradition for Megs and Mitch. They'd taken poetry on every climbing expedition since and read it together in their tent at night.

As for the book of sexual fantasies…

She'd turned the tables on Mitch with that one.

Megs moved to Mitch's left leg, repeated the stretch, her thoughts drifting to that terrible night, to the memory of rage on her mother's face.

It had been fifty-one years since her mother had thrown her out, and the woman hadn't gotten in touch with her or offered an apology, not even when Megs made the covers of magazines for summitting Everest and winning the world championships in sports climbing. As for Wayne…

Well, karma had come for him. He'd gone to prison, where the other inmates had beaten him to death. Child molesters weren't popular behind bars.

Fabiola entered the room, a look of concern on her face. "Radiology is coming to get another chest X-ray. Mitch's fever has spiked, and the doctor is concerned he might have pneumonia from the vent."

"Pneumonia." Megs knew that pneumonia was a common complication of being on a ventilator. "Isn't he still on antibiotics?"

"Yes, but some bugs have become resistant."

It was the start of a day of complications.

The X-rays showed pneumonia. Not long after, his subclavian line stopped working and had to be replaced. Then his oxygen levels began to dip, probably from pneumonia. Then word came back that the bacteria in his vent was, indeed, resistant to the antibiotics they'd been giving him.

Megs sat in his room or stood at his bedside, holding his hand, explaining what was going on as if he were conscious. But she couldn't forget what Dr. Schwartz had told her, his words on repeat in her mind.

With this kind of severe injury, he's got about a forty-percent chance of a favorable outcome. It's not just the injury. There are also potential complications.

This could *not* be the point when the odds kicked in and everything went south. Mitch had been making progress. He didn't need setbacks.

Keep fighting, love. Keep fighting.

The hours ticked by, Megs holding tightly onto any bit of positive news that came her way. His fever was responding to medication. They had the right antibiotic now. The new subclavian line was working. His eyes were open. Best of all, that big, beautiful heart of his—the heart that had carried him to the summits of all fourteen of the world's highest mountains and had loved her so well—was still beating inside his chest.

It was close to suppertime when Kurt came to see Mitch.

Megs gave him a quick update. "He's had a rough day."

Kurt looked at her through eyes so like his father's. "And for you, I'd say. Come with me down to the cafeteria. Have a cup of coffee. Take a break."

They rode down together in the elevator.

"I noticed that the boy in the room next to Mitch's is gone. Did he get better—or are you allowed to say?"

Kurt pressed his lips together, shook his head. "He didn't make it."

Megs' heart sank. She'd been better off not knowing. "How can you do this job—so much human suffering, so much grief, so much anguish."

He touched a finger to the white of his clerical collar. "It has something to do with this. It's faith."

"Huh." She didn't know what to think about that.

They found a table in the cafeteria away from others.

Megs started to tell him about the journal entry where Mitch and Dean had gone to San Francisco and had dinner with his aunt and uncle—leaving out the sex books, of course—but Kurt stopped her.

"I'd love to hear about it some other time. I'm here because I'm concerned about *you*. This is some hard stuff you're going through, and today was a tough day."

The sincerity of his words and the compassion in his eyes made it impossible for Megs to pretend or to offer some trademark smart-ass reply.

She drew a breath, tried to find the words. "Mitch is the only man I've ever loved. He's been the best part of my life since I was sixteen. This is going to sound pathetic, I know, but I ... I don't know how to live without him."

Kurt took her hand. "That doesn't sound pathetic at all. That's how it is when we love someone with our whole being. The price of deep love is, unfortunately, deep pain."

━━━

BY THE FOLLOWING DAY, Mitch's condition had improved somewhat. His oxygen levels were normal again, and his fever wasn't as high. His gaze moved over the room, though it remained unfocused.

"Good morning, love." Megs took his hand, rubbed his knuckles with her thumb. "How are you doing? I had a pretty good night. No erotic dreams, though."

His gaze drifted in her direction, his eyes still unfocused.

Was he responding to her?

She moved to the other side of the bed to test this theory. "Rain is coming down this morning. The Gazette ran a story about you in today's edition, and she's bringing me some copies."

His gaze slowly drifted her way once again, his head turning as much as it could in the collar. Still, he didn't look directly at her.

She went on. "I hadn't planned on doing an interview, but I had a run-in the other night with a reporter from a webzine and decided I needed to give the press something. It looks like Riana from PT is here."

"Good morning! It's time for more stretches."

By the time the staff had completed all of Mitch's routine care, it was almost noon. Megs picked up the journal and scanned the next few entries, laughing as she settled in with the recorder.

"Knock, knock!" Rain peeked her head inside.

"Look, Mitch, Rain is here." Megs set the journal aside.

"Hey, Mitch. We're all praying for you." Rain held out several copies of the *Gazette*. "Here you go. You're on the front page, Mitch. I brought extras in case you wanted to share them with the nursing staff or his doctors."

Then Rain held up a paper bag. "I also brought lunch —pesto-crusted salmon salad, your favorite."

"You are a saint!"

"Oh, hardly. But you're welcome."

Megs took the newspapers and the paper bag. "You're saving me from that stuff they call salad down in the cafeteria."

Rain laughed. "Thank Rico. When he heard I was coming to see you, he quickly put this together."

Rico was the head cook at Knockers, a former felon who'd learned to use knives for cooking instead of violence while in prison and had made a good life for himself in Scarlet. But that was Joe. He was a staunch believer in second chances.

"Thank Rico for me."

While Megs ate her salad, Rain shared the news.

"Conrad seems to be managing the Team well. They got toned out twice yesterday—once to rescue a woman who twisted and broke her ankle on Longs Peak and once to evacuate a kid who fell thirty feet while free soloing on some rock formation in the Indian Peaks Wilderness. From what I overheard, it went pretty smoothly."

"They had a busy day." It felt strange not to be a part of it. "You're pretty good with the lingo for someone who doesn't climb."

"Hey, I've been waiting on Team members since the early days. You'd be surprised what you overhear when you're the one bringing the beer."

"I can only imagine."

Rain reached for a copy of the *Gazette*. "When I read the article this morning, I was blown away by everything you and Mitch have done together. All of the world's highest mountains. Climbing in Patagonia. Winning world championships. The lives you've both saved. What a life you two have made together! I don't know if that brings you comfort or if that makes this harder."

Megs remembered what Kurt had said yesterday

evening about great love and great pain. "I don't know. Probably both."

Rain seemed to consider this, her gaze warm with sympathy. "Oh! I almost forgot. The Scarlet Springs Fire Department is doing a shirtless calendar to raise money for Mitch's fund. It was Vicki's idea."

"A shirtless calendar? Like a *beefcake* calendar?" Megs' expression must have been comical because Rain laughed. "Did you hear that, Mitch? Scarlet FD is getting naked for you—or half-naked anyway. I might have to buy one of those."

"They've already got a half-dozen orders from the women on Knockers' staff—Marcia, Cheyenne, Sam, and the rest." Rain stood. "Speaking of Knockers, I should go. I need to get back to help with afternoon prep."

Megs hugged her. "Thanks for coming. We appreciate the company—and the food. Tell everyone hello for us."

After Rain had gone, Megs settled down next to Mitch with the journal and the recorder, laughing to herself about the calendar. "When you told me you wanted to settle in your small, close-knit hometown, I had nightmares of something like Mayberry—or my awful hometown. But Scarlet Springs is too damned crazy to be either of those."

Now, she couldn't imagine living anywhere else.

She skimmed through Mitch's journal, searching for another entry to record and found herself smiling at his growing sexual frustration. "It was your fault. You were the one determined to wait until I turned eighteen."

But now that she was older and at least somewhat wiser, Megs understood what he'd done for her. He'd put her need to grow up ahead of his need to get laid.

But, oh, she hadn't made it easy for him.

MITCH WOKE to the unmistakable scent of sizzling bacon, crawled out of his tent wearing only a pair of gym shorts, and found Megs in a tank top and cutoffs making breakfast on her little camp stove. "Good morning. God, that smells good. You always have the best food."

She lifted her gaze to meet his, her hair braided. "That's because I have a job."

Though Mitch refused to sleep in the same tent—a man could only endure so much temptation—he had moved his tent next to hers. It had become part of their routine to eat breakfast together and talk about what they wanted to climb that day. For Mitch, the first meal of the day was always a package of instant oatmeal with instant coffee, while Megs tortured him by making real food— eggs, bacon, pancakes, sausage, hash browns.

"It just so happens I'm making this for you." Her gaze was back on the cookstove, but that smile was still on her lips. "It's my way of saying thank you."

Was there something different about her this morning?

He must be imagining things. "Thank you?"

"Yes." She divided the eggs and bacon between two plastic camping plates and handed one to him, leaning in close and speaking in a whisper. "*I did it.*"

Distracted by the food, he picked up a piece of bacon with his fingers, took a bite, tried not to moan. "Did what?"

She looked into his eyes, color in her cheeks. "I made myself come."

Mitch forgot the bacon and eggs. "You made yourself … Oh!"

Blood rushed to his groin, his brain going blank.

She sat back on her heels, plate in her hand, her face glowing. "It was … incredible. It's taken me a couple of weeks. I've been trying every night. It's kind of hard for me to relax enough, but last night I finally did it."

"Right on!" Mitch's mind filled with images that shouldn't be there, images of Megs alone in her tent, experimenting with her body—and the ache in his groin grew sharp. "That's ... great news."

Damn!

A part of him wanted to laugh. No one would think anything of a man making himself come. But he knew from his human sexuality and psychology classes that it wasn't as easy for women to come—especially not those who'd been sexually abused.

Her smile faded, newborn sexual confidence melting into vulnerability. "I thought you'd be happy for me. Do you think I'm ... a slut or something?"

"God, no! I don't think anything like that." He reached out, ran his thumb over the curve of her cheek, touched that she'd trusted him with something so private. "It's *your* body. You need to understand how your body works. I was just surprised. That's all. That's not what I was expecting you to say first thing this morning."

She gave a little laugh. "I suppose not."

He looked down at his plate. "And you thank me by sharing your food. I wasn't even there."

Those sweet lips curved into a knowing smile. "Oh, yes, you were. I always fantasize about *you*."

That's what was different. Megs was no longer an inexperienced, uninformed girl. She had crossed a threshold. She had knowledge now.

And Mitch had a full-on boner.

"Isn't it incredible?" She poured herself a cup of coffee. "It feels so *good*, like heaven packed into just a few seconds."

Had he done the right thing? He was certain much of

society would think it wrong of him to give her those books, to encourage her to learn about her sexuality. For lots of people, masturbation was still taboo, especially when it came to women.

He thrust his doubts aside. These were new times. Megs had to learn somehow. Besides, he hadn't touched her beyond an occasional kiss since the moment he'd found out she was sixteen. More than that, she had no one else. Alone in this world, she'd built a wall around herself to keep herself safe, and for some reason, she'd let him in.

She stared at him, suddenly serious. "Does it feel the same for a man?"

He laughed. "I've only ever been a man, so I can't compare."

"I want to hike up the slabs to Half Dome."

And just like that, they were back to climbing.

"That's a tough hike."

The slabs were so steep that there were fixed ropes to keep climbers from falling before they reached the rockface.

"I want to free climb the Regular Northwest Face. I think we can do it."

Mitch almost choked on his coffee. "You want to *free climb* Half Dome?"

The route had first been climbed over a stretch of five days in the late 1950s with the help of aid equipment, but no one had yet done a free ascent.

"I thought we could try out some of the lower pitches, get a feel for the rock, and see what we think."

"Right on." Mitch tossed back the last of his coffee, inspired by Megs' ambition. Who else thought up projects like this? Why not Mt. Everest? "Let's do it."

Chapter 12

MEGS TOOK A BREAK FROM READING, set the journal and the recorder aside. "I'm not sure how you put up with me for the rest of the summer. What did you call it? The Summer of Blue Balls. Once I discovered that I had the power to turn you on, I used it. I guess it felt empowering —a change from being abused. You have the patience of a saint, Mitchell James Ahearn."

She remembered that recon hike up the slabs—what climbers now called the Death Slabs. Once they got there and looked up at the route, she'd known they could do it. They'd already put up several first free ascents, climbing all over the Valley, and she wasn't going to let anything stop them.

They'd hiked back to Camp 4 that evening, fired up by the new challenge and hungry for supper, only to find Gridwall and Accardo there.

"You told them that if they violated my space or said anything disrespectful again, you'd beat the shit out of them. I thought Gridwall was going to cry. He all but got on his knees to apologize."

Mitch's gaze was turned her way again, his eyes more focused.

Was she imagining this?

"Mitch, can you hear me?"

The hand she was holding tightened as if he were trying to squeeze her fingers. It lasted only a second, almost like a twitch. But that hadn't happened once in the four days she'd been here. Had he done that on purpose?

Megs' pulse spiked. "Mitch, can you squeeze my hand?"

His grip once again tightened. It was stronger this time, though still fleeting.

Heart racing, Megs pushed the call button.

Fabiola had just gone home, and Kim, an RN she hadn't yet met, walked in.

Doing her best to stay calm, Megs explained what had happened. "I can't be sure he squeezed my fingers in response to what I said. It could have been a reflex. But he hasn't moved his hands at all before now."

"That's interesting."

Megs had expected the nurse to sound more excited.

Kim checked Mitch's various monitors. "Radiology is on its way to do another chest X-ray. I'll let his neurosurgeon know. I think his pulmonologist is making rounds soon, too."

Megs went to the cafeteria to grab a coffee and some yogurt, then went back to Mitch's room to find radiology had gone and Mitch's pulmonologist, Dr. Aulakh, examining Mitch. He shook Megs' hand and jumped right in. "The chest X-rays show improvement in both lungs."

Thank God.

"That's good news."

"His lungs aren't yet clear, but the antibiotics are doing their job."

"I'm glad to hear it."

He turned and put his hand on one of Mitch's monitors. "The system we use for ventilators tracks a variety of readings that are crucial for patient care. Mitch is breathing above his set rate, which is encouraging. That means he's taking some breaths without the prompting of the ventilator. Based on that data and other factors—his blood gases and the improvement he has shown overall—I'm hopeful we can begin weaning him off the ventilator as soon as his pneumonia has cleared."

Megs then described what had happened. "He hasn't squeezed my fingers once these past few days. Also, he's been turning his head toward the sound of my voice."

She tried to prove this by speaking with Mitch, but this time Mitch didn't move, his face turned away from her.

Had she imagined it earlier?

She tried not to feel discouraged. "Are you trying to make a liar of me, love?"

Dr. Aulakh chuckled. "That's the frustrating thing about the minimally conscious state. Sometimes they respond, and sometimes they don't. It can be very discouraging for family members who are hoping to see quantifiable progress. Did Dr. Schwartz give you the brochures? You should ask him for one the next time you see him."

Damn the brochures anyway! Couldn't people just talk to her?

Then it hit her. "Wait. Did you say minimally conscious state?"

Wasn't that the next level of recovery?

But Dr. Aulakh had already left the room.

Megs waited impatiently for a good hour or so before Dr. Schwartz appeared. When she saw he was wearing surgical scrubs, her impatience vanished.

Mitch isn't the only person whose life he's trying to save.

125

Dr. Schwartz spoke with the nursing team at length, read through Mitch's chart on a computer at the nurse's station, then finally walked into the room. "I hear there was some excitement today."

Once again, Megs described what had happened, Dr. Schwartz listening, a thoughtful frown on his face. "Is he in a minimally conscious state now?"

Dr. Schwartz examined Mitch, then turned back to Megs. "I believe we're seeing a steady progression toward consciousness. His intracranial pressure continues to decrease. He's taking some breaths on his own. This is good progress. We'll be watching him closely—with your help. Keep doing what you're doing. I saw there was progress with his pneumonia, too."

Megs had to ask. "When will we know his life is out of danger?"

"We're not there yet, but everything is moving in the right direction. You need to prepare yourself for the long haul."

———

MITCH PULLED their haul bag up to the ledge known as Big Sandy, set protection for it, then took a long, deep drink. He couldn't remember the last time he'd felt so exhausted or excited. "Look at this view."

They'd taken turns leading and were now seventeen pitches up Half Dome, a mere six pitches from becoming the first people to free climb the Regular Northwest Face. They'd had a few hairy moments, but they'd taken their time and worked through them. They would bivouac here for the night and head for the summit of Half Dome early tomorrow morning.

Roped in, Megs sat, dangled her legs over the edge,

water bottle in her hand, the sunset turning her hair to gold. "Isn't it beautiful?"

"Beautiful." He checked his protection and sat beside her, taking her hand in his. "I've spent three summers climbing here in the Valley, but this has been the best summer of my life. You showed me I'm capable of doing more than I knew."

She rested her head against his arm. "You respected me and accepted me when the others saw only a girl."

He kissed her hair. "I think they've come around. You're a girl who can climb."

A helicopter flew by in the distance, stopping to hover when it came parallel with their position.

Megs stared. "Are they filming us?"

"I think they are." Mitch chuckled. "We're going to be on the news."

They waved to the helicopter, then broke into the haul bag for some calories and water, talking about the day's climb as they ate and drank. Then for a time, they sat together in comfortable silence.

"You know how the world goes quiet when you're climbing? One moment you're aware of everything, and the next, it's like you're floating in sunlight. One move leads to the next. Your body gets lost in some kind of dance with the rock. You're not who you were a moment ago. Now, you're breath and sweat and movement. And all the struggle, all of the fear and bullshit—it just disappears."

Mitch looked at the beautiful girl beside him, her words putting a hitch in his chest. She'd just described the sublime experience of climbing in a way that he, with his reading and college education, couldn't. "Walt Whitman must be getting to you."

She laughed. "Maybe."

They watched the sunset, then turned on their head-lamps and set up their bivy for the night, checking their protection before stretching out beside each other, the ledge just wide enough for them to lie down side by side.

Mitch drew her against him, his chest her pillow, the feel of her precious. He didn't need sex to feel close to her. Somehow, it was enough just to be with her, talk to her, hold her.

God, he was going to miss her.

He hadn't told her yet, but school started in a few weeks. Soon, he would have to drive back to Stanford and settle in for his senior year. He would much rather remain here, living like a dirtbag, if it meant he could spend every minute of the day with Megs.

"Look at the stars. They're so bright here. I can even see the Milky Way."

He pointed. "There's Venus. That's Cassiopeia over there."

They talked about the stars, UFOs, and NASA's decision to end the Moon missions last year. But they were both fatigued from today's climb, and soon the conversation stilled.

"Mitch?"

"Yeah?"

"I want this summer to last forever."

He held her closer, kissed her temple. "So do I."

They both fell into an exhausted sleep.

———

MITCH WOKE AT FIRST LIGHT, smiled to see the sky above him and the Valley below. There weren't many people who'd spent the night on Big Sandy.

Beside him, Megs stirred, opened her eyes, kissed him. "Good morning."

They ate a quick breakfast, slamming down as much water and as many calories as they could, talking about what stood between them and the summit. Megs would lead Pitch 18, and they would alternate to the top.

"I think you should take the last pitch. You should be the first one to top out—provided we make it. This was your idea."

"Are you sure? It doesn't matter to me."

"I'm sure."

They packed up, sorted out their protection, and left Big Sandy behind.

The next three pitches were tougher than they'd imagined, both of them struggling for holds on the granite. After that, they came to a small ledge.

"Thank God." Megs worked her way along it to a tight chimney that was anything but secure. She stopped, caught her breath. "I just need to think this through."

Once she found her footing, she battled her way up it.

It was like watching an artist at work. Her motions were efficient and graceful, her breath catching every so often.

Then it was Mitch's turn.

He could only be impressed as he grunted his way up. "This... isn't... my... favorite... part... of this ... climb."

He led the next pitch over an exposed and insecure slab, switching to a belay stance so that Megs could lead. "Finish this."

As she neared the top, Mitch could hear the voices of tourists on the summit.

"Oh, my God! There's a woman climbing up here! Look!"

"How is she doing that?"

"That makes me dizzy!"

Then came Gridwall's voice. "Move back, everyone. Give them room! Get away from the edge! Come on, folks!"

Megs topped out to applause, then belayed Mitch. Adrenaline rushing through his veins, he finished the pitch, dragging their haul bag up behind him.

When his feet stood on solid ground, Megs jumped into his arms. "We did it!"

He held her tight, kissed her deep and slow, the moment too sweet for words.

Tourists. Photographers. A microphone in their faces.

"How does it feel to be the first people to free-climb Half Dome?"

Megs glowed. "It feels great."

Mitch couldn't quit smiling. "It's another beautiful day in the Valley."

"Give them room! Come on!" Gridwall stepped forward, a huge smile on his face, a large paper bag in hand, the other dirtbags trailing behind him. "Way to go! I figured you would be hungry and thirsty, so I brought sandwiches and water."

Megs cracked open her water, chalk on her nose, sweat beaded on her forehead. "Gridwall, you're not such a jerk after all."

MEGS HELD MITCH'S HAND, the joy of that memory bringing a bittersweet ache to her chest. "It means a lot to me that you wrote more about the connection between us than you did the nuts and bolts of the climb. That's what I remember, too."

The two of them lying side-by-side on Big Sandy,

talking about the stars. Mitch holding her all night. Gridwall bringing his peace offering.

"That's the climb that set the Valley on fire."

As a result of the news coverage, new faces had begun to arrive in Camp 4. Inspired by Mitch and Megs' success on Free Spirit and Half Dome, the dirtbags had started finding their own routes and putting up first ascents all over the Valley. The free-climbing revolution was on.

"We ended up in newspapers and on television. We both thought that was the end of it, but we were wrong. It was the beginning of…"

Megs' words trailed off as Kim walked in, a bag of IV antibiotics in hand. "I couldn't help but overhear. I read the news article about Mitch. You two are famous. What an incredible life you've had together. I can't imagine traveling to all of the places you've been or doing the things you've done."

Then she lowered her voice to a whisper. "I'm afraid of heights."

"You save lives for a living. That does more good for the world than climbing."

Kim shook her head, checked the subclavian line. "The world needs people like you to inspire us. The rest of us sit at desks or slog our way through the workweek. You give us reasons to dream. You take us places we would otherwise never go."

"Thanks." Megs had never thought about it like that. "That's kind of you to say."

"What was your toughest climb?"

That was easy.

"Without a doubt, it was K2. That's the world's second-highest Himalayan peak after Everest. That trip nearly broke me. It was so cold, and the climbing was brutal. I wasn't sure we'd make it."

Almost 30 percent of climbers who attempted K2 died.

"Why did you do it?"

"Good question. We've been sponsored by various climbing gear companies since our twenties. Part of the deal is coming up with exciting projects. Mitch and I tried not to let our egos drive us, but we just *had* to tick the boxes and climb all of the eight-thousand-meter peaks."

"Which was your favorite?"

"Everyone expects me to say Everest, but Everest is overrated—too many people, corpses, oxygen bottles, and trash." Megs thought about it. "Honestly, I think it was our first ascent of the Regular Northwest Face on Half Dome that I was just reading to Mitch. It's not that difficult, really, compared to other projects. But there's nothing like being the first to do something when others believe it can't be done."

That's when Megs noticed. Mitch was looking right at her. "Mitch?"

There was a grimace on his face, as if he were in pain. He bent one leg, squeezed his eyes shut, then opened them again.

Megs' pulse raced. "Tell me you saw that. He bent his leg, and he was looking right at me. Then he opened and closed his eyes. I think he's in pain."

"Yes, I saw it." Kim hurried out of the room. "I'll page his doc. He might need pain relief now."

Mitch grimaced again, moaned, stretched out his leg.

Megs held tightly to his hand. "I'm so sorry, love. I bet you've got the world's worst headache. She's going to get the doctor. I'm right here, okay? They'll give you something for pain."

Could he understand what she was telling him, or was he trapped inside himself, confused and aware only of pain?

It took the neurosurgeon on duty a brief eternity to answer the page. When he arrived, he went over Mitch's chart and then examined him.

"Though there's some disagreement, there's good evidence that people in a minimally conscious state can feel pain. I've ordered morphine for him, though we want to be careful not to overmedicate him. That can have adverse effects that set him back."

"We don't want that." Megs also didn't want Mitch to suffer.

"We'll do what we can to keep him comfortable."

"Thank you." When the doctor had gone, Megs stroked Mitch's arm. "They're bringing you pain meds. You get the hard stuff."

Kim walked in with a syringe and injected the morphine into his line. "This should bring immediate relief. We'll monitor him closely."

Within seconds, Mitch's face relaxed, his eyes drifting shut.

Megs let out a breath, relieved. "You rest now, love. I'm right here."

Chapter 13

MEGS COULDN'T BRING herself to leave Mitch's side. Now that he was conscious enough to feel pain, she wanted to be there to make sure he got his morphine on time in case the nurses got busy or forgot. Debby, Jackie, Fabiola, Kim, and the other RNs were excellent at their jobs, but no one loved Mitch the way she did.

The night came with the same care routine as the daytime, meaning she got very little sleep. But by morning, there was no doubt in anyone's mind that Mitch had progressed to a minimally conscious state. He tracked Megs with his gaze. He rubbed the bandages over his clavicle. And once, when Megs laughed at a joke, he smiled.

Megs' heart skipped a beat. "You're smiling."

Dr. Schwartz made his rounds early. "We're taking him to the OR to remove his intracranial catheter today. The pressure has continued to decrease, so it's time."

Megs stayed with Mitch until they rolled him away, then made the short drive back to the hotel, where she slept for a few hours. When she woke, it was already mid-afternoon. She took a quick shower, updated their social media accounts, and answered emails from Conrad and Rain.

Megs' phone buzzed.

It was Gridwall. "How are you holding up, Megs?"

"I'll be okay."

"Hey, it's me. I know you better than that. Mitch is everything to you."

This was true.

What could Megs say? "I'll be fine when Mitch is fine."

"Fair enough. What can we do to help?"

"Help me put together a 'wear your fucking helmet' campaign. Mitch would be dead without his helmet. So many younger climbers think helmets are uncool. I guess they ruin their selfies or some shit. So many climbers refuse to wear them."

"Kids today are stupider than we were."

Megs couldn't resist. "Oh, I wouldn't go that far. We helped invent this insane sport, remember?"

Gridwall chuckled. "I'll get in touch with the rest of the dirtbags. We'll get on it and come up with some kind of PSA. Maybe I can get a sponsor to help us."

"Thanks, Jim. You're a good friend."

Back in the ICU, she found Debby on duty and Mitch unconscious.

Or was he sleeping?

"We had to sedate him. He's progressing, but he's not aware enough to understand that he can't mess with the subclavian line or the vent. Also, he's been fighting the ventilator, trying to breathe on his own. We have to ensure his care, and sometimes that means sedation."

"I understand." Megs took Mitch's hand, waited until Debby had left them alone. "I hear you're causing trouble, giving the nurses a hard time. But to be honest, you look more like yourself without a catheter sticking out of your brain."

It was a big step, but they still had so far to go.

She told him about Gridwall's call and her idea for a helmet campaign. "If we can get some of the big gear brands to join us, we ought to be able to reach a lot of people."

She shared the news with Rain via text message, then dozed in the chair—until radiology came with their mobile X-ray unit to check his lungs once again. "You're going to get superpowers from all these X-rays, love."

When the X-ray tech had gone, Megs walked back to Mitch's bedside.

He watched her, his gaze aligning with hers.

Was her Mitch in there? What must he feel right now? What was he thinking? Was he afraid? Did he have any memory of what had happened?

She took his hand, kissed it. "This must be confusing as hell, but you're getting better. Every day, you're getting better, Mitch. So many people around the world are pulling for you, praying for you. Try to relax and let your body do what it needs to do to heal, okay?"

His forehead furrowed as if he were trying his best to comprehend her words.

"Can you understand me? Squeeze my hand if you understand me."

His fingers tightened—and held.

Not a reflex. Not a coincidence.

Megs' throat grew tight. She squeezed back. "You're the strongest man I know. You will get through this. I'll be here the whole time."

She would have picked up the journal to read to him again, but he didn't let go of her hand, holding on as if he didn't want her to leave his side. She spoke softly to him for an hour at least, telling him about the headlines, the weather, the results of his latest X-rays when she had them.

"Your lungs are clearing up. You'll be able to get this damned vent out soon if you keep that up. Do you know how much I miss the sound of your voice?"

Jackie came with his next dose of sedative. "Say goodnight."

"Sweet dreams, love."

Soon, his eyes drifted shut.

She picked up the journal and the recorder and scanned the pages. "Oh, God. The day your father and uncle showed up and demanded you come home. I didn't make it any easier on you, did I? In my defense, I *was* a teenager."

She turned on the recorder and began reading.

TWO DAYS after their successful free ascent of Half Dome, Mitch was lying on the boulder at the tarn, Megs beside him, the two of them holding hands and watching the clouds drift across the sky. He pointed. "That one's a chicken."

"Ahearn, man!" Gridwall ran out of the trees. "Some square with glasses and a crew cut who claims he's your old man is waiting for you in camp with some dorky-looking guy he says is your uncle. He's come to take you home, man."

Mitch sat up. "Is this some kind of joke?"

Gridwall looked dead serious. "He saw the news coverage of you on Half Dome and says your mother wants you to spend the rest of the summer before classes start at home. I guess you freaked her out."

Megs sat up, too, her eyes wide. "You don't have to go,

do you? You're twenty-one. You're a legal adult. He can't tell you what to do."

"He can when he pays my tuition." Mitch laced up his boots.

"But the war is mostly over, right? They've stopped calling guys up." She reached for her socks and boots. "You don't need college, so you don't need his money."

Mitch helped Megs to her feet. "I didn't go to college to escape the draft, Megs. I went because I wanted an education. If I drop out, I'll dishonor every man who fought—and my father would probably disown me."

Megs looked both frightened—and furious. "You're going to let him drag you away? You're going to leave me?"

Mitch drew her into his arms. "I don't want to go. It's just until next June. Then we'll both be in the Valley again —and you'll be a few months away from turning eighteen. When you do—"

"Next June is ten months from now!"

"You're going to be okay without me. You were okay before, remember?"

"I wasn't nearly as happy. I'm going to miss you, Mitch."

"You can write me letters."

"Will you write back?"

"You bet." Then Mitch turned to Gridwall. "I've got a message for you and the rest of the dirtbags. Can you deliver it for me?"

Gridwall nodded, seeming happy to be trusted with something. "Yeah, man."

"If any of you disrespect Megs, touch her in any sexual way, offer her alcohol or drugs, or get her into any trouble, I will hunt you down and kill you. There won't be anything left but blood and hair. You dig me?"

Gridwall's expression was so grave Mitch might have laughed. "Yeah."

Megs glared at Gridwall. "You won't have to kill them. *I'll* do it."

Gridwall chuckled. "Yeah, you probably would."

Now that they'd settled that...

The hike back to Camp 4 was hell, anger at his parents making Mitch's pulse pound, Megs doing all she could to talk him into telling his father to shove it.

"You could do what Gridwall does and hide. Gridwall can tell him we didn't find you, that you're off somewhere climbing. He's good at lying, right? If your dad can't get a hold of you, he can't threaten to take away your tuition money."

Gridwall nodded emphatically. "Good idea. Yeah, I can do that."

Oh, Mitch was tempted.

"I need to graduate. When I've got my degree, I'm moving out." He would do what Megs did—hold a string of seasonal jobs that enabled him to buy gear and gas and keep climbing.

Then it hit him.

What if she didn't wait for him? What if she found some other man, one who didn't care about consent laws who was willing to do what he hadn't? What if she fell in love with someone else and forgot about him entirely?

He stopped. "Gridwall, you go on ahead, tell them we're coming—and deliver my message. I'm dead serious, man."

"Yeah, yeah. You'll kill us. Got it."

When Gridwall had gone, he took Megs' hands. "Megs, I know ten months is a long time, especially when you're only sixteen. But I'm making you a promise, okay? Are you listening?"

"Yes."

"On my honor, I promise that I won't date or sleep with any other woman while we're apart. The next time I have sex, it will be with *you*—if you still want me on your eighteenth birthday."

"If I still want you? You're all I think about—well, you and climbing."

That made him laugh.

"I promise I won't sleep with anyone, either. You're the only man I want, and you're leaving." She looked like she might cry.

"You're going to be okay."

"Are you sure you'll come back? You won't fall in love with some pretty co-ed?"

He wanted to tell her that he couldn't fall in love with anyone else because he was already in love with her, but something stopped him. "I've never met anyone like you, Megs. You're the freshest breath of fresh air on this planet. You have nothing to fear from any other girl. Any chick who wants to be *my* girl has to free climb Half Dome."

That made her smile.

He held her hand all the way back to camp, stopping before they reached the clearing to hold her tight and give her one last deep, slow kiss. "I'll see you in ten months. You be here in camp by the end of May next year, and I'll see you then."

"I'll be here."

His father and Uncle Frank were waiting by his father's black Buick, looking comically out of place. While Megs went to sit with Gridwall and the dirtbags, Mitch broke down his tent, packed his gear, and said one last goodbye.

"See you next summer. Until then, climb on!"

Cheers, fists in the air.

"You know it, man!"

"Right on!"

"The dirtbags rule!"

He started toward the car, but his father's snort of disgust stopped him. "Put on a shirt, son. Is this how you walk around—half-naked?"

The dirtbags, shirtless apart from Megs, laughed.

Genuinely angry now, Mitch yanked a shirt out of his pack and pulled it over his head. "Happy now?"

"Watch your tone!" Uncle Frank snapped. "You scared your poor mother half to death messing around on that cliff. What were you thinking?"

"We made history." Mitch stashed his gear in the trunk.

"The history of stupid stunts, perhaps."

Mitch ignored his uncle's insult, looked back at Megs.

She was standing now, the grief of the world on her face.

He blew her a kiss. "Remember the promise."

She nodded, her lips curving in a sad smile.

He climbed into the car.

His father started in on him right away. "You need to get your head on straight. If you want a girlfriend, there are plenty of nice girls at Stanford, girls from good families, girls with the sense not to camp in the wilderness with a bunch of men. First this rock-climbing nonsense, and now you're hanging with loose women."

Mitch snapped. "It's fine with me if you think climbing is a waste of time, but you will *not* say another unkind word about Megs. She's *not* loose. She's sixteen and a virgin, for God's sake! Not another word about her. Do you understand me?"

"Don't talk to your father like—"

"Shut up, Uncle Frank! Jesus! This doesn't involve you!"

"Don't you raise your voice to your elders, son, or—"

"Or what? You'll disown me? Maybe I'll disown *you*." Mitch didn't care what his father said. "I'm an adult. I can make my way in this world without you. I'd rather climb than go to school anyway. There's only so much shit I'm willing to take from you and Mom before I decide it's not worth it. You leave Megs out of this. Got it?"

They drove all the way to Stanford in silence.

MEGS FLIPPED to the back of the journal and found all of the letters she'd sent him during those ten long months. She read through a few of them, smiling at the teen angst that radiated off the pages. Then she tucked them away once more.

"I still have your letters, too. I think they're in a shoebox in my closet. I checked the mailbox at the lodge every day that fall. If there was a letter from you, I was happy. If not, the entire day sucked. There was no in-between."

She'd stayed in Yosemite until the weather had turned, putting up new routes with Dean, Gridwall, and the others. Then she and Dean had driven down to Joshua Tree National Park, where it was warmer. She'd applied for a job cleaning rooms at a hotel in Twentynine Palms, but then something had happened that she could never have imagined.

"We were in camp, getting ready to climb, when a man in a Porsche drove up and asked if I was Megs Hill, the girl who'd free climbed Half Dome. I thought the dirtbags were going to beat the shit out of him at first."

The man turned out to be François Charbonneaux, the famous climber from the 1950s who'd first climbed the Regular Northwest Face. He now owned an outdoor clothing company and was quite wealthy. He'd offered Megs and Dean five hundred bucks a month just to wear his line of clothing when they were climbing.

"I thought he was insane, but Dean knew who he was. He negotiated the deal for us. The next thing I knew, I was wearing all of this hip climbing stuff. That was the end of waiting tables and cleaning hotel rooms. François came back to Joshua Tree to climb with us. He brought a photographer and did a photo shoot for a catalog."

That had been Megs' modeling debut and her first sponsorship. François had wanted to offer Mitch the same deal, but Mitch hadn't been there. He and François had connected the following summer.

"I was able to climb full-time, but it wasn't the same without you. Dean and the others were good, but they weren't you. I suppose it's like having the perfect dance partner and then having to dance with someone else. It works, but it doesn't feel right."

Her seventeenth birthday came and went, the dirtbags sticking a lit match in a bran muffin as a treat. That winter, Megs had pushed herself until her taped fingers bled, demanding more of herself, teaching herself new climbing moves and techniques.

"It wasn't really about climbing. I was just trying not to miss you."

Then Christmas had come.

One by one, the dirtbags had left to spend the holiday with their families—all except for Gridwall, who wasn't welcome at home. Megs had expected to spend another Christmas alone. She had resigned herself to a Christmas Eve of stars and instant noodles, when Dean pulled up in his van and told her to pack her shit and climb in.

"God, that was a fun trip. We sang along to his eight-track the entire way. I'd never been to the city. I was so excited to see the Golden Gate Bridge."

But Dean had been plotting with Mitch.

"I didn't notice that we'd driven to Stanford. When we turned that corner and I saw you waiting on the sidewalk in front of your parents' house, I couldn't believe it."

Megs could still remember the elation she'd felt at that first sight of him, their first kiss, the feel of his arms around her, the scent of his skin. "We kissed in the back of the van while poor Dean drove to his sister's place in the city. To be fair, four months is a long damned time when you're seventeen—or twenty-two."

Dean's brother Chris, and his sister-in-law, Renee, had welcomed them like family, giving Megs the guest room while Dean and Mitch slept on the family room floor. They'd even had gifts for them.

"They gave me one of those newfangled climbing hexes. You gave me another book—Kerouac's Scattered Poems. That was the first Christmas since my father's death where I felt like I had a family. You and Dean had become my family—and the dirtbags, too." Megs laughed. "Gridwall and the others were the dysfunctional cousins."

They'd spent ten whole days together from Christmas Eve through New Year's, sharing a kiss at midnight, starting 1974 together.

"You leaned in close, nuzzled my ear, and said, 'This is the year you and I become lovers.' I melted. Damn. That still gets me."

Then, all too soon, it was time to go. Dean drove Mitch back to Stanford to face his parents' anger for having ditched them. Megs kissed him goodbye. Then she and Dean made the long drive back to Joshua Tree.

Grief broadsided Megs as it often did when she

thought of Dean, her throat going tight. "He was like a big brother to me and a good friend to you."

Heart heavy, Megs set the journal aside and went to stand next to Mitch once more, taking his hand. "I miss him. I know you do, too."

She set Mitch up with the recorder, waited until he got another dose of morphine, then kissed his cheek and headed back to the hotel to catch up on sleep.

Chapter 14

MEGS SAT in the hospital lobby, enjoying another lunch from Knockers, while Rain, Sasha, and Rose shared the news from Scarlet.

"Last night's Town Council meeting was chaos." Rain shook her head, frustration on her face. "You'd think that last year's fire would have taught people the importance of fire mitigation. We've removed all the trees close to our house."

"That's only because you're smart." Megs wasn't surprised to hear the Town Council was getting pushback from the proposed fire-mitigation ordinance. "Some people don't have the common sense that God gave a goose."

Rose shrugged, the tassels of her black lace shawl swinging. "People are connected to trees. We evolved in trees. Trees were sacred to the Celts. Trees connect us to our past and our spiritual side."

"You know what else trees do?" Megs had never had much patience with Rose's brand of New Age bullshit. "They catch fire and burn."

Rain pressed her lips together, clearly trying not to

laugh. "If you'd been there last night, you'd have shut down that nonsense."

"I'll have another chance." Of that, Megs was certain. There was no shortage of nonsense in Scarlet. She turned to Sasha. "How's the Team?"

"Conrad is doing a fantastic job. He's a good leader. Everyone has pulled together. We're putting in extra hours and making sure everything gets done the way you'd do it —gear inspections, inventory, debriefings."

Megs felt a sense of pride. The Team was their baby—hers and Mitch's. They'd put everything they had into it in Dean's name, and now it was strong enough to go on without them. "Please thank everyone for the extra effort."

Then Rose brought Megs up to date on the gossip. "Bob Jewell drove to Food Mart wearing only flip-flops, underwear, and his wife Kendra's floral bathrobe to get some salsa for his breakfast eggs. I was there and saw it myself."

"That sounds like Bob." What else could Megs say?

"Marcia, the bartender at Knockers—"

"I know who Marcia is."

"She's dating the drummer from the Mudbugs. I saw them together after the show. They were kissing. Marcia has a *lot* of extra second-chakra energy, so…"

Jesus, help me.

Megs might or might not have rolled her eyes. "Good for Marcia."

Apparently realizing Megs wasn't interested in people's private lives, Rose changed tack. "How is Mitch? When are we going to see him? I brought sage and my eagle feather to hold a healing ceremony for him."

Megs shared a glance with Rain. "He can't have visitors in the ICU."

That wasn't true, but Megs didn't want Rose anywhere

near Mitch. Though Rose meant well, she didn't know how to keep her mouth shut. She would share every detail of what she saw with anyone who asked—and anyone who didn't.

Mitch deserved better than that.

Sasha asked the question Megs hadn't answered. "How is he?"

"He's making steady progress. He squeezes my hand when I ask him to. He follows me with his gaze, and, yesterday, he smiled."

Sasha's face lit up with hope. "He smiled?"

"Oh, Megs!" Rain raised her hands to her face, and for a moment, she looked like she might cry. "Thank God!"

"They're going to start weaning him off the ventilator soon, possibly even this afternoon. They say he's recovering rapidly—more quickly than they had anticipated. That's a good sign."

"Do you think he'll ever be the Mitch we love again?" Rose's question, asked in an innocent voice, hit Megs hard.

"Rose!" Rain glared at her.

Megs' temper sparked hot. "He'll always be the Mitch *I* love no matter what."

"Yes, of course, he will." Rose squeezed Megs' hand.

Sasha's eyes narrowed. "He's like a father to me. Nothing can change that."

"He would be touched to hear you say that, sweetie." Megs glanced at her watch, got to her feet. "I need to get back upstairs. I want to be there when they start weaning him off the ventilator."

Megs thanked them for coming and said her goodbyes. She hadn't yet reached ICU when her phone buzzed with a text from Rain.

I'm so sorry, Megs. I won't bring her
again.

Megs replied.

It's not your fault. Thanks for lunch. It
was good to see you and Sasha.

Back in the ICU, she found Mitch awake, earbuds in his ears. She removed them, turned off the recorder, her heart swelling to see him looking straight at her. She took his hand. "Rain was just here with Sasha and Rose. Sasha said you're like a father to her. I told her you'd be touched to hear that."

She brought him up to date on the news, stopping when Debby appeared.

"Okay, it's time. I'm going to set the ventilator for a spontaneous breathing trial—what we call an SBT. The machine will still give him oxygen, but it will stop breathing for him. He'll have to initiate breaths himself."

"What happens if he doesn't?"

"I don't think that will be the case, but if it is, an alarm will go off, warning us, and we would cancel the trial and put him back on his previous settings." The monitor beeped as Debby programmed it. "The machine will collect a lot of data that the doctor can use to decide what happens next. Here we go."

A series of beeps and then…

Debby watched the monitor for a moment and then smiled. "For now, he's breathing on his own."

Megs stood beside him, watched his chest rise and fall, her hands wrapped so tightly around his bedrail that her knuckles turned white. "You're doing it, Mitch. You're breathing."

Five minutes.

Ten minutes.

Debby came in to check his progress. "You know, you should breathe, too."

Megs exhaled. "Right."

Mitch's eyes drifted shut, but his chest continued to rise and fall.

Debby left the room again.

Megs talked to Mitch, tried to encourage him. "One breath at a time, love."

Fifteen minutes.

Twenty.

Megs watched the time pass, Rose's words still in her mind. "I'll love you no matter what. Do you hear that? Even if you can't walk, can't talk, can't climb, I will love you. You've given me the best years of my life. If it were me in that bed and you standing here, you'd say the same thing."

Twenty-five minutes.

Beep. Beep. Beep.

Megs jumped, saw that Mitch was still breathing.

The time had run out.

Debby returned. "I would call that a successful trial. We'll put him back on his previous settings now so he can rest. This was hard work for him."

"Thank you so much, Debby."

"You're welcome—both of you." Debby reset the ventilator. "We'll start doing several of these each day until we're certain we can extubate him."

Megs kissed Mitch's forehead. "I am so proud of you. I always have been. You rest, and I'll read."

She and Mitch were about to be reunited in his journal —but it wasn't going to go the way he had expected.

MITCH ARRIVED at Camp 4 in his new 1970 VW camper van, expecting to find Megs waiting for him, but her car wasn't there. Neither was Dean's.

He parked, grabbed his backpack, and walked over to the dirtbags, who were hanging out at the picnic table.

"Hey, Ahearn!"

"There's the college grad!"

"Welcome back, man!"

"Hey, Gridwall. Accardo. Cook. Yoder. Ansel." He lowered his pack onto the bench. "Has anyone seen Megs or Dean?"

Gridwall grinned. "Can't wait to see her, huh?"

Mitch didn't see the point in pretending. "You could say that."

In fact, he was aching to see her again, aching to touch her, to hear her voice, to see her smile, to kiss her.

"I haven't seen them since I left Tahquitz Rock," Accardo said.

"She said in her last letter that she'd be here a week ago."

"Maybe she lost track of time." Yoder took a hit, passed a joint to Cook.

"Maybe." Mitch set up his tent in the camping spot he'd shared with her last summer, unable to shake a sense of misgiving.

She ought to be here. She'd said she would get here early so she wouldn't miss a moment with him. Megs didn't say things she didn't mean. It wasn't like her or Dean not to show up on time.

He counted the change in his pocket, glanced through his wallet for Chris and Renee's phone number, then got back in his van and drove to the Village. He found a payphone, dropped in a dollar's worth of quarters, and called them.

"That will be one dollar and fifty-five cents, please," a voice said in his ear.

He dropped in the additional change, hoping Chris or Renee was home and would answer quickly.

"Calder residence."

"Chris, it's Mitch calling from Yosemite. Megs and Dean haven't—"

"Thank God! She's in Palm Springs. She had a bad fall."

Blood rushed into Mitch's head. "*What?*"

"Dean is with her. It sounds like she was pretty beaten up. She has a broken arm, a mild concussion, and a few bruised ribs. Dean said she was testing some new gear, and it failed. They're at the Palm Springs Suites in Room Two-Oh-Four. She was discharged from the hospital a few days ago, but Dean didn't think she could handle a long drive."

"When did this happen?"

"About a week ago. Dean called your parents and left a message with your mom."

A week ago, Mitch had been home. His mother hadn't passed the message along. Well, he would deal with her eventually.

Damn it!

"Thanks, Chris. I'm on a payphone. If they call again, tell them I'm on my way."

"I will. Drive safely!"

"Thanks." A knot in his chest, Mitch climbed back into his van, drove back to camp, and shared the news. "She was testing some new gear, and it failed. I'm headed to Palm Springs."

Gridwall shot to his feet. "I'm coming with you.

Someone has to make sure you stay awake and follow the speed limit."

"Okay, but no weed or LSD or bullshit like that."

"Fine." Gridwall ran back to his tent.

By the time he returned, wearing a clean shirt and a pair of jeans, Mitch had his gear together and was ready to go.

It was a six-hour drive, but Gridwall proved to be a capable navigator—and better company than Mitch had imagined. It was almost ten when they reached the hotel. They made their way through a vacant lobby to the elevator.

"They're in Room Two-Oh-Four." Mitch punched the button for the second floor a half-dozen times in quick succession.

"You're going to see her in just a minute, so take it easy."

Gridwall was right.

Mitch drew a deep breath.

The elevator doors opened, and Mitch saw that their room was just across the hallway. "There it is."

He knocked.

Dean opened it, glared at him. "Where the hell have you been, man?"

"My mother didn't give me the message. I found out what happened when I called Chris to see if he knew where you two were."

"Jesus!" Dean stepped aside. "She's in bed. She's having a hard time sleeping because of the pain in her ribs. They gave her narcotics, but…"

Mitch walked down a short hallway, found Megs propped up on pillows, her hair tousled, yellowing bruises on her cheek, her left arm in a cast. "Megs, honey?"

She opened her eyes, smiled. "Mitch! You came. Hey, Gridwall."

Gridwall spread his arms wide, grinned. "No fear. Uncle Jim is here."

Mitch resisted the urge to draw her into his arms. Instead, he kissed her cheek, sat down beside her, took her right hand. "I'd have come sooner, but I just found out this afternoon. I'm so sorry."

Her smile crumpled, despair in those gray eyes. "I can't climb for six weeks, maybe longer."

"The important thing is that you're going to be okay." He wanted to ask her what had happened, but he could tell she was exhausted. "You need to get some rest. We can talk about what happened tomorrow."

"I can't sleep. My ribs hurt too much to lie down, and these stupid pillows don't stay fluffed. They sink and don't hold me up."

"I have an idea. I'll be right back." Mitch made a pit stop in the bathroom then got a drink of water. Back at Megs' bedside, he stripped down to his jeans. "We'll scoot you forward, and I'll climb in behind you. You can use me as a pillow."

"Okay."

He helped her inch forward, her little gasps of pain cutting at him. He piled the pillows high against the head-board, then sat, his back against the pillows, his legs on either side of Megs. "Lean back against my chest. Nice and easy. There you go."

"I'm so glad you're here," Megs said in a sleepy voice. "I missed you so much."

"I missed you, too. I'm sorry I wasn't here sooner." He looked over at Dean. "Is it time for another pain pill?"

Dean turned out most of the lights. "Not for another hour."

Damn.

"You just sleep now, okay?"

She held his hand. "Okay."

Dean had already claimed the other bed, so Gridwall took the sofa. "Anyone have a pillow they can spare? Not you, Ahearn."

"Sure." Dean threw a pillow at him.

"Thanks." Gridwall pointed. "She's already asleep."

Mitch drew the blankets up to Megs' chest and then met Dean's gaze. "Tell me exactly what happened."

"She climbed thirty feet up to test that new hex for her sponsor. She let herself hang from it. It broke, and she fell. I thought it was over. She was unconscious at first. I carried her back to my van, put her in the back, and drove her to the ER. She woke up on the way in a lot of pain. They had to set her arm and kept her for observation."

"She climbed *thirty* feet and hadn't placed other protection?"

Dean shook his head. "It was an easy route, one we've both free soloed before. We both thought she was safe. She was just testing that hex. That turned out to be a big mistake. The moment she put her weight on it, it broke."

"Yeah." Mitch kissed the top of her head, the thought that he could have lost her making his heart ache. "A big mistake."

"YOUR MOTHER LIVED to regret not delivering the message, didn't she? You called her from the hotel and let her have it. You stood up for me." Megs tucked her receipt bookmark into the journal, certain Kurt would like to hear this story. "That was the first time you and I slept together. I don't think it lived up to either of our expectations."

Not by a long shot.

They'd spent a week at that hotel, the three men taking care of her—giving her meds, getting water and food for her, making sure she was as comfortable as she could be. "I've never felt more protected or loved. It was ridiculous, really, but sweet."

Once the swelling had gone down in her ribs and she was able to lie down again, they'd packed everything into Dean's and Mitch's vans and had made the long drive back to Yosemite, Megs riding with Mitch, and Gridwall with Dean.

She'd spent the next four weeks in a hotel room pouting because she couldn't climb, and everyone else was sending new routes left and right.

Megs laughed at the memory. "I was afraid there wouldn't be anything left in the Valley for me to climb."

But, of course, once she'd healed and returned to Camp 4, she'd found plenty of unclimbed rock still available. She'd had to take it slow at first, building up the strength in her left arm, getting back into climbing condition after six weeks of inaction.

"God, it felt good to climb with you again."

François had shown up in the Valley when he'd gotten the news of her fall. He'd paid her medical and hotel bills and had taken her to see a specialist for her arm, apologizing profusely since it was his hex she'd been testing. He'd looked into it and found out that the contractor manufacturing the hexes for him had used a cheaper metal alloy. But the greater mistake had been hers—climbing more than twenty feet with no protection apart from a new, unproven device.

"People wonder why I'm so uptight about safety." Megs knew that Team members thought she was a pain in the ass when it came to safety protocols. "I learned the hard way that when you cut corners, you cut your chances for coming out alive."

But her focus on safety hadn't saved Mitch, not this time.

God, she wished she'd decided against Painted Wall when they'd read the beta for that route. It warned climbers that the rock was chossy and loose. If only they had decided to climb somewhere else…

Regret gains you nothing.

Mitch looked up at her, a confused and pleading look in his eyes, his fingers tightening around hers without Megs having to ask.

"I'm here, love. Are you in pain?" Megs hit the call button.

He tried to push the vent away.

"Don't do that. You need that for now." Megs caught his other hand, restraining him just as Debby came in. "He just tried to pull the ventilator out."

"Time for more sedative." Debby injected the meds into his subclavian line.

Almost immediately, Mitch relaxed, his eyes drifting shut.

"What about pain meds?"

"I think we can give him another two mgs of morphine. I'll be right back."

Megs stroked Mitch's cheek, his eyes opening to look up at her once again. "You're fighting so hard to get out of there, aren't you? I can't imagine what it must be like. Do you even know who and where you are? My poor love."

Debby returned promptly with the morphine. "The doctor has him scheduled for another breathing trial in about a half-hour. So I don't want to give him too much morphine because that can suppress his breathing."

"I understand." Megs explained to Mitch what was

about to happen. "They're trying hard to get this vent out of you and get you breathing on your own again. I know that's what you want, too."

Megs found herself growing tense as the time for the next SBT approached.

He'll do fine. He did just fine before.

Debby came back almost exactly a half-hour later, programmed the monitor, and the second SBT began.

Megs watched Mitch's chest rise and fall, her gaze darting now and again to the timer on the monitor. Once again, Mitch completed the trial with no problems.

Debby was pleased with the data on the monitor. "I think he'll be extubated sometime in the next several days. He's come such a long way in such a short time. That's probably because he's so healthy and strong."

"Did you hear that? You might get that vent out in the next few days." Megs watched Debby leave the room, then took Mitch's hand again and lowered her voice to a whisper. "I'll make you a deal. You get that vent out, and I'll read you the X-rated parts of your journal."

Chapter 15

THE NEXT FEW days were too busy for Megs to read to Mitch. According to Dr. Schwartz, he was progressing rapidly and was now in a confusional state. He was conscious enough to know that something was wrong, but he couldn't yet understand what was happening. This made him a handful.

Megs had stayed overnight two nights in a row because the nurses said Mitch was calmer when she was there. He hated the ventilator, and more than once, she'd been forced to hold him down while the nurses sedated him so that he couldn't interfere. It broke her heart to see him so distressed.

They'd reached the point this morning where Dr. Schwartz decided they either needed to give him a paralytic and morphine to restrain him—or they should try to extubate him. Given that he met most of the criteria for ending intubation and that the paralytic would surely be traumatic for him, Megs had pushed for the latter.

Now she sat in the ICU waiting area, watching the

clock, while Mitch's medical team did one last trial, which would hopefully end with them removing that damned vent. She tried to distract herself by checking email and sending a few text messages, one to Rain to update everyone in Scarlet and one to Gridwall. Then she noticed the date on her calendar app.

October 2.

October already? Her birthday month.

It had been eight days since the accident, eight long days since she'd heard Mitch's voice speak her name or seen that teasing glint in his eyes, eight days since she'd taken for granted that her future would include him.

It seemed much longer than that.

Megs was beginning to understand what Dr. Schwartz meant by preparing herself for the long haul. Mitch hadn't returned to full consciousness yet. He didn't seem to know where he was, sometimes looking about his room with wild eyes, as if the place were filled with monsters the rest of them couldn't see.

Almost an hour had gone by before Kim came to get her, a broad smile on her face. "He's breathing on his own."

Relief rushed through Megs, bright and sweet.

"Thank God!"

"We sedated him, but he should be coming out of it soon." Kim explained that being intubated could affect a person's ability to speak and often left their voice sounding rough for a time. "Of course, a brain injury can also affect speech."

Megs found Mitch asleep, oxygen mask on his face. She rested her hand on top of his, and for a time, she just watched his chest rise and fall.

It felt like a miracle.

Megs sent a quick text to Rain and Gridwall.

```
He's breathing on his own.
```

Rain's reply was immediate.

```
Thank Heaven!
```

Gridwall's came a few minutes later.

```
That bastard! I knew he'd pull through.
I'll let the others know.
```

Megs laughed, slipped her phone into her pocket, and found Mitch awake and watching her through tired eyes. She took his hand again. "Hey, there. They took the ventilator out, and now you're breathing on your own. Can you understand me? Squeeze my hand if you understand me."

He squeezed her fingers, his lips pressing together. "Mmm."

Megs' pulse skipped. "Megs. I'm Megs. Is that what you're trying to say?"

His brow furrowed, whether from pain or anger, she couldn't say. "Mmmmeh."

She laughed out of sheer joy. "Yes! Megs. That's it. You'll get it."

He looked into her eyes, and she could see he was frustrated. "Mmmeh."

"I know this is hard, love, but you've spent the past week in a coma. It's going to take some time before you're whispering sweet nothings in my ear, but that's okay. You've fought a tough battle, so just rest."

He seemed to relax, his hand still holding hers, his gaze fixed on her.

"You don't remember what happened, do you?" She didn't think it would hurt to tell him. "A chunk of rock fell when we were climbing on Painted Wall. It missed me, but it hit you. It broke your helmet, one of your cervical vertebrae, and your clavicle, and it left you with a severe head injury. You've been in a coma for a week, but you're … coming out of it now."

Her throat went tight on those last few words. A week ago, she hadn't known whether he'd ever wake up again.

"I suppose now is a good time to tell you that I love you. And also that I've been reading your journal. I've been recording what you wrote and playing it back to you." She lowered her voice to a whisper. "I made you a promise. I told you that if you got off that ventilator, I would read you the sexy parts. What do you think of that?"

She went to retrieve the journal, but he held on tightly to her hand and didn't seem to want to let go. The journal could wait.

She caught him up on the news from Scarlet—all of the fundraising efforts, the Town Council meeting, the Team functioning well without them. But he'd begun to grow restless, and she thought she knew why. "You're in pain, aren't you?"

He moaned, closed his eyes, shifted his legs.

Megs pushed the call button. "We need some pain meds."

Kim walked in a few minutes later. "Time for more morphine."

Megs watched Mitch's eyes drift shut, the strain on his face easing. "You rest, love. You just rest."

"Speaking of rest…" Kim pinned Megs with her gaze.

"I'll head to the hotel soon. I just want to read to him first. And, Kim, can you close the door behind you?"

Megs had a promise to keep.

MITCH'S PAIN LESSENED, and he floated in a world that was blurry around the edges. He knew who he was. He knew his name, and he knew when people were talking to or about him, though it all seemed far away somehow.

He knew *her* name, too. He knew that he loved her, needed her, wanted her close to him. But when he had tried to say her name, he hadn't been able to do it.

Anger. Confusion. Frustration.

This wasn't right. He couldn't say why, but it wasn't. He was trapped in a strange place, and he didn't know how to get out. He had questions but no answers.

But when she held his hand, when she smiled at him, when she told him she loved him and read these stories that he somehow already knew, things made sense for a while.

━━

MITCH POURED himself a second cup of coffee, his breakfast eaten, camp waking up around them. "And then what did I do?"

"You kissed me with your tongue—down there."

Sweet Jesus.

Wouldn't he just love to do that?

This was how every day started now. Megs shared what she'd read in that book of sexual fantasies or, worse, shared her fantasies *about* him. It was her revenge for his making her wait until her eighteenth birthday.

But Mitch would not let her break him.

He took a sip of coffee, waited until he could speak with clinical detachment. "What does that mean—kiss you with my tongue?"

His question caught her off-guard, as he'd suspected it

would. Yes, she had learned a lot, and she could make herself come. But reading about sex was very different from the actual event, and she had no real experience.

She stammered. "I … uh… It means you gave me oral sex."

He put a thoughtful frown on his face. "Oh, I get that. I'm just not sure what exactly I did with my tongue."

"Well, I guess you did what you'd do with your dick."

"So, I thrust my tongue inside you?"

She nodded. "Then I came."

Who was he fooling? She was *killing* him.

Well, two could play at this game, and he had more experience than she did.

He finished his coffee and set the cup and empty plate inside the plastic tub they used to wash their dishes. "That's not how I would do it."

She cocked her head, a look of confusion on her face. "It's not?"

"Nope." He took her empty plate from her hand, set it in the tub, and drew her onto his lap, his hands on her hips. "First, I would push your knees back to your chest. I'd want a really good look at you."

Her pupils dilated.

"Then I'd run my tongue over you, taste you."

She frowned. "What if I don't taste good?"

He couldn't help but laugh. "Oh, you will. You'll taste exactly how you're supposed to taste—like musk and heat and sex."

She shivered, her nipples pebbling against her halter top.

"When you were used to the feel of my tongue, I would use it on your clit. First, I would stroke you and flick you until you started to moan. Then I would suck on your clit, draw all of you into my mouth, let my lips stroke yours.

After that, I would slide my fingers inside you and thrust hard."

Her hips moved in a circle, proof that he was turning her on. "Then what?"

"You would come. My lips would be covered with your wetness, and your taste and scent would be all over me. Then I would bury my cock inside you and make you scream."

She circled her hips again, a look of pure sexual frustration on her pretty face. "That's not fair. Now you've got me all hot."

"How is that not fair?" He laughed. "Haven't you heard? Turnabout is fair play. Maybe you need some time alone in your tent."

She glared at him, a smile tugging at the corners of her lips. "You're a mean, hard man, do you know that?"

"I'm definitely hard, thanks to you." He stood, helped her to her feet, adjusted himself—and saw her look. "I'll wash the dishes while you think about what you want to climb today."

"I want to climb *you*."

Satisfied that he'd won this round, he carried their sauce pot to the water spigot, filled it, then brought it back and set it on the camp stove to boil. Megs sat on a nearby log, looking at a topo map, her blond hair spilling around her bare shoulders.

It was only mid-August. How was he supposed to last until October 24?

Here he was in one of the most beautiful places on earth, being paid to do what he loved, and all he could think about was Megs. She filled his head during the day. She made his blood run hot. She hijacked his dreams at night.

God, he wanted her. He wanted her so bad it hurt.

Mitch poured the steaming water over the dishes and added a few drops of dish soap. Then he fished their sponge out from the bottom of the bin and washed the dishes.

He'd been planning. Of course, he had. He wanted to make sure their first time together was as perfect as it could be. It would be her birthday, too, so it needed to be extra special.

He'd bought a box of condoms from a pharmacy before coming to Yosemite. He'd also gotten her a few birthday presents—a new book of poetry, flowers, and a new internal frame pack from François' company. But he hadn't yet decided where they should stay that night.

He didn't want her first time to be in a tent or the back of his van. That wasn't classy or romantic. At the same time, he wasn't sure if it was legal for unmarried couples to get a hotel room together in California. He knew it was illegal in some states. Hell, having sex outside of marriage was still illegal in some states.

It was 1974, but some people still lived in the Dark Ages.

He also worried about Megs. She'd been molested as a younger teen. He didn't need a degree in psychology to know the experience might affect her more deeply than she realized. The last thing he wanted to do was dredge up bad memories for her.

He wanted her first time to be perfect.

Megs looked up from the map. "Why don't we check out Middle Cathedral Rock? Gridwall and the guys put up a few first ascents there last year, but I'll bet there are more. Let's see what we can find."

"Sounds good." He finished the dishes, and they pulled their gear together and piled it in the back of his van.

Megs shoved her backpack inside. "Just so you know, I'm grumpy."

"It's called sexual frustration." Mitch didn't bother to hold back his grin. "Now you know how I feel."

Her lips turned down in a perfect pout. "But you've already had sex."

"Sure." He shut the van's doors and pressed his forehead to hers. "But I haven't had sex with *you.*"

———

MEGS REMEMBERED THAT DAY. She had pushed him to the brink, tried to get him to change his mind. She'd known she was making life hard for him. But he was determined at age twenty-two not to be the dirty old man who led the teenage virgin astray.

At the time, it had irritated the hell out of her. But now, she respected him for it. If he'd done what she'd wanted him to do and had sex with her that first summer, she wasn't sure their relationship would have lasted. By making her wait, it gave their friendship and mutual respect time to grow. It had also given her time to grow as a person. By the time they finally *did* have sex, the tension had been thick enough to cut with a knife.

Megs couldn't help it. She flipped forward through the journal, skipping over dozens of pages and many fantastic climbs in search of his entry for her eighteenth birthday. "I hope you didn't skip it or just write, 'We balled.' I want details."

Not that she didn't remember what happened that night. It had been magical, a rite of passage, a sexual initiation at the hands of a man who had loved her even then. It was one of her favorite memories, and she wanted to see it all through *his* eyes.

And then she found it.

She perused the page, then smiled at Mitch, who was awake but drowsy from morphine. "Oh, my. You *did* include the details."

When he saw her smile, he smiled. Of course, it might have been a reflex, him mimicking what he saw. Still, the sight of it put an ache in Megs' chest. They had always had a strong emotional connection. Nothing, not even this terrible accident, had been able to change that.

"Are you ready for this? It's pretty explicit."

Megs began to read.

━━━

MITCH DROVE under the shelter of the cabin's carport and parked. "Here we are."

The cabin belonged to François, who had invited Mitch to stay here with Megs when he'd heard Mitch was looking for a special place to celebrate Megs' birthday.

Megs looked up at him, surprise on her face. "Are we staying here?"

"It's ours for the entire weekend."

"Far out!" She opened the door and hopped to the ground.

Mitch drew a breath, anticipation twined with nervousness in his belly. After more than a year of waiting, of wanting her, of burning for her, tonight was the night. He wanted it to be perfect.

They got their backpacks from the vehicle and walked up the steps of a wide wrap-around deck to the front door. Mitch unlocked it, opened it, and let Megs enter.

"Oh, wow!"

He smiled to himself. "Nice, isn't it?"

He'd had the same reaction this afternoon when he'd dropped off the food, flowers, and other things they would need for the weekend. The place wasn't a rustic cabin at all, but a luxury mountain getaway.

They set their packs down inside the door. Mitch followed Megs as she walked from the living room, with its fireplace and leather furniture, to the modern kitchen, and then to the primary bedroom, which had its own fireplace, a king-sized four-poster canopy bed, and an en-suite bathroom.

"Did you see that?" she pointed toward the bedroom. "There are mirrors on the underside of the canopy. How silly! Who cares what they look like when they sleep?"

Mitch burst out laughing. "I don't think that's why the mirrors are there."

Megs frowned as if puzzling through this, then her eyes went wide. "You mean they watch themselves when they…?"

"Yeah." He couldn't help but find her innocence cute. "Keep looking. You haven't seen everything yet."

There was a guest bedroom, a wine cellar, and, outside the back door, a Jacuzzi with a sunset view of the mountains.

Megs played with the dials on the Jacuzzi, starting the jets. She laughed, ran her fingers through the bubbles, the happiness on her face putting a hitch in his chest. "This place has everything."

"I think you missed something." He led her back inside, stopping beside the dining room table with its bouquet of roses.

"Are the flowers for me?"

He glanced around. "I don't see any other birthday girls."

She found the little card, opened it, read what he'd written aloud. "'Happy Birthday to the brightest star in my sky.' Oh, Mitch, I love them—and the card. It was so sweet of you to set this all up."

She stood on tiptoe and pressed a kiss to his lips.

He drew her against him, kissed her in a way he hadn't allowed himself to kiss her since the day he'd said goodbye last summer. Oh, she tasted sweet, his blood going hot at the first brush of her lips. He wanted more than that—but not yet.

He broke the kiss. "It's not your birthday—not until midnight."

She moaned in frustration. "You're not seriously going to make us wait until midnight, are you?"

"It's not easy, but you're worth it." He let her go. "I got us steaks for supper. How about we grill them on the deck?"

They made dinner together—grilled T-bones, baked potatoes, and salad, with ice cream for dessert—but Megs insisted on loading the dishwasher alone since she'd never used one before.

"How does this work? Oh, I see. Right on!"

They sat on the deck to watch the sunset, deer grazing in the meadow downhill from the cabin, the scent of fall in the air. Then Megs stood and undressed, exposing her sweet body to his gaze.

"I'm going to try the Jacuzzi."

Damn.

The breath left Mitch's lungs, and for a moment, he could do nothing but stare. Her smooth skin. Her small, sweet breasts. The curves of her hips. Her round, athletic ass. Those slender legs.

She stepped down into the water. "Oh, this feels so good!"

Before he knew it, he was on his feet. While she watched, he stripped down to his skin and followed her into the hot tub.

Chapter 16

SOMEHOW MITCH MANAGED to keep his hands to himself, despite the beautiful, naked almost-woman beside him. They stayed in the Jacuzzi until their fingers and toes grew wrinkled and the sky was full of stars. Then they came inside, walking hand in hand, naked and wet.

Mitch took a shower first, shaving away the day's stubble. He couldn't imagine that whisker burn would feel good on Megs' inner thighs. Then he slipped into one of two blue velour robes hanging in the bathroom and went in search of Megs.

He found her wrapped in a towel in the living room. "Your turn."

"Nice bathrobe."

While she showered, he got things arranged in the bedroom—condoms, champagne on ice, candles, a book of poetry by Kahlil Gibran. Then he started a fire in the bedroom fireplace and glanced at his watch.

10:30

An hour and a half to go.

Good grief.

Was he nervous?

Hell, yes, he was.

Megs walked into the bedroom, her long hair damp, the robe far too big for her, its sleeves hanging beyond her fingertips. "Candles and champagne. This is romantic."

He drew her into his arms. "I have waited so long for this night. I want to make it special for you."

"You already have."

He kissed her, exploring her mouth with lips and tongue, until his blood ran hot. Then he drew her over to the bed, picked up the book, handed it to her. "I bought you this for your birthday."

She ran her hand over the cover. "The Prophet by Kahlil Gibran."

"He wrote amazing poetry, some of it about love. I thought you'd enjoy it."

She looked up at him. "Thank you."

They read poems together every night back at Camp 4, so they climbed into bed and took turns reading to each other, his arm around her shoulder, her head resting against his chest.

"You bookmarked a page." Megs turned to that page.

"I'll read this one." He took the book from her. "Love has no other desire but to fulfill itself. But if you love and must needs have desires, let these be your desires: To melt and be like a running brook that sings its melody to the night. To know the pain of too much tenderness. To be wounded by your own understanding of love; And to bleed willingly and joyfully."

"That's beautiful." Megs took the book and set it on the nightstand.

"Don't you want to hear the rest?"

"I'm done reading about love, Mitch. I'm tired of waiting. Kiss me."

Technically, the law prohibited *penetrative* sex, so Mitch would just have to make the foreplay last until midnight. Well, no problem there.

"Come here." He drew her onto his lap and, remembering the past abuse she'd suffered, did his best to set the tone. "I want you to enjoy tonight, Megs. I don't want to rush it, and I don't want to do anything that makes you uncomfortable. We'll start slow, okay? If you want me to stop, I'll stop."

"Okay."

He tugged on the velour belt of her bathrobe, let the fabric fall from her shoulders to reveal her naked body. "You are so beautiful."

"You really think so?" There was the vulnerability she always tried to hide.

He cupped her breasts, ran his thumbs over her nipples, and watched them draw tight. "I've wanted to touch you like this for so long."

She sucked in a breath, her eyes drifting shut, her hands coming to rest on his.

He kept it up, encouraged by her response, plucking her nipples, pinching and rolling their tips between his fingers. Then, needing more, he wrapped an arm around her waist, drew her closer, and sucked one puckered nipple into his mouth.

Hell, yes.

"Oh!" She gasped and arched into him, her hands sliding behind his neck to hold on as he teased her and laved her with his tongue.

But there was more to her breasts than nipples.

He licked the sensitive underside of one breast, nipped the sides with his lips, grazed the tip of her nipple with his teeth, gratified by her little whimpers and moans. He shifted to the other breast, lavishing the same attention on it until her fingers were clenched in his hair. And then he just had to kiss her.

He raised his head, looked into sweet gray eyes that had gone smoky, then claimed her mouth with his, bearing her back onto the bed.

For the first time, he didn't hold back, but kissed her the way he'd wanted to kiss her since that day at the lake. And, oh, God, she kissed him back, giving as good as she got, the two of them sparring for control, neither of them willing to yield.

He broke the kiss, smiled down at her. "Damn, girl."

She tugged at his bathrobe. "I want to feel you."

Mitch was only too happy to oblige. He sat back on his heels, untied the robe, and let it fall to the floor, his gaze raking over her, an emotion stronger than desire hitting him in the solar plexus. "*Megs.*"

Her gaze slid over him, fixing on his erect cock. She sat up, ran her hands over his pecs, her thumbs grazing his nipples. "I love the way you feel—so hard."

He sucked in a breath, watched her expression change as she explored him, her hands moving to his abs and then down to his erection.

She got a feel for him, moving her hand along his length. "Is this right?"

"Let me show you." He placed his hand over hers, tightening her grip, his breath catching when she got it right. "Just ... like ... *that.*"

He let her play, his hips thrusting into her fist.

But this was moving too fast.

He drew her hand away. "I don't want the party to end before it starts. Lie down."

She did as he asked, watching him, her hair fanned against her pillow.

He picked up her foot, kissed her sole and each of her

toes, working his way over the bridge of her foot to her ankle and then the inside of her calf.

"That tickles."

"It does?" He nibbled his way up the inside of her leg, his fingers caressing the sensitive back of her knee.

By the time he reached her inner thigh, her eyes were closed once more, one of her hands fisted in the sheets.

Anticipation was one hell of an aphrodisiac.

He kissed his way to the top of her thigh, her scent filling his head, sending a jolt of pure lust through him. Then he remembered the fantasy she'd shared this past summer, so he kissed her curls, letting his tongue slide into her cleft to tease her clit.

Her breath caught, and her body arched.

God, she tasted good.

But when he raised himself back up and picked up her other foot to start over, she moaned in frustration. "That's not what you said you would do."

"Patience. There's a lot more of you to taste."

And a half-hour still until midnight.

———

A KNOCK AT THE DOOR.

Megs stopped reading just as Kim opened the door. "The lab is here for another blood draw, and I need to change out his antibiotics."

More than a little turned on by what she'd just read, she had to bite back a smile. "Do what you need to do."

Mitch watched her, something akin to fascination in his eyes. Did he understand what she was reading? Did he remember that night?

Kim hooked up the new bag of antibiotics. "How is he doing?"

"He seems to be doing fine. I'm still reading. We haven't finished yet." Megs almost laughed out loud at her own words.

Kim headed toward the door. "I'll be back in about an hour with more meds."

"Thanks."

Then the lab tech came with a cart to draw blood from his subclavian line.

"Thank you." Megs' gaze met Mitch's as the tech left them alone again, closing the door behind him. "Now, where were we?"

———

"PATIENCE. There's so much more of you to taste."

Mitch's heart pounded as if he were climbing a 5.12. After waiting for so long, tonight was the night. It almost didn't seem real. He had half expected her to give up on him when he was away at school and find another man, someone who would be only too willing to take advantage of her.

But here she was, naked and warm and *his*—at least for tonight.

She let out a breath, her hands fisting in the sheets again, as he tasted his way up her other leg, lingering on her most sensitive places. When he reached the top of her thigh again, he did what he'd done before, licking her, taking a hit of her.

She bucked, moaned.

But he wasn't finished.

He kissed his way over her hips, her belly, her ribcage, and her breasts once more, before finally nibbling his way along the column of her throat.

"Mitch! You're torturing me!"

"Oh, honey, I'm just getting started." He kissed her again, let his hand explore her breasts and belly, moving downward in slow circles, savoring the silky feel of her skin.

Then he cupped her and felt a thrill at the way her hips rose to meet his touch. "Show me what you like."

She wasn't shy, but reached down to touch herself, and he felt a sense of pride that she could claim her sexuality without awkwardness.

He watched, the sight of her pleasuring herself making him burn. Then he nudged her hand aside and took over, stroking her clit with his fingers. "Like this?"

"*Mmm, yes!*" She bent one knee and let it fall open to make room for him.

"That's right, love. Open up for me."

Once he was sure he had the hang of things, he built on the motion, exploring her, going for variations on a theme—a little more pressure here, a teasing caress there, a finger circling the entrance to her vagina.

God, she was wet.

Damn.

Oh, he wanted to slide a finger inside her, but he couldn't—not yet.

He lowered his mouth to one breast and feasted on her, his hand still busy between her thighs, need for her thrumming in his chest.

She whimpered, moaned his name, her thighs spreading wider, the fingers of one hand clenching in his hair, the nails of the other biting into her own thigh. "*Mitch.*"

It turned him on to see her so turned on—and to know *he* was responsible.

But he'd gotten a taste of her, and he was hungry for more.

He raised himself, sat back on his heels, and caught her legs behind her knees, pushing them back until they almost touched her shoulders. Then he slowly and deliberately lowered his gaze to her most private flesh. "Oh, Megs."

The sight of her sent blood rushing to his already rock-hard cock, made his balls draw tight and his brain go blank. He tried to remember what he'd told her he would do to her. Then he knelt between her thighs, lowered his mouth to her, and licked, groaning as her taste danced over his tongue.

"*Mitch.*" She moaned his name, her fingers sliding into his hair.

He stroked her where she was most sensitive, his tongue playing with her clit until her every exhale was a ragged moan, her fingers pulling at his hair. Then he did what he'd said he'd do—and sucked her clit into his mouth.

"Oh, *God!*"

He stroked her with his lips and tongue, suckled her, her hips lifting to meet his caresses, forcing him to hold her in place.

That's when he noticed the time.

Oh, thank God.

One minute to midnight.

He stopped, reached for a condom, smiling at her protests.

"You can't stop now!"

"Who's stopping? We're counting down the last minute to the end of your virginity." He held out the condom. "Want to help?"

She sat up, her hair a glorious tangle. "Hell, yes!"

He showed her how to do it, let her roll the condom down his length. Then he stretched out on his back and reached for her, helping her to straddle him. "You're going to control the pace. You decide how much of me to take inside you and how fast. Do what feels good."

"Will it hurt?" Her gaze met his, a mix of desire and nervousness in her eyes, her hands splayed on his chest for balance.

"It might. You can always stop." He glanced at his watch, followed the second hand. "Five... four... three... two... one. Happy Birthday, love."

He held his cock in place for her, one hand on her hip, as she settled herself above him. He hoped she was aroused enough that this would be easy.

As soon as she began to take him inside her, she tensed, sucked in a breath, her eyes going wide. "Oh!"

So it *was* painful.

Damn.

"You don't have to—"

"I'm okay. It wasn't that bad."

Mitch held himself still for her. "Relax. Take it easy."

She exhaled, her eyes drifting shut.

Then slowly, inch by inch, Megs took him inside her.

SWEET JESUS.

It had been almost two years since Mitch had been with a woman, the tight, hot feel of her stealing his breath. He willed himself to relax and to focus on Megs and not on the thrum of his own need. "Give yourself time to get used to me being inside you."

She opened her eyes, the erotic smile that played over her lips making his heart thud. "This is the best birthday present ever."

Then she began to move slowly up and down.

Mitch savored the sight of his cock moving in and out

of her, pleasure unfurling along the base of his spine. But he doubted this would be good for her.

He grasped her hips to still her. "My cock isn't a pogo stick, love. You don't have to bounce up and down. Do what feels good to *you*."

He watched, awed by her as she experimented, searching for her own rhythm. It was like watching a flower open, seeing her transform from teenage girl to fully sexual woman. It meant more than he could say that she had chosen *him* for this moment.

First, she moved her hips in circles. Then she tried rocking herself against him, her breath catching when she found her sweet spot. "This feels *so* good."

Mitch caressed her breasts, palming them, teasing their tight nipples. He focused on her and not the ache in his groin, keeping his hips still, giving her the time she needed. "God, you're beautiful."

She moved faster now, her eyes squeezed shut, her nails biting into his chest, her breath coming in shudders as she rode him.

He reached between her thighs to stroke her clit, then tried to match her motions with quick, shallow thrusts.

"Oooh, *yes*." She moaned out his name. "Mitch!"

Desire for her beat in his chest, the sexual anguish on her face driving him crazy. She was strung out on him, caught in that space where pleasure was torment, every exhale a moan. Then she sucked in a breath—and shattered.

"Mitch!" She cried out, bliss shining on her sweet face.

She was a glimpse of heaven, the sight of her overwhelmed by sexual pleasure putting an ache in Mitch's chest.

He was lost in her, in love with her, and there was no turning back.

He kept up the rhythm with his fingers until her climax had passed and she collapsed, spent, against his chest. Then he held her, kissed her hair, his senses full of her, his cock still hard and buried inside her.

She raised her head, her eyes still smoky, her hair a tangled mess. "Sex is the best thing *ever*. It's even better than climbing."

Well, that didn't hurt his ego.

"Better than climbing?" In a single move, he flipped her onto her back, smiling at her surprised gasp. "That's good, because it's not over."

He wrapped her legs around his waist, looked into her beautiful eyes. Knowing she might be sore, he started with slow, deep thrusts. "How does that feel?"

"Perfect." She ran her hands over his pecs to his shoulders. "Don't stop."

Mitch wanted this to last, but endless months of longing for her had taken their toll, his self-control dangerously close to unraveling. "I've waited so long for this, so long for *you*."

Harder, faster.

He could tell from her face and the way her nails dug into his shoulders that she was aroused again, too. Well, he couldn't leave her wanting.

He shifted his position, tried to graze her clit with his cock on each deep thrust, his control worn down to a single thread, orgasm building deep in his belly. But he had to hold on. He had to hold on for Megs.

She moaned, her eyes drifting shut again. "Oh!"

Harder, faster.

He was hanging on by his fingertips now, so close to that bright edge. He willed himself to relax, held himself deep inside her, grinding his pubic bone against hers.

Oh, yeah, she liked that.

Her breath came in pants now, her heels pressing hard against his ass as if to hold him in place. "So... good... so... good. *Mitch*!"

She arched beneath him, crying out as orgasm claimed her again.

At last, Mitch let himself go, driving into her hard, every thrust taking him higher until he plummeted over the edge, falling with her into paradise.

They lay there, Mitch still inside her, as their heartbeats slowed.

He had to say it. "I love you, Megs."

She moaned, but it was a sad sound. "I love you, too, and it scares the hell out of me. *Please* don't turn out to be a jerk."

He chuckled. "I'll do my best."

———

MEGS CLOSED THE JOURNAL, a rush of emotion making her chest feel tight. She took Mitch's hand, spoke to him even though he was sleeping. "You wanted that night to be special, and it was. It was one of the most incredible nights of my life. The great mystery of sex turned out to be even more magical than I had imagined."

She knew from speaking with other women that it didn't always go like that. Many women didn't climax the first time. Some found it painful. Others thought the whole experience had been awkward and embarrassing.

"You have always put me first, even when I didn't. If that's not love..." She set the journal aside, turned down the lights, drew the blanket over the sheet. "By the way, I looked in those mirrors. I watched you when you were on top, and, damn, it was erotic."

The sight of his muscular ass clenching as he drove himself into her was on her Top 10 Sexual Thrills list.

But it was late, and she desperately needed a full night's sleep.

She kissed his cheek. "You're still that man, you know —the one who made my first time perfect. In my eyes, you always will be."

She left the hospital, went back to the hotel, and fell asleep, still in her clothes.

Chapter 17

AFTER A GOOD NIGHT'S SLEEP, Megs showered and got back to the hospital for an early meeting with Dr. Schwartz. "I haven't seen Mitch yet today. How is he?"

"Mitch has made truly remarkable progress." Dr. Schwartz pulled off his surgical cap, his mask still hanging from around his throat. "I evaluated him this morning, and he is fully conscious now. His pneumonia is gone, and he's breathing well on his own. We're transferring him out of ICU today and putting him on the neurology floor. You asked when he would be out of the woods. I think we're there."

Megs closed her eyes, exhaled, relief flowing through her, as sweet as honey. "That's good to hear. Thank you."

"He'll get a full evaluation, but he has deficits. So far, we know it has impacted his ability to speak and his short-term memory. It has probably affected his balance and ability to walk, too."

"How likely is he to see improvement?"

"I'm sure he'll see some improvement, but it's hard to say how much. Here's what I do know—it's going to take time, and it's going to be frustrating for the two of you, but especially for him."

"Oh, I'm sure of that. Mitch is used to doing things that most people can't even imagine doing. To find himself limited…" Megs searched for the words. "It's going to be a new experience for both of us."

Dr. Schwartz went over the short-term plan—evaluate him for deficits, get him eating again, perform his cranioplasty. "I'm hopeful that we can move him to an acute recovery center in the next couple of weeks to start intensive therapy. In the meantime, we'll do our best to keep him comfortable and support his progress."

Megs stood, shook Dr. Schwartz's hand. "You're a hero in my eyes. Thank you for saving Mitch's life."

Dr. Schwartz smiled. "I love happy endings. We don't always get them, and that makes them all the more precious."

Megs made her way to Mitch's room and found him trying to feed himself red Jello with a large-handled spoon, Riana, the physical therapist, sitting beside him.

Riana smiled. "Speaking of Megs, here she is."

Mitch looked up, and the blob of red Jello fell onto his tray. "Nnno."

"Hey, there, love. How's the Jello?"

Mitch frowned. "Nnnoo."

Riana tried to encourage him. "Hey, most of it is getting into your mouth. That's not easy, especially when you're wearing a collar."

Megs understood that Mitch was frustrated, but, damn, he'd come so far so quickly. "I'll help him if you've got other patients to see."

Riana stood. "He's got some new exercises. I printed them out and left them for you at the nurse's station."

"Thank you. We appreciate your help."

Megs sat beside Mitch. "You haven't eaten food since we had that snack on the ledge on Painted Wall. Do you remember?"

His brow furrowed. "Nno."

He struggled, making other sounds that weren't words, then he dropped his spoon, clearly angry.

Megs took his hand. "You remember me, right?"

He nodded, the motion hampered by his collar. "Mmmek."

"That's right." She couldn't help but smile. She hadn't been sure she'd ever hear his voice again. "Eight days ago, you and I were on vacation at the Black Canyon. We wanted to climb Painted Wall. Do you remember?"

He pondered that, a sad expression coming over his face. "Nnno."

"We were just beneath the Roofs of Mordor, a big overhang, when a huge flake of rock broke off. It hit the overhang and shattered. One of the pieces struck your helmet, fractured your skull, a vertebra in your neck, and your clavicle. You had a hematoma on your brain. You've been in a coma since then, and for a while, it looked like you might die. Do you understand all that?"

He stared at her as if she were talking about someone else.

Then Megs had an idea. She hit the call button. "Hey, it's Megs Hill. Can someone bring us a mirror? Yes, a mirror. Thanks."

Mitch's expression told Megs that none of this made any sense to him.

She squeezed his hand. "You'll see."

A few moments later, a nurse she hadn't met walked in with a hand mirror. "Here you go. Just call me when you're done."

Megs held it so that Mitch could see himself. "The

falling rock hit your head and fractured your skull. They had to do a craniectomy to remove the hematoma, stop the bleeding, and save your life. That bit of your cranium is what's stitched into your abdomen. Yeah, I know. That's completely insane."

He stared at his reflection, reaching with one hand to touch the collar, then the bandages on his clavicle, and then his head. Finally, his gaze moved to Megs, and he made sounds that weren't words but conveyed shock and sadness.

Then the sounds coalesced, became her name. "Mmmek."

She lowered the mirror, set it aside, and held him as best she could. She knew she would probably have to tell him all of this many times in the days ahead, but that was okay. "I know it must be scary and confusing to wake up and not know how you got here. You had a traumatic brain injury, and for days I thought I was going to lose you."

Enough with the dark stuff.

She smiled, and it came from her heart. "But look at you now. You survived what most people wouldn't. You're out of your coma, and you're going to get better. You've got some things you need to re-learn, and I'll be here to help you."

He seemed to relax, his gaze dropping to the spoon. It was a struggle to pick it up and hold onto it, but he managed it. Then, with a look of determination on his face, he scooped out some Jello and carefully brought it to his mouth.

Megs cheered for him. "See? To be fair, Jello wobbles. It can be tricky shit to keep on a spoon even if you haven't had your head smashed by a rock."

Mitch laughed, the sound giving Megs' heart wings.

HIS HEAD ACHING, Mitch watched the lights pass overhead as they wheeled him from one room to another, the medical staff talking to each other about him.

"We removed his subclavian line. He's got an IV. He just had two mgs of morphine before we brought him down. He had some clear liquids for breakfast, but nothing since."

"He's scheduled with PT and OT later today."

"These two bags hold his belongings."

Voices swirled around him, passing over him like the lights, not all of the words making sense, his mind on the reflection he'd seen in that mirror. He was that man—the one with the bandages on his head and the collar around his neck.

He'd recognized his face, though it was thinner. Something had happened to him. He must have fallen. He couldn't remember.

Megs had explained. She could tell him again.

Where was she?

"I'm Debby, your ICU nurse." A woman with brown hair and a warm smile patted his arm. He thought she might be the same woman who had helped Megs get him into this hospital gown. He'd been surprised to find he was naked. "I'm so happy you're doing better, Mitch. You take care of yourself, okay?"

Mitch wanted to answer, to say something, but the words weren't there.

Why was he in the hospital?

Where was Megs?

MEGS SAT in the financial counselor's office, an itemized hospital bill and a stack of brochures on the desk before her. These brochures were about acute recovery facilities. This one covered the process for getting Social Security. Another went over Medicare and what it had to offer. Yet another listed resources for making one's home accessible and finding equipment like wheelchair-friendly vans and lifts.

"I need to read all of this, fill out all of these applications, find a good facility for Mitch, and arrange to have him transported there—and do it all now?"

"I know it's overwhelming." Lora, the financial counselor, was very good at sounding understanding and looking sympathetic while still demanding money. "Just take it one application at a time. How were you planning to pay today?"

And there it was—the monetary side of US healthcare raising its ugly head.

Their insurance hadn't paid anything yet but would pick up much of the bill. But once Mitch was discharged and entered the rehab facility, their share of the cost would skyrocket. Of course, they had savings—retirement funds —but the better acute recovery centers cost more than ten thousand bucks a month.

"I can transfer some funds over and pay by debit card." She would have to call Scarlet Springs Savings and Loan to do that. "I need to step out and make a phone call."

Lora smiled. "Of course."

Megs stepped out of the office and made her way to one of the exits. She walked out into the cool October wind, looked up the number, and called the bank. "Hey, it's Megs Hill. Can I speak to Karl?"

Karl, the bank manager, knew her. She was pretty sure he wouldn't have any problem helping her over the phone.

"Hey, Megs. We're all so sorry about what happened to Mitch. How is he doing?"

"He's awake now, and they've moved him out of ICU." She explained the situation, told him how much they owed the hospital so far. "We've got more than enough to cover that in our retirement accounts. I need to transfer the money into checking so I can pay with by e-check."

"Why, yes, you do have more than enough to cover it, but there's another account—one set up by the folks of Scarlet—and we can tap into that first."

Megs was reluctant to do that. "I don't know. It would be great if those funds went to benefit the whole town."

"The money is earmarked for your use in these regrettable circumstances. Joe was extremely clear about how the money was to be spent."

If anyone in Scarlet could be more stubborn than Megs, it was Joe.

"Is there enough?"

"Why, yes. There's more than a hundred fifty-thousand in that account right now. So, why don't you tell me what you need, and I'll move it over for you."

A hundred fifty-thousand?

That was enough to cover the hospital, several months of rehab, and some alterations to their home.

Megs' throat grew tight. She waited a moment, then gave Karl the information he needed. "Thanks, Karl. This really helps. I'm deeply grateful."

"It's my pleasure. And please tell Mitch we're all pulling for him."

"I will." Megs ended the call.

To think that she'd once been reluctant to move to Scarlet…

She walked back to Lora's office, a great weight lifted off her shoulders.

Thank you, Joe and Rain. Thank you, Scarlet Springs.

———

BY THE TIME Megs left Lora's office, it was mid-afternoon. As she rode in the elevator, she wondered whether she should discuss Mitch's long-term care with him. He was already coping with so much. Was it fair to ask him to participate in these decisions? Was he cognitively able to discuss such things? Would it cause him unnecessary stress?

He'd awakened to find himself and his life almost unrecognizable. She wasn't even sure he had fully understood what she'd told him. With his short-term memory issues, he might not remember anything they'd discussed.

On the other hand, she didn't want to leave him out of decisions that directly impacted his life and well-being. That would infantilize him, depriving him of agency when making decisions might help him feel in control again.

When she reached his room, she found him awake and looking stressed. He lay with the head of his bed raised, getting oxygen through a cannula, anxiety etched into his face. Or was that pain?

When he saw her, he held out his hand. "Mmmek."

She knew him well enough to read the look in his eyes. *Where have you been?*

"I'm sorry. The hospital wanted to talk money." She would bring up rehab facilities some other time. She moved the chair close to his bed and threaded her fingers through his. "I hope they haven't worn you out. Are you in pain?"

"Nnnoo."

"Good." She caressed his hand.

She'd spent the past eight days in a monologue with someone who was in a coma, hoping the sound of her voice would help him. Now that he was awake, she wasn't sure what to say, especially since he might not remember any of it. She decided to keep the conversation light, to focus on daily life. If he was anxious, it might ease his mind to hear of normal, everyday things.

She thought back to the day of the accident and tried to remember all the news she'd shared with him when he'd been in a coma. She told him about all of the good wishes, Rose's gossip, and the fundraising. "The Timberline Mudbugs even put out a special mixtape of your favorite tunes. Isn't that cool?"

She navigated to the Mudbugs' website, found the mixtape, and read off the songs they had included, then played his favorite, holding his hand as she sang along.

Mitch seemed to relax, one of his feet keeping time.

When the song was over, Megs stood. "Where did they put your journal? I've been reading it to you. Do you remember what I read to you last night?"

He looked completely baffled.

"I read your entry from my eighteenth birthday. Do you remember what happened the night I finally turned eighteen?"

His lips curved in a slight smile.

"You *do* remember. Good. I'll never forget." She kissed him before sitting, journal in her lap. "We spent the next couple of days at François' cabin, drinking his wine, soaking in his hot tub, making good use of that bed with its mirrors. Do you remember the mirrors?"

Mitch nodded stiffly, his smile wide now.

"From then on, the Seventies were basically fucking and climbing." She thumbed through the entries. "Oh, yes, here's the time we got busted by a ranger for illegal parking while having sex in your van. That was fun. And then the first time we made love up at the lake. Our free climbs all over Joshua Tree that fall. Do you remember those?"

Mitch's eyelids seemed to grow heavy, but he nodded.

She kept turning the pages. "Oh, yeah. Remember that day when François showed up in Joshua Tree? I thought he was going to demand that we pay for all that wine. Instead, he wanted to fly us to Europe and sponsor some climbs there. We got to take one other person, and we chose Dean. Gridwall was bummed."

Italy, Germany, France, Spain—they'd climbed in all the hottest places with Dean, with François, his wife, Melody, and a photographer, Greg, tagging along. François had been trying to glamorize the sport of climbing, while promoting his line of sportswear. It made business sense for him to try to launch a trend—and it worked.

"That trip piqued our interest in alpine climbing. Dean talked us into climbing the Eiger and the Matterhorn, and we couldn't get enough." She turned the pages. "I see you made lists of the gear we took in our packs. It wasn't exactly ultra-light climbing in those days, was it?"

They'd left Yosemite and started climbing big peaks, bagging the most challenging alpine climbs in Europe, the US, and Patagonia, before attempting the 8,000-meter mountains in the Himalayas.

"Meanwhile, Gridwall and the other dirtbags were putting up incredible first ascents in Yosemite." She laughed. "I'll admit it. I was a little jealous. No matter where we traveled or what we climbed, I loved Yosemite best."

She looked up, saw that Mitch was exhausted. "We'll read more later."

She set the journal aside, opened the foldout chair, and stretched out for a nap beside him.

Chapter 18

MEGS SAT BESIDE MITCH, holding his hand, wishing she could do more to help him through what had to be one of the most difficult days in his life. "She did say that she's seen people recover completely. It's going to take time, but if anyone can do it, you can. I believe in you, Mitch."

Dr. Linda White, the neurologist who'd evaluated him this morning, had diagnosed Mitch with non-fluent aphasia, which meant he could understand language, but couldn't put words together to speak. He'd also been diagnosed with deficits in short-term memory, balance, and, to a lesser degree, his fine and gross motor skills. She had referred him to a speech-language pathologist to help him learn how to speak again, a physical therapy team, and an occupational therapist.

It had been a lot for Mitch to take in all at once.

He sat, silent, his expression unreadable, his fingers twined tightly with hers.

Megs knew that it could have been worse. He could have lost his ability to comprehend language at all. He could've lost his ability to make sounds, smile, and even swallow. He could have lost all of his fine motor skills. He could have lost his ability to take a single step. He could have died. But she didn't think that hearing this would make the journey ahead easier for him.

"I'm excited to see those communication apps that Dr. White recommended. They'll make it easier for you to share what's on your mind. Rain is picking up a tablet for you to use. Do you remember Rain?"

He tried to say her name, a furious expression on his face when he managed only to make a *Wr* sound.

Megs could see that her Susie Buttercup routine—all this positivity—wasn't helping him. "I cannot say how sorry I am you're in this shitty situation, Mitch. I'd do *anything* to change it for you, but I can't. It breaks my heart to see you suffering like this. It was bad fucking luck that the rock fell when it did, and now you've got a long struggle ahead of you, one that you didn't choose. I *hate* that this is how it is for you now, and I know you hate it, too."

The two of them had never faced anything like this.

Then again…

"Do you remember when we climbed K2? We got pinned down by some of the worst wind and cold we've ever encountered near The Bottleneck. We still had about ten hours of climbing to reach the summit. I was chilled to the bone, exhausted. I was coughing and was worried about high-altitude pulmonary edema. Dean had lost feeling in his toes. I thought we were going to be a statistic —part of the twenty-five percent of climbers who die up there."

Megs couldn't do the physical misery justice, not with words. She'd have to resort to interpretive dance or primal screams. Climbing K2 had been the most brutal experience of her life. But she'd gotten through it—thanks to Mitch.

"*You* got me through it, remember? You told me that this mountain was a climb like any other climb. You said we would succeed one step at a time like we always did. No matter how painful it got, we would focus, keep our minds sharp, reach the summit— and go home alive."

She shifted so that Mitch could see her face and took both of his hands in hers. "Mitch, love, you have been in the Death Zone. When we arrived here at the hospital, the doctor told me you had only a forty-percent chance of surviving. Only *forty* percent. That's worse than the odds on K2 or Annapurna."

She let that sink in. "You pulled through, and now you need to finish *this* climb. It's not going to be easy, but you need to do what we did then—focus, keep your mind sharp, and take it one step at a time. I'll be right here."

She saw despair in his eyes—despair, fear, anger.

Then his gaze softened, and he nodded.

A knock at the door.

"Come."

Kurt stepped in, held his hand out for Mitch. "Hey, Mitch. I'm Kurt Calder, Dean Calder's son. I heard you got evicted from ICU. I came to introduce myself and see how you're doing."

Mitch gaped at him as if staring at a dead man.

"He's Dean's son—Kurt. He's a chaplain here at the hospital. He came to visit you several times in the ICU."

Mitch's gaze moved from Megs to Kurt, and he smiled. It was clear he understood—though he probably wouldn't remember.

Megs brought Kurt up to date on Mitch's prognosis and told Mitch that she'd read Kurt parts of his journal that had involved Dean. "I told him you wouldn't mind."

Kurt thanked Mitch. "I got to see a side of my father I'd never seen. I'd be interested in anything you feel like sharing. I know my sister would, too."

"Do you have time for me to read another entry now? Mitch, would that be okay with you?"

"I would love that." Kurt pulled over a chair.

Mitch nodded.

Megs reached for the journal, looked for an entry featuring Dean. "Oh, hey, here's the day we summited Mt. Everest."

Megs began to read.

———

May 11, 1978
Camp 4, South Col
Mt. Everest

MITCH CHECKED his crampons to make sure they were tight, their headlamps bobbing in the starlit darkness of Camp 4. Dean stood beside him, ready to move on. Megs was still inside the tent, taking extra care with her feet, which had become painfully cold on yesterday's ascent from Camp 3.

A few minutes later, she joined them. "Let's move."

Mitch insisted on checking her crampons first.

"Did I tie my shoes right, Daddy?" She put on the mask that would warm air before she breathed it.

Mitch did the same. "Yes. Good girl."

Megs hadn't said anything, but Mitch knew she must be feeling the pressure. If they were successful today, she would be the first American woman to summit Mt. Everest —and the first woman to summit without guides or supplemental oxygen.

The three of them had chosen to tackle the mountain without oxygen, believing that climbing with oxygen could make a person overly confident. Without the artificial boost, they would know exactly how well their bodies were handling the altitude—and would have to be honest about their ability to climb. As for guides, how could they say they had climbed any mountain if someone carried their gear and went ahead of them to make the path safer and more accessible?

It was probably all ego and bullshit, but it sounded good to the reporters.

It was 9 PM. when they started their summit attempt, the sky full of stars. Their goal was to be off the summit well before 2 p.m. tomorrow so they would be back at Camp 4 by late afternoon, well before any sudden storm could move in.

They were in Everest's Death Zone now—above 26,000 feet—so none of them had the energy or breath to spare for conversation as they started up the steep Triangular Face toward an area called The Balcony. Mitch and Dean had talked it over privately. They had agreed that Megs should lead and set the pace. She was tougher than either of them, but she also had a shorter stride and smaller lung capacity.

Still, she set a brisk pace through the bitter cold, the three of them finding a rhythm, syncing their steps to their breathing.

Step, inhale. Step, exhale.

They took each step with care, each of them carrying an ice ax in case they needed to stop a fall. One slip, and they could easily plummet to their deaths.

Step, inhale. Step, exhale.

And so it went for hour after hour.

When they reached The Balcony, they stopped to

PAMELA CLARE

hydrate and get some calories before tackling the Southeast Ridge Slabs—a steep section along a stone ridge with fixed ropes. A slip in either direction would be fatal.

Megs munched granola. "Four hours. Not bad."

Mitch drank. "Not bad at all."

But Dean stood there looking over at Lhotse. "Look at this view."

The snow was such a contrast to the darkness that the shapes of neighboring peaks were easy to make out.

When they felt rested, they started up the Slabs, clipping carabiners to the fixed rope and taking each step carefully. Much of the snow had blown away here, leaving sections of rock with scant coverage and making their crampons slip. It was a bit like walking on a beach—at more than 27,000 feet altitude.

Step, inhale. Step, exhale.

This section was more challenging than Mitch had imagined, in part because of the limited snow coverage, but also because they were gaining altitude with every stride, the lack of oxygen a strain on mind and body. His quads, glutes, and hamstrings burned, his heart thudding in his chest. The cold gnawed at his fingers, toes, and the small amount of exposed skin on his face.

Step, inhale. Step, exhale.

They couldn't see the true summit from here, just the South Summit, which was far below their ultimate goal. Still, Mitch kept looking up, the part of him that wasn't occupied with the physical struggle in awe of the mountain. The Sherpa name for Mt. Everest was Chomolungma —Mother of the World.

It was a fitting name.

But right now, Mama was kicking their asses.

"It's like I always say." Dean trudged along behind

Mitch, as out of breath as Mitch and Megs. "Stick with the pain… and the pain will stick with you."

Megs burst into laughter, the sound still magical to Mitch after four years together. "Don't you dare make me laugh!"

They took another break on the South Summit, catching their breath as well as they could, giving their muscles some calories and electrolytes, taking in a view that few people would ever see.

Mitch checked his watch, saw that it was just after 4:30 in the morning. "That was three hours. We're making good time. How are your feet?"

Megs looked up at him, her mask concealing her expression. "What feet?"

Shit.

They decided Dean should lead them from there to the summit. Climbing Everest had been his dream. He set out at a moderate pace, and they quickly reached the bottom of the infamous Hillary Step, where the climb became vertical and technical.

Dean clipped into the fixed rope and, using a stem stance, made his way over the section of exposed rock, Megs following, Mitch taking up the rear.

That's when it hit him.

They were doing it. They were going to summit Mt. Everest.

But the hard work wasn't over. For the next forty-five minutes, they slogged over a steep, snow-covered ridge, fatigue setting in, the air desperately thin as they neared 29,000 feet in elevation.

Step, inhale, exhale. Step, inhale, exhale.

Mitch's mind began to grow dull, strange dream-like thoughts drifting through his head. He had to work hard to focus on each step as they moved upward.

Step, inhale, exhale. Step, inhale, exhale.

And then they were there—at the top of the world.

They took off their masks and gaped at the unbelievable sight around them.

The summit itself was small compared to the rest of the mountain. Buddhist prayer flags, faded from the sun, fluttered in the breeze. To the east, the sun had begun to rise, making the snow glisten pink.

Adrenaline and elation pushed the dullness from Mitch's mind. He had never imagined when he was a kid that he would climb Mt. Everest one day. But here he was, with the woman he loved and his best friend, watching the sunrise on the top of the world's highest mountain.

Megs turned in a slow, careful circle. "My God, would you look at that?"

Dean glanced around, tears spilling down his cheeks. "We did it."

Megs drew the two of them into a group hug, their down suits, gloves, and packs making it awkward. Her voice strained, whether from the lack of oxygen or because she was on the brink of tears, he couldn't say. "There's no one I'd rather share this moment with than the two of you."

"Yeah." Mitch couldn't agree more.

Dean cleared his throat. "I don't know where I'd be without you two."

They stayed on the summit for an hour, taking photos of the three of them together and the landscape below, drinking in the scenery that they knew they would likely never see again. Then they started the dangerous descent back to Camp 4.

MEGS CLOSED THE JOURNAL, a bittersweet ache in her chest.

God, she missed Dean.

Kurt blinked away the sheen of tears in his eyes. "Thank you for sharing that, Mitch, and thanks for reading for us, Megs. I'm so grateful that it's all written down. All I've heard about that climb is what my father told my mother. This gave me a much better idea of what it meant to him."

Megs understood that. "I think Everest mattered more to him than any of the other eight-thousand-meter peaks, even more than K2, which was a much tougher climb."

Kurt nodded. "My mother told me that he climbed to exorcise demons from the war. She said it was on Everest where he finally broke free. He believed that if Everest hadn't destroyed him, nothing would."

Mitch looked like he wanted to say something, grief in his eyes. His lips moved, but no words came out.

Megs rested her hand on Mitch's thigh, tried to be his voice. "Regardless of the anguish he suffered as a result of the war, your father was a strong man and brave. *Nothing* broke him. We loved your father, Kurt. He was our best friend."

Kurt nodded, smiled. "Your friendship meant the world to him."

Megs remembered the mayhem that had ensued when they'd returned from Nepal. "Reporters were waiting for us when our plane landed in Los Angeles. Remember that, Mitch? Everyone wanted to do a story on the first American woman to summit Everest. One reporter asked you and Dean why you had decided to climb with a woman."

Mitch rolled his eyes.

"How did you answer that?" Kurt asked Mitch.

Megs answered. "Mitch said something like, 'This

woman is one of the best climbers in the world. We're lucky she let us climb with her.' Your father said, 'We needed someone who would know when to stop and ask for directions.'"

Kurt grinned, making eye contact with Mitch. "Good answers."

"Then someone asked if we felt we were too good to climb in the US, given how much time we spent abroad. I told them we didn't feel that way at all. We were just doing our best to avoid disco."

Kurt laughed at this. "And who can blame you?"

"The three of us already had a variety of sponsorships —gear, energy bars, clothing. We were making good money climbing right at the time when the sport exploded. Companies started signing us to do ads—and not just us. The dirtbags had been doing some pretty amazing climbing in Yosemite. By the end of the Seventies, most of us had landed lucrative advertising contracts."

She smiled as she remembered. "Your father did commercials for running shoes, though he'd never been a runner. Baker, who'd gotten into free soloing, did ads for shaving cream. Cook did a series of ads for Chevy pickups. President Carter pardoned draft dodgers, so Gridwall was off the hook. He stumped for some electric razor. Accardo had a contract for some goofy breakfast drink. Mitch did commercials for watches."

"How about you?" Kurt asked.

"Mostly deodorant and feminine hygiene products. 'Do you ever worry about body odor or feeling fresh while climbing Mt. Everest? No? Neither did I.'" Megs couldn't help but laugh at the absurdity of it.

Kurt laughed, too, but Mitch looked tired now.

Kurt must have noticed because he glanced at his

watch and stood. "Thanks for the visit. Can I come see you again, Mitch? Would that be okay?"

Mitch nodded, held out a hand.

Kurt grasped it, placed his other hand on top of it, and said a brief prayer. "I'm so glad to see you back with us. Please call if you need anything."

Megs stood, gave Kurt a hug. "Thanks for stopping by. Come again soon."

Kurt closed the door behind him.

"He really does look like his father, doesn't he?"

Mitch looked perplexed, and Megs realized he might not remember that Kurt had just been in the room—or know who Kurt was. He tried to speak, making only unintelligible sounds, his anger with himself heartbreaking to witness.

Megs took his hand once more. "Please don't be hard on yourself. I can't imagine how frustrating this is, but your inability to speak isn't a moral or intellectual failing. You almost *died*, and you're doing the best you can. It won't be like this forever. It *will* get better. But you should rest now."

She left his side long enough to close the blinds and retrieve her phone, which she set to play their favorite classical music playlist, the one they often listened to at night before bedtime. Then she sat beside him once again and held his hand while he drifted into an uneasy sleep.

Chapter 19

MEGS SAT in the surgery waiting room, going over different acute rehabilitation facilities with Rain and watching the surgery board. Dr. Schwartz had said the cranioplasty would probably take two hours. So far, an hour had passed.

"I really liked this place." Rain set a different brochure on the table. She'd spent the past week touring various facilities, asking for information. "It's in Boulder, which means you're just down the canyon. It's got some new weightless technology that assists people in re-learning how to walk. The rooms are nicer and feel more like family suites than hospital rooms. They have pool therapy, private treatment rooms, and an award-winning speech-pathology team."

"How much does it cost?" Megs was afraid to ask.

"Almost fourteen thousand."

Megs almost choked. "Per *month*? Jesus fried chicken!"

The couple sitting across the room looked up from their phones, disapproving expressions on their faces.

Rain waved off the expense. "Helping Mitch heal is all that matters."

Megs looked at the photos, liking what she saw. "And you prefer this place over the ones in Lafayette and Aurora?"

"Definitely. The place in Lafayette had small, dark rooms and felt very clinical. The one in Aurora smelled like unemptied bedpans and is a lot farther from home."

Megs wrinkled her nose. "Okay, you've convinced me. Thanks for visiting these places. I suppose I should've done it, but I didn't want to leave Mitch."

"It was no trouble. Your place is here. Sasha wanted to come with me, but the Team got toned out."

Megs looked at the brochure for the Boulder facility again—the Front Range Rehabilitation Hospital. "I guess I need to fill out an application."

"It's available online. You should be able to use Mitch's tablet for that. How does he like the communication apps?"

Megs had to laugh. "The first thing he made the new program say was, 'This is stupid.' Not being able to communicate is really difficult for him."

"It would be difficult for anyone." Rain reached into her enormous handbag. "I brought those books of poetry —Walt Whitman and Kahlil Gibran."

Megs took the books from her. "Thanks so much. Mitch and I have a tradition of reading poetry to each other before we go to sleep. We started doing that back in the dirtbag days in Yosemite, and we never stopped."

"That's awesome—or should I say *far out*?"

"Listen, whippersnapper, that expression was cool in its day." Megs reached over and squeezed Rain's hand. "You and Joe have gone above and beyond to help us. I don't even know how to thank you. I will always be grateful."

"You're welcome." Rain squeezed back. "Here's the thing, Megs—I know you'd do everything you could to help us if our positions were reversed. Remember when we got eight feet of snow in just a few days and my roof caved in?"

"I surely do. That's what finally got you and Joe together. I think the whole town was grateful."

Rain laughed. "Well, before Joe and I got together, you had the Team out there clearing snow off people's roofs so it wouldn't happen to anyone else. I've heard stories about Moretti going from rooftop to rooftop on skis."

"I think they enjoyed themselves a little too much that night."

"And then there was the time when Hawke asked you to tone out the Team to clean his cabin before he got there with Vicki. You, Sasha, and Mitch went over and cleaned up his pigsty so that he could make a good impression."

"We still rib him about that."

"The point I'm trying to make is that you and Mitch do nothing every day but save people. We'd be a sad town full of petty, little people if we didn't repay that love. You two are a huge source of pride for Scarlet."

The doors from the OR opened, and Dr. Schwartz walked out, a broad smile on his face. "It's done. It went well. It was completely textbook."

He motioned Megs to a private room to talk.

Rain said goodbye, leaving all the materials she'd picked up with Megs. "Let us know how it's going."

"Thanks, Rain." Megs hugged her and then followed Dr. Schwartz, remembering the last time she'd stepped into this particular room with him. They hadn't known then whether Mitch would survive. "How's he doing?"

"He's doing really well. As you know, it's early to be doing a cranioplasty. Most doctors wait for the three-to-six-month mark. But there are a host of complications that are lessened in cases where we can perform cranioplasty early."

He explained how he'd used the bone he'd removed from Mitch's cranium along with a custom-made titanium plate to cover the small area where the bone had shattered. "It's a serious surgery and comes with several significant risks, possibly the greatest of which in his case is infection. He's getting IV vancomycin, and, of course, we still have him on anti-seizure meds. We'll keep him in ICU for the next couple of days and then move him back to the neurology floor. If all goes well, we should be ready to transfer him to an acute rehab facility next week. Have you picked one out?"

"We were thinking of the Front Range Rehabilitation Hospital."

"That would be my choice for him, as well."

That was reassuring.

"Can I go see him?"

"He's still in recovery. I'll have someone come get you when he's back in ICU."

Once again, Megs found herself thanking Dr. Schwartz. "If you're ever in Scarlet Springs, stop in at Knockers or come by The Cave—that's what we call Team HQ."

"Thanks. I might take you up on that."

———

MITCH GRADUALLY BECAME aware of his surroundings. A persistent beep. Women's voices. *Her* voice. His own moans.

"Are you in pain?" Warm fingers held his hand.

He had a headache, and his abdomen hurt, too.

"I'll get him some morphine."

"Thanks, Debby."

What had happened? Had he fallen again? He had fallen—or maybe it had been a rock. He couldn't remember. He'd been in the hospital.

"Here's the morphine."

When he opened his eyes later, he found Megs sitting beside him.

"Hey, handsome. The surgery was a success. Your skull is back on your head and out of your abdominal wall."

What the *hell* was she saying?

"Dr. Schwartz said it went well." She smiled. "You've got a little titanium plate, too. I guess I can call you a metalhead now."

He couldn't quite comprehend why that was funny.

"If all goes well, they'll transfer you out of ICU tomorrow evening, and we'll be able to move you to a rehabilitation facility in about a week."

A rehabilitation facility.

Fear snaked through Mitch, cold and dark.

What was wrong with him? What if he never got better?

Before he could work out the answer, he was asleep once more.

━━

MEGS WALKED beside Mitch's wheelchair as they left the hospital, the nurses who had cared for him so diligently these past three weeks standing near the exit and applauding for him. Did he understand why they were cheering?

Megs thanked each of them as she passed. "These

nurses saved your life. They're happy that you've recovered enough to leave the hospital."

Mitch waved, a baseball cap covering his shaved head and scar, the cervical collar still around his neck. He had been excited to get out of that damned hospital gown and into real clothes and, apart from helping him with balance, he hadn't needed her help getting dressed.

The LPN who pushed the wheelchair stopped outside the van. "Here's your ride."

Two paramedics greeted them and helped transfer Mitch into a new wheelchair, steadying him so he wouldn't fall. "Ready to go?"

"Yeah." Mitch nodded.

That was one of this week's new additions to his vocabulary.

Megs knelt so he could see her face. "I'm going to get into my SUV and follow you to the new place. These guys are going to take care of you. I'll be right behind you, and I'll see you soon."

"Yeah."

She hurried to her car, which already held Mitch's belongings and her bags from the hotel, and followed the transport toward I-25. Some part of her couldn't believe they'd come this far, that they were leaving the hospital.

She drew a breath, allowed herself a moment to feel nothing but gratitude.

Damn, they'd gotten lucky.

It wasn't a long drive—maybe forty minutes. Still, it felt strange to be away from Mitch for so long. She knew the medical staff in the van would take care of him, but, given his short-term memory problems, she wasn't sure he understood what was happening. She didn't want him to think she'd abandoned him or disappeared.

Megs turned the radio to her favorite classic rock

station and started to relax as she sang along to the Doors, the Guess Who, and James Taylor. She might have said that today's music *sucked* by comparison, but Lark, Rain's older daughter, had recently said that hating modern music was a sign that someone was truly growing old.

So Megs wouldn't say it. Oh, *hell*, no. She would just think it.

She was singing along to Boston's *More than a Feeling* when she reached the top of McCaslin Mesa on Highway 36. She stopped singing, her heart seeming to swell. The Rockies stretched out before her as far as the eye could see, first the foothills with their green pine forests and then the snow-capped high peaks. Scarlet Springs was tucked in at the base of those high peaks just up Boulder Canyon. They weren't quite home, but at least they could see the mountains now.

She followed Mitch's transport van into Boulder, turning into the facility's parking lot. Immediately, she could see where some of that money went. The grounds were immaculately landscaped, the building artfully designed.

She climbed out, grabbed Mitch's stuff, and walked over to the van where the paramedics were unloading Mitch. She kissed his cheek, pointed. "See the mountains? We're closer to home."

His gaze fixed on the high peaks, and he drew a deep breath, the sight as stirring for him as it was for her. "Mmmow…"

"Mountains. You almost got it."

While staff settled Mitch in his room, Megs spent the next hour filling out paperwork, getting a permit for her vehicle, meeting the medical staff who would care for Mitch, and listening to the director go over the rules. Megs would have to sign in and out any time she entered or left the facility. The front door would be locked at 10 p.m., after which no one would be admitted. Mitch would have meals with the other residents in the cafeteria, and Megs was welcome to join him. His treatment schedule would be available online and would also be posted inside his room.

Megs did her best to absorb all of this and carried a folder full of documents to Mitch's room on the second floor. The place was plain with a few generic-looking prints on the walls, a TV, a chest of drawers, a few chairs, a nightstand, and a double bed. The bathroom was accessible with grab bars and a shower with a bench.

Mitch sat in his wheelchair in the middle of the room, looking lost.

"What do you think of your new digs?" Megs sat on a chair beside him. "This is the acute rehabilitation hospital. Now, you can finally focus on getting better. They said I can be with you during treatment. I can also stay overnight."

Mitch tapped in a message on his tablet. "When do we go home?"

He'd been playing with the voices, and this one had an English accent.

"I liked the Aussie accent better." She took his hand. "I don't know when we'll go home. This must be overwhelming, but this place can give you the kind of treatment you need to recover. The faster you recover, the sooner we'll get to go back to Scarlet. I know you can do this, and I'll help in every way I can."

There came a knock at the door, and a young Latino stepped into the room. "Hey, Mr. Ahearn. I'm Rodrigo Pérez, a member of your physical therapy team. Are you ready to get to work?"

Mitch seemed to steel himself, his jaw set. "Yeah."

Megs rested a hand on his shoulder. "That's my man."

MITCH STEPPED CAREFULLY into the shower, Megs beside him to hold him steady. He was mentally and physically exhausted from his first day at this new place. He accepted Megs' help turning on the water.

"Is that too hot?"

"Nnno."

Megs closed the shower curtain. "I'll be right here if you need me."

He sat on the shower bench because of his balance and let the water sluice over his skin, the hot spray soothing muscles that were sore from…

He wasn't sure why they were sore. From the accident that had landed him here? From his injuries? From today's therapy?

"That weightless treadmill was interesting. They were all very impressed with your level of fitness."

Mitch had already forgotten about that, but now that she mentioned it, he, too, had been impressed with the machine. They'd told him they would take that data to create therapies specific to his problems. But would any of it work? Or would he always be like this—dependent, unable to speak, fragile?

He took the soap and a washcloth and scrubbed his skin clean, finally able to get his incisions wet. He rinsed and then reached for the shampoo. Then he remembered he didn't have hair yet. He had asked Megs to buzz off the long parts to make it the same length as the area around the incision. He stuck his head beneath the spray for a rinse and tried to figure out how to turn off the water.

"Do you need help?"

"Nnno." By the time he was dried off and in a pair of

pajama bottoms and a T-shirt, he was both exhausted—and too keyed up to sleep.

Megs helped him get settled in bed, arranging the pillows so that they supported his neck and arm on the side with the fractured clavicle. A nurse came for vitals and to dispense meds. Then Megs dimmed the lights and sat in the chair beside him.

She picked up the Walt Whitman book he'd given her so many years ago.

"Nno." He pointed to his journal.

She set Walt aside, picked up the heavy, leather-bound tome, and went to the bookmark. "We left off with Everest. After that, there were more Himalayan climbs—Cho Oyu, Shishapangma, Lhotse, Makalu, Nanga Parbat, Annapurna, and the others. I don't feel like reading about K2, if that's okay with you."

"Yeah." Mitch was fine with that.

K2 had been sheer physical misery. He'd always told those who asked that the Savage Mountain, as K2 was known, hadn't killed them because they were too damned stupid and stubborn to die.

Having summitted all the world's highest peaks, Dean had left professional climbing after K2. A short time later, he met and married Beth. They had settled in Ridgeway, Colorado, on a small ranch, while Mitch and Megs entered the world of competitive sports climbing. They'd won the men's and women's world championships in their first year, setting money aside for when they could no longer climb.

She turned the pages, and something fell out and onto the floor. She bent down, picked it up, unfolded it, and laughed. "Oh, my God! You kept a copy—the infamous nude cover. I want to read that. Is that okay with you?"

Mitch smiled, nodded.

"I need to get a drink of water. Do you need water?"

She checked his plastic pitcher and carried it out into the hallway.

She'd been so patient with him, so thoughtful. Though he remembered very little, he knew she'd been beside him through this entire ordeal. He also knew that, in some ways, this had been more difficult for her than for him. He didn't remember the accident that had put him here, but she did. He knew that, whatever had happened, she'd been the one to pull him through. He could see the ordeal written in her eyes every time she looked at him.

She returned quickly, set his pitcher on his bedside table, and sat in her chair, water bottle on the table beside her. "I remember when François called and told us that Sports magazine wanted us for an interview and cover shoot. You asked what they had in mind. We both thought they'd want photos of us climbing. François said they wanted us to be completely nude. You were hesitant, but I was all for it."

If he'd been able to, Mitch would have told Megs that he hadn't been surprised at her reaction. She'd always been willing to throw caution to the wind, especially if there was any chance of upsetting gender stereotypes or pissing off society's prudes.

"When the magazine hit the shelves, the press went crazy. I guess you could say the cover went viral, though the phrase didn't exist back then. People's big objection wasn't that we were naked, but that your hands were touching my breasts."

Megs took a drink and began to read.

Chapter 20

November 1985

MITCH AND MEGS arrived at the studio in New York City to find it different from what they'd imagined. Much of it was just empty space like a vacant warehouse, with chairs, ladders, and huge rolls of paper or cloth—he couldn't tell from a distance. Bars crossed the ceiling, supporting large lights.

"There they are!" Myrna, the art director, walked toward them, clipboard in hand, her heels clicking on the tile floor. Her face was carefully made up, her curly hair held aloft by what must have been a gallon of hairspray. "Let's introduce you to Rod, our photographer, and I'll show you to the dressing room."

"More like the *undressing* room," Megs whispered.

Rod was a tall man, maybe in his late 40s. Dressed only in black, he wore his dark hair in a mullet, gold chains around his neck. He greeted them each with a hug and a kiss, as if they were old friends. "Mitch! Megs, darling! I'm so glad you're here! Isn't the weather awful? It's so cold and gray."

Mitch could see that Megs was fighting not to laugh.

She took off her down jacket. "We've seen worse weather."

"Of course, you have." He went over what would happen during the shoot. They would try a variety of poses, looking for something exciting and provocative. "No breasts, dicks, or pussies will go on the cover for obvious reasons. We have ways of hiding those lovely bits—text, airbrushing, artfully placed shadows. It's a closed set today, so no one who shouldn't be here will walk in on us."

Myrna led them back to the dressing room, where they found robes. "Can I bring you herbal tea or coffee or something stronger?"

Mitch answered this time. "No, thanks. We're fine."

"Okay." Myrna glanced at her watch. "When you're ready, just head to the left and take a left again, and you'll find our makeup artists and stylists. Let me know if you need anything."

Makeup artists? Stylists?

"I've got a question." Megs put a hand on her belly. "I've got recent scars from getting my tubes tied. They're small but—"

"Lucky you! No worries. We can airbrush that out."

François, who'd become their de facto agent and fixer, had connected them with a doctor in Canada willing to do the surgery when they hadn't been able to find anyone willing to sterilize a 29-year-old, unmarried, childless woman in Colorado.

For Megs, it meant being able to enjoy sex without worrying about an unwanted pregnancy. For Mitch, it meant no more condoms.

"Thanks, Myrna."

Inside the dressing room, they found a bouquet of flowers sitting on a glass table, cold bottles of water beside it, fluffy white bathrobes hanging on a hook.

Mitch found all of it surreal. "I think I prefer being photographed while I'm climbing. Stylist? What do they plan to do with my hair?"

Megs stood on tiptoe, rubbed the top of his head, his hair cut short. "Braid it?"

They stripped down to their skin, hanging their clothes on hooks.

Megs looked at Mitch's dick. "The first thing everyone is going to do is check out your penis. Men, women, children, pets, the fly on the wall—they're all going to stare. I might stare, too."

Mitch's dick wasn't *that* big. "Ten bucks says they'll try very hard not to look."

"You're on."

They spent what felt like an inordinate amount of time with two makeup artists. It was a new experience for Mitch to wear mascara, eyeliner, and lip tint.

Megs seemed to find it all funny. "Don't you look pretty? I'm jealous."

"Are you kidding?" Terri, Megs' makeup artist, put the finishing touches on Megs' lips. "God, I wish I had your arms. They're so sculpted. You look beautiful!"

"You do." Mitch had to agree—but it wasn't the makeup.

Megs had always been the most beautiful woman he'd ever seen—fit, strong, sharp-witted, with the face of an angel.

Myrna led them to the set, where Rod stood on a ladder, adjusting lights. On one end of the room stood the biggest fan Mitch had ever seen. Hanging from the ceiling was a long blue curtain that would serve as their backdrop.

Camera hanging from a strap around his neck, Rod told them how this would work. "You're not professional models, I know. So what we'll do is turn on the fan to catch your hair and then run through a series of poses while I shoot. I'll ask you to move this way or that, to lift your chin or shift your arm. Let's just see how it goes. What kind of music would you like—disco, R&B, jazz?"

Megs looked up at Mitch, and he could see she was close to laughter.

Mitch fought to keep a straight face. "We don't need music."

But Rod apparently did, and soon *Last Dance* was playing. "You can leave your robes on that sofa."

They did as they were asked and then stood stark naked in front of about fifteen people, Megs' hair flying into Mitch's face, the two of them fighting not to laugh when everyone's gaze went straight to Mitch's dick.

Myrna wasn't even coy about it. "You are one lucky woman."

"Don't I know it?" Megs said, then whispered, "That's ten bucks."

Rod put them through a series of poses, clearly not satisfied.

Then Megs had a suggestion. "Can we try this?"

She turned to Mitch and told him to stand behind her and reach around to hold her breasts while she used her hands to cover her pubic area.

Well, Mitch would never turn down a chance to hold her breasts.

Rod stared at them for a moment, then looked through his lens and started clicking. "Beautiful! Beautiful! I love it! Intimate. Strong. Provocative."

All Mitch could think about was Megs and how good it felt to be the man who went home with her. Being naked with her in front of an audience made his blood run hot, and he had to fight not to get an erection.

Afterward, they put on their robes and walked back to the dressing room.

The moment the door closed, they were on each other, tearing off one another's robes. There was no need for foreplay or finesse. Mitch backed Megs up against the wall, lifted her off the floor, and slowly buried himself inside her, thrusting deep. The two of them came hard and fast—and in complete silence.

Afterward, a driver took them back to their hotel, where they started from scratch, taking time now for tenderness, indulging themselves, prolonging one another's pleasure.

Mitch drew Megs against him, kissed her. "I love you."

She snuggled into his chest. "I love you, too, but you still owe me ten bucks."

MEGS LOOKED up to find Mitch looking angry, distraught. "What's wrong?"

He tapped a message into his tablet. "What if I can't?"

"What if you can't?" It took her a moment. "What if you can't have sex?"

His gaze met hers, despair in those brown eyes.

Megs hadn't imagined her heart could break more for him, but it did.

She set the journal aside, sat on the bed beside him, took his hand. "I won't love you any less, if that's why you're worried. You've been through a terrible ordeal. You're on a lot of medications, and those narcotics and anti-seizure meds can make it hard to get an erection.

None of the medical staff have suggested this will impact you sexually in the long run. Give yourself time to heal."

He tapped another message into the tablet. "I want to try it."

"You want to try to have sex—*now*?"

He answered without the tablet this time. "Yeah."

She supposed some people would find it scandalous—having sex in a rehab hospital. Though why shouldn't they? Mitch was injured. He wasn't dead.

Still, she hesitated. "I don't want to hurt you. You've just been through a second major surgery, and you've got a broken neck and a clavicle that hasn't healed."

Megs thought about it. "I suppose I could go down on you."

He tapped in another message. "Yes, please."

"Change the accent back to Australian, and ask me again." She was just teasing him now, but he did what she asked.

"Yes, please."

"Okay, then." She walked to the door, locked it, then made her way back to the bed, taking off her clothes. She knew how visual he was, how much looking at her body aroused him. "Don't put any pressure on yourself, okay?"

She knelt beside him, drew down his covers.

He reached out, cupped one of her breasts, fondled her. It was the first time he'd touched her sexually since the night before the accident, pleasure sliding through her. But this wasn't about her.

She tugged off his pajama bottoms and pushed up his T-shirt, his body with its new scars so precious to her, his gaze raking over her.

"I know every inch of you." She started slow, leaning down to kiss his chest, those firm pecs with their dusting of graying curls. She teased his nipples, kissing them, licking, sucking them into her mouth—and delighting when she felt his abs clench. "I love every inch of you."

His fingers slid into her hair. "Mmm."

It was the first sound of pleasure he'd made in so long.

She didn't look at his penis. She didn't want to put pressure on him. Instead, she caressed and kissed his chest, her lips pressing against his heartbeat before shifting to kiss and taste his biceps. "God, I love your muscles."

She wasn't just saying that. She'd always loved his body —all that muscle and soft skin, his flat, dark nipples, his sculpted chest. "My man."

She kissed and nibbled her way down the center of his belly, giving each muscle of his six-pack lavish attention before moving on to nip and lick his obliques. "My favorite muscle."

She could have wept honest-to-God tears when she saw his erection, not for herself but for him. She kissed her way around it, then, uncertain how long it would last with those meds in his bloodstream, she took him in hand and stroked.

"Did you ever pay me that ten bucks?"

His answer was a soft chuckle.

She lowered her lips to his cock, swirled her tongue over the swollen head, then took him into her mouth, sucking, bringing him fully erect. She knew his body well and knew what he liked most. Holding onto the base of his cock with one hand, she moved the other up and down his length in tandem with her mouth.

Mitch sucked in a breath, his fingers drawing tight in her hair.

And her pulse skipped—not from desire, but from joy for him.

Focused entirely on his pleasure, she built on her

rhythm, swirling her tongue around him as she moved, going faster when little thrusts of his hips demanded it.

God, she loved him—her other half, her heart, her delight.

She knew how to read him. He was close now, his balls drawing tight, one hand clenched in the bedsheets, the other fisted in her hair.

He came with a groan, his hips lifting off the bed, come spilling over her hand as she finished him.

Heart soaring, she reached for the tissues, wiped them both clean, then helped him pull up his pajama bottoms once more. "Well, I guess that answers *that* question."

He reached for her, relief and love shining on his face.

"I can't sleep in your bed. It's against the rules."

He raised a middle finger to the ceiling, a fierce expression on his face.

"In that case…" She slipped into bed beside him, pressed her cheek to his chest, one strong arm holding her close. "I'm so glad you're still here with me, Mitch. Whether you learn to speak or climb again, I'm so grateful that you're alive."

When he'd fallen asleep, she got out of bed, dressed, and unlocked the door. Then she lay down in her foldout chair, her heart brimming with gratitude.

Thank God.

⸻

THAT FOLLOWING SUNDAY, Megs drove back to Scarlet Springs with Mitch's blessing. He'd made it through his first week of rehab and was already showing improvement with speech and balance.

"Go," he'd said when she explained she needed to do laundry.

Then he'd tapped a message into the tablet, asking her to be back for dinner.

"You got it."

It felt strange to enter their home after so long away. The place felt frozen in time somehow. And yet, there was proof that others had been here. The gear she and Mitch had taken on vacation was laid out neatly in their gear room. Someone—probably Rain—had stacked the mail on the kitchen table.

She lugged their dirty clothes to the laundry room, sorted it all into piles, and started the washing machine. She was in the middle of opening the mail when someone knocked on the door. She had hoped to slip in and out of town without being noticed. But Scarlet had only about 1,500 residents, and her SUV was parked in the driveway for the first time in weeks. Someone was bound to see it.

Megs opened the door to find Winona Belcourt, who was now seven months along with her first child. She and her husband, Jason Chiago, lived in a house down the mountainside and were Megs and Mitch's nearest neighbors.

Her face lit up. "Megs! You're home?"

Megs ushered her inside and closed the door behind her. "Just for today. I need to do laundry and catch up on mail. How are you?"

Win touched her hands to her bulging belly. "I'm feeling good, though I'm tired sometimes. I got an intern from CSU to help manage the clinic."

"That's smart. Have a seat. Can I make you some tea?"

Win shook her head. "You do what you came to do, and I'll make the tea."

"The tea bags are in the cupboard to the left of the stove." Megs went back to opening mail, the two of them talking about little stuff—Win's wildlife clinic, the growth of aspen on the slopes that had burned in the big fire more than a year ago, Win and Jason's growing list of baby names.

"We're trying to decide whether to go with Lakota and Tohono O'odham names or whether to mix those with English names."

"You could alternate—Lakota for one, Tohono O'odham for the next."

"That's a cool idea."

"Oh, I'm full of cool ideas. Just ask me."

Another knock.

Sasha bounded through the door, her hair in braids, a ski cap on her head. She hugged Megs and Win. "Is he coming home?"

"Not yet." Megs gestured toward the table. "Win has some tea almost ready. Sit down. Tell me what's going on."

Sasha was training hard for the next round of world championships. The Team was operating smoothly. "Conrad is almost as strict as you are."

"Almost?" Megs teased. "I'll have to talk with him about that."

Then Sasha and Win asked about Mitch.

Before Megs could answer, there was another knock.

Lexi waddled in, out of breath. "You're home?"

"Not exactly." Megs glanced at her belly. She looked so uncomfortable. "You'd better have that baby soon, or you're going to pop."

"Tell me about it." Lexi sat. "This is my last. Never again."

Another knock, and Vicki and Rain joined them, both bringing treats—a pie from Knockers and some freshly baked scones from the local coffee shop.

Winona made more tea, and they settled in the living room.

Megs updated them on Mitch's condition. "I can see a big difference already in his confidence, in his vocabulary and speech, and his balance. Yesterday, he walked on the treadmill with minimal support from the harness. He has a long way to go, especially with speech. He gets so frustrated, and I can't blame him."

Lexi took a small slice of pie. "When do they think they can discharge him?"

"They're hoping to discharge him by the middle of next month, but they can't yet say whether he'll go to a long-term facility or whether he'll be able to come home and get therapy on an outpatient basis. He could easily spend six months or more in rehab."

Everyone looked surprised except Vicki.

Eric Hawke, her husband, had been badly burned on one leg while fighting to save Scarlet from the big fire. He'd had a dozen surgeries and months of painful rehab before he'd finally returned to work at full capacity as the town's fire chief.

Vicki sipped her tea. "How are *you*, Megs?"

The question caught Megs off guard.

She didn't often talk about her emotions with anyone other than Mitch. Still, she answered as honestly as she could, determined not to break down. "I ... I don't know. I keep telling myself I'm fine as long as he's fine, that the better he gets, the better I get. But this hit me hard. It's going to be a while before I truly feel like myself again."

The women stayed, helped with the laundry, then left her to pack up, sending their best wishes to Mitch. Megs thanked them, once again wondering why she hadn't wanted to move to Scarlet.

She drove back down the canyon, not wanting to be late for dinner. She parked outside the facility, carried in the duffel bag of clean clothes, and signed in at the front desk. Then she made her way to his room to find that dinner had just started and he was in the cafeteria. She set the duffel down on his bed and hurried to join him.

But when she walked in, the place was dark.

"Mitch?"

The lights came on, twenty or so voices shouting, "Surprise!" as well as they could—victims of strokes, brain tumors, and head injuries sitting around a long table, some in wheelchairs, all with their best smiles on their faces.

Then Mitch stood, love shining in his eyes, a cupcake in his hand, a single candle sticking out of it. "Ha... happ ...y Bir..thday."

Happy Birthday?

"Oh!" She made eye contact with everyone at the table, people in rough circumstances, each of them eager to feel and share joy again. "Thank you, all! Would you believe that I completely forgot?"

The gleam in Mitch's eyes said quite clearly, "I didn't."

Chapter 21

MITCH STRAPPED into the harness for the treadmill, then waited for Rodrigo to double-check it. His walking ability and balance had improved enough that he could probably do this without the harness. But then he'd climbed with a helmet since the 1990s and had only needed it once.

Rodrigo did a safety check. "You're going to be doing all the work this time—no support. Okay, you're good to go."

Rodrigo started the treadmill, increasing the speed gradually until Mitch was walking at a fast clip. "Now I know how you got to the top of Mt. Everest, man. You are one determined dude."

Then Rodrigo tapped a button, and the theme song from *Rocky* came over the room's sound system, Rodrigo singing along. "That's you, Mitch! Guts and glory."

Mitch couldn't help but smile despite a sense of embarrassment. A few months ago, walking on a treadmill without support wouldn't have meant anything to him. Now, it meant everything. His care team had decided last week that he could be discharged tomorrow and finish his rehab on an outpatient basis.

He'd worked hard these past couple of weeks, buoyed by Megs' love and her faith in him. He didn't know where he'd be right now without her—her smile, her support, her strength beside him. Every day, he reminded himself what she'd said about his rehab being a kind of climb. Step by step, day by day, he was healing.

Knowing he could still make love to Megs had made him feel whole again. They'd always had an incredible sex life, and losing that part of himself, that part of who they were together, would have been hard for him to face. He couldn't wait to sleep in his own bed with her beside him, though, honestly, it had added a little spice lately to wonder whether one of the medical staff was going to catch them screwing in his room.

Megs was in Denver this afternoon, filming her part of the public service announcement that she and the dirtbags were making together. That was Megs—always fighting to turn tragedy into a chance for good. If it saved a single life, then perhaps everything they'd gone through would serve some purpose.

When the session was over, he helped Rodrigo remove the harness and stepped down from the treadmill.

Rodrigo gave Mitch a fist bump. "Congratulations on your last PT session with me. It was a real pleasure getting to meet you. It's not often we have celebrities here."

"Thank you, Rod…reego. I am … grateful."

"Before you leave, can I come by and get your autograph?"

Mitch nodded. "Come … visit … us in … Scar… Scarlet."

"I might take you up on that."

Mitch went from there to his speech therapy session,

which was as frustrating as ever. Yes, he was putting more words together, but it was still a struggle to communicate. While Megs seemed to read his mind—she'd always been far more sensitive than most people knew—that wasn't true of the rest of the world. Going home meant facing his disability in a way he hadn't so far.

Wilma Atcitty, his speech pathologist, was more upbeat. "I know you don't think you're improving, but you've come so far in such a short time. You're going to love your new therapist. I've worked with Angela before. And now for your favorite part of the day—singing."

God, no more children's songs.

"No Twinkle, Twinkle Little Star." He sang that last part.

"Okay, Mr. Picky, what do you want to sing?"

Strangely, it was much easier for Mitch to formulate words when he was singing than when he was trying to speak. He'd thought that it was just the fact that he already knew the lyrics. But Wilma said studies showed that it was the rhythm that helped in cases of non-fluent aphasia like his.

He handed her his phone, the music app open and Simon and Garfunkel's *Sound of Silence* queued up. "This."

Wilma raised an eyebrow. "You've got a strange sense of humor, but I like it."

Though he messed up the lyrics a few times, he was able to sing along much better than he would have been able to recite the words. They were on the last verse when Wilma smiled at someone and Megs' sweet soprano joined in, her hand coming to rest on Mitch's shoulder as they finished the last words.

Wilma applauded. "Well done."

When the session was over, Wilma took Mitch's hand. "I know that what you're going through is hard. It's normal to grieve when we lose a part of ourselves. But from my perspective as a professional, you're doing well. You've got a chance at regaining normal speech. If you don't, life will be different, but it can also be good. As my Navajo grandma liked to say, 'Don't let the tears in your eyes keep you from seeing the future.'"

"Your grandma sounds like a wise woman," Megs said.

Wilma nodded. "She was."

On the walk back to Mitch's room, Megs shared the news. "Lexi finally had that baby boy. Nine pounds, five ounces. They named him Kit after an ancestor of Austin's who was sheriff of Scarlet back in the day. Kit Michael Taylor."

Mitch liked that name. "Nice."

"Also, the dirtbags are coming to see you—if that's okay. I told Gridwall you might not be up for that, but he wants to see you. I think your accident shook him up."

Mitch wasn't sure he was ready for the full-on insanity of a dirtbag reunion. He'd be the only one who couldn't climb, who couldn't belay, who couldn't even share his thoughts or feelings without difficulty. Then again, it had been so long.

"Br-ring it... on."

———

MEGS DROVE up the canyon to Scarlet Springs, Mitch in the passenger seat, the two of them holding hands. "How does it feel to be going home?"

"Good."

When they'd left Scarlet for their two-week climbing vacation, the aspens had been golden, and the air had been warm. Now, it was November, and the aspens were bare, a dusting of snow on the ground, the high peaks solid white.

But for Mitch, this journey involved so much more than time and space.

She could tell that he was a little nervous, no doubt worried about how people would react to his speech challenges. "I let Rain and a few others know that you're going to need peace and quiet to finish healing. I expect that will hold folks at bay for a whole ten minutes or so."

Mitch chuckled. "It's oh… kay."

She hadn't warned him he'd be getting a hero's welcome. She'd texted Sasha and Rain to let them know they were on their way up the canyon. Word had gotten around. Ten minutes ago, Rain had sent back a photo of people lining the streets or standing in their driveways, waiting to welcome Mitch home. The sight had put an honest-to-God lump in Megs' throat.

"I've called a Team meeting for tomorrow evening. You don't have to be there if you don't want to be. I just want to go over the past couple of months and decide how we're going to handle things moving forward."

She wouldn't be able to be on call around the clock like she'd been before the accident. Mitch couldn't drive for six months to a year, and he had speech pathology and physical therapy appointments. Given that he was also at risk of seizures and stroke, she didn't want to leave him alone for long stretches. Though she could carry out her administrative functions, Conrad or someone else would need to fill in for her when it came to managing rescues for the next several months.

They were close now, the canyon narrowing, the turns growing tighter. They came around the last curve and passed the sign for Scarlet Springs, the reservoir to their left, the Indian Peaks rising above the town.

Scarlet Springs Town Limit

Population: 1,492 Elevation: 8,936
Home of the Rocky Mountain Search &
Rescue Team

Megs slowed the vehicle. "They repainted the sign. Do you see that?"

Rain hadn't told Megs about this.

Mitch squeezed her hand. "Nice."

A tribute to the Team mattered more to Megs than any personal recognition. She and Mitch had poured everything they had into the organization, growing it from a few volunteers into a world-class rescue operation. By acknowledging the Team, the town was acknowledging their combined life's work.

Then it began.

Townsfolk stood at the end of their driveways, shouting words of welcome and waving as Megs and Mitch passed. It hit Megs square in the chest, made her throat tight. She couldn't imagine how Mitch felt. This was *his* hometown.

She slowed down, giving Mitch time to see everyone, hear their greetings, and wave back. It wasn't easy for him to turn his head wearing that collar. "You've had so many people praying for you."

They headed downhill and through the roundabout into the center of town to find the sidewalks on either side of the street lined with people.

"Sweet baby Jesus." Megs glanced over at Mitch, met his gaze, saw the emotion in his eyes. "This town loves you."

"You, too."

Normally, she would have turned off at the roundabout to head up the mountain to their home. But if she did that, most of the people who'd come out in the cold to greet Mitch wouldn't get a chance to see him.

"What do you say, love? Is it time for a victory lap?"

"Yeah."

She went around the roundabout, where Bear stood, waving, a big smile on his bearded face, and headed into town proper, driving slowly. "What's Hawke doing with the big fire engine?"

Parked on a side street, it was just sitting there. Had there been some kind of emergency, a car accident?

As they drew near, the lights came on, and, with a squawk of the siren, Hawke pulled out into the street ahead of them, followed by Deputy US Marshal Jason Chiago in his service vehicle, his overheads flashing, too.

Megs swallowed—hard. "I think you're getting an escort."

Mitch looked this way and that, clearly overwhelmed by the response, his eyes suspiciously bright. "Wow."

Everyone had turned out. Joe and Rain with Lark and little Angel. Rico. Cheyenne, Marcia, Libby, and Sam from Knockers. Rose. Bob and Kendra Jewell, and beside them Lexi with tiny Kit, all bundled up. The staff of Food Mart. Naomi, Winona, and Old Man Belcourt. Esri, the Team's trauma therapist. Jesse and Ellie Moretti with their twins Daniel and Daisy and toddler Dylan. Vicki standing with her two little ones and her mother-in-law, Robin. Wendy from the newspaper with her camera. The guy with the bushy beard who owned the marijuana dispensary. Last of all, outside the front door of The Cave—the Team's headquarters—stood the Team members, applauding.

At the edge of town, Megs followed Hawke and Chiago, turning around in the firehouse parking lot and heading back for a second pass, Mitch waving to friends and neighbors he'd known his entire life.

When they reached the roundabout this time, Megs turned her SUV homeward, honking a farewell to their escort. She turned into their driveway, parked close to the house, then leaned over and kissed his cheek. "Welcome home."

———

GOD, it felt good to be home. The comfort of familiar spaces. A fire crackling in the woodstove. The stillness.

While Megs ordered dinner from Knockers and put together a grocery list, Mitch did his best to settle in. He put away his clothes, opened his mail, downloaded almost two months' worth of emails, and visited their social media for the first time. Then, overwhelmed by the thousands of supportive posts from followers from around the world, he wrote his first post since September.

I am home at last. My heart is full of gratitude for all the support, prayers, and good wishes you've sent my way. I will forever be grateful to the Black Canyon rangers, the Rocky Mountain Search & Rescue Team, and my doctors, nurses, and thera-pists for all they did to save my life. Most of all, I'm grateful to my beautiful partner, Megs Hill, for her unfailing love and strength.

Where would he be without her?

He'd been thinking about their life together a lot these past weeks. He supposed that was natural after a person came face-to-face with death. He'd thumbed through his journal, reading random entries. It hadn't been hard to see the impact that Megs had had on his life these past forty-eight years. With her passion for life and adventure, she had lifted him up, bringing out the best in him, enabling him to become far more than he'd have been without her.

It had made him think about their future. At best, they had maybe thirty years left. That might seem like a long time, but he knew how quickly the years passed. It seemed to him that it was just yesterday when they'd been in the prime of life and hanging in Camp 4. He wanted whatever time they had left together to be special. Most of all, he wanted Megs to know how precious she was to him, how much he loved her.

Megs poked her head into his office. "Dinner just arrived. You hungry?"

"Yeah." He shut down his computer, his head aching from the screen time.

They talked over the day while they ate, Mitch savoring Megs' company and his first good meal in what seemed like ages. Words came slowly for him, but Megs was patient. She was also perceptive.

"Are you feeling okay?"

"My h-head ... ay... ay.. aches." He set down his fork, unable to finish.

"You've had a busy and exciting day. You should rest."

Megs cleaned up while Mitch took pain meds, then she helped him get settled, propping up the pillows to support his neck and head. "Do you want me to turn out the light and let you sleep?"

"No. I ... wan... want you... to... r-read." He pointed to his journal.

"Okay." She changed into her pajamas, made them each a cup of herbal tea, and sat down beside him with the journal. "You bookmarked a spot. Is that what you want me to read?"

"Yeah."

"You're not sick of the sound of my voice?"

He chuckled at that ridiculous idea. "N-never."

She opened the journal. "Oh, wow. Right. Okay."

The entry he'd marked was the day she'd shattered gender stereotypes and enshrined herself as one of the greatest climbers of all time by becoming the first person to free climb The Nose on El Capitan. For a moment, the world had stood in awe of her. From that day forward, the woman he loved had ceased being just another celebrity rock climber and had become a legend.

She began to read.

Chapter 22

June 10, 1993

MITCH HIKED with Megs toward the base of El Cap in the pre-dawn dark, wondering whether the two of them ought to be committed. Megs said she needed a challenge, but this was more than that. What they were about to attempt was insane.

No one had free climbed The Nose, and Megs was determined to be the first.

He and Megs had spent the past two months preparing, reading everything they could find about the route, going over every one of more than thirty pitches, looking for ways to outsmart the rock, analyzing their past climbs. They had climbed until their fingers bled, pushing themselves to peak fitness. They had even calculated calories and how much water they would need to drink. Megs believed they could do it, and, after working through every detail, Mitch was crazy enough to agree.

Gridwall caught up to them, Accardo, Baker, Cook,

and the others jogging behind him. "You don't have to do this."

"Just leave it, man."

Mitch had said the same thing to Megs last month. They'd gotten into a huge fight when he'd tried to explain the concept of survivor guilt.

Gridwall wasn't giving up. "We lost Calder. We can't lose you, too."

Megs stopped, turned to face Gridwall. "You're not going to lose us. We're going to climb clean, and we're going to stay safe. If we get in over our heads, we'll bail."

Gridwall didn't look convinced. "You should at least be prepared to bivouac with extra food and water."

But Megs was done talking and had moved on.

Mitch understood Gridwall's misgivings. He and Megs had only a day's worth of food and water packed. If they got stuck up there, they were going to get hungry and thirsty fast.

"All right, then." Gridwall stopped. "If I can't talk you out of it, I'm going to hike up to the summit of El Cap. I'll have food and water and a first aid kit waiting for you when you top out. We'll set someone in the Meadow with binoculars to watch your progress."

"Sounds good." Mitch followed Megs.

Gridwall shared his plans with the other dirtbags, and they all turned and started back toward camp.

Twenty minutes later, Mitch stood with Megs at the base of The Nose. Mitch looked up, three thousand feet of stone towering above them. That wall would either make them—or break them.

The plan was for Megs to lead all of the pitches, with Mitch cleaning their gear from the route as he moved. When Megs reached the end of a pitch, she would belay him, and he would return the equipment. If she got stuck, she would wait for him.

They geared up—harnesses, rope, racks—and then it was time to go.

Mitch took up the slack, a nervous knot in his belly. "Belay on."

"Climbing."

"Climb on."

For the first few minutes, Mitch was sure they were making the biggest mistake of their climbing careers. But once they got going, his worries faded, pushed aside by the thrill of watching Megs climb. He was with one of the world's greatest climbers on what was arguably the world's greatest rock climbing route, trying to do the greatest thing that anyone had ever attempted here since the original first ascent.

They sailed through the first seven pitches, taking a break to hydrate before working their way up the Stove Leg Cracks, inconveniently wide fissures in the rock that had repulsed more than a few ambitious climbers. The next three pitches flowed together, the two of them taking advantage of fixed bolts and old pitons left by the previous generation of Yosemite climbers. When they came to the ledge at El Cap Tower on Pitch 15, they stopped for lunch, the sun high in the sky.

Megs looked out over the Valley, seeming more like herself than she'd been in a while. "I'll never get tired of this view."

He took her hand, squeezed. "Neither will I."

They didn't linger, but pushed on for some of the best climbing Mitch had ever experienced, from the Texas Flake to the Boot Flake and on to the King Swing.

Megs used the rope to make an enormous pendulum swing to her left, reaching for the edge of an arete. She missed on her first attempt, and Mitch found himself watching the rope above her, hoping it wouldn't fray. The second time, she used her shoes to stick it, pulling herself across the rock with minuscule fingerholds until she finally grasped the arete.

Mitch exhaled—and then it was his turn. With his longer reach, he was able to grab the arete on the first try. It only made him admire Megs more.

They set off again, working through each successive pitch—the Great Roof, the Pancake Flake, a couple of crack systems. The rock grew hot from the sunshine, shadows shifting as the sun moved across the sky. Then came Pitch 27.

They had identified this as the crux pitch. If they succeeded here, nothing would stop them. If not, there would be nowhere to go but down. There were no holds, and the existing crack was too small to set protection. Other climbers might have drilled holes in the rock here and hammered in bolts, but that went against his and Megs' shared ethos of climbing the rock without altering it.

Mitch forgot to breathe as Megs moved into the pitch, using her knees, her elbows, her shoulders, her butt, her entire body to create the counter-pressure she needed to inch slowly up the wall. No one climbed like that—no one in the world.

What had he done that Megs had fallen in love with *him*?

It was only after he'd grunted and fought his way up the pitch that he knew they were going to make it.

With just a handful of pitches left and the sun setting, they took a quick hydration and calorie break, put on their headlamps, then set off again.

Mitch knew Megs must be tired because he certainly

was, his hands raw, his forearms pumped, his body fatigued from continual exertion. But there was no stopping either of them now, the summit a handful of hours and pitches away.

The sun set. Darkness came over the Valley. They kept going.

Running on adrenaline fumes, they pushed themselves beyond exhaustion and pain, focused only on the rock, the next move, the next piece of protection.

Voices came from overhead, the summit near.

"There they are!"

Megs belayed him to the finish just below the summit so they could top out together. They reached the summit just after midnight to find Gridwall and the other dirtbags waiting for them, along with a few other climbers who'd wanted to watch, a ranger, and a news crew with lights and a big camera.

Cheers. Camera lights flashing. The warmth of the campfire.

"We're here on the summit of El Capitan, three thousand feet above the valley floor, where just moments ago, climbers Megs Hill and Mitch Ahearn became the first people to free climb The Nose in a day."

While the reporter continued to speak, Gridwall drew them both into an awkward embrace, tears streaming down his cheeks. "You fucking did it!"

MEGS CLOSED THE JOURNAL, set it down on the bedside table, the words Mitch had written dredging up emotions she'd tried to bury. "You were right. It was survivor guilt. I hated knowing that Dean was gone—and that I had played a role in his death."

"I know." Mitch's gaze went soft. "Not… our… fall… fault."

Megs crawled into bed beside him, turned off her lamp, and rolled onto her stomach so she could make eye contact. "I still miss him."

"M-me, too."

"He would have been so happy for us. Free climbing The Nose was the greatest achievement of our careers."

It had also been their last climb as professionals. They hadn't planned it that way. That's just how things had unfolded.

"I never liked getting all of the credit for it. You climbed every inch of that with me. We topped out together."

Mitch tucked a strand of hair behind her ear, smiled. "Your … cray… crazy idea. You w-wen… went… first."

"We were a team. We've always been a team." Then she remembered the question he'd asked himself. "As for why I fell in love with you, that's easy. You're incredibly hot. More than that, you stood up for me. When everyone else treated me like 'the girl who thinks she can climb like a boy,' you took me seriously. From the moment you told the others to let me take a shot at White Lightning, I knew you believed in me. Plus, you're a damned good climber—and you fuck like a god."

If he hadn't had a headache, she would have suggested they put his God-given talents to use and screw each other to sleep. But she knew he needed rest.

Mitch grinned at that last part, but his grin faded, his expression growing serious. "Why not … Dee …Dean?"

"Why didn't I hook up with Dean instead?" That was easy. "He wasn't attracted to me, and I knew you were. He thought of me as a kid. He might have been only six years older than you, but to my teenage self, he seemed *old*."

Mitch laughed. "L-luck-y for … me."

⸻

MITCH COULDN'T BELIEVE how good it felt to see Gridwall, Accardo, and Cook again. They arrived at the house via Las Vegas on Friday afternoon, Gridwall behind the wheel of a rented Lamborghini in lemon yellow.

Like Mitch and Megs, they'd gotten older. Accardo had packed on a few pounds, while Gridwall seemed thinner. Cook, who'd once had a long ponytail, was now bald. Then again, so was Mitch, his hair only stubble, his scar still visible.

"For a man who got his brains bashed out, you look damned good, my friend." Gridwall drew Mitch into a bear hug. "God, you scared the shit out of me."

"Good … to see you… Jim." Mitch had made progress, but speaking was still a challenge for him.

"Where's your more beautiful half? Megs, honey, there you are. Come give your old Uncle Jim a big hug."

Megs hugged him, kissed his grizzled cheek. "Good to see you. Thanks for making the trip. Hey, Accardo. Cook, I'm so glad you came. Come inside. I want to introduce you all to someone."

Kurt and his wife, Jennifer, had arrived about an hour ago. They were spending the weekend in the mountains and would be joining Megs and Mitch and the dirtbags at tonight's big celebration for Mitch at Knockers.

Kurt stood when they walked into the living room.

Gridwall, Accardo, and Cook gaped at him.

Gridwall held out his hand. "You can only be Dean Calder's son. I see your daddy on your face."

Kurt shook his hand. "And you're Jim Gridwall. This is my wife, Jennifer."

When the introductions were done, they shared a decade worth of news over a lunch of Vicki's Chicago-style deep-dish pizza that Megs had ordered from Knockers.

Gridwall had six grandkids that he shared with his ex-wife Elaine and had earned a fortune from the rock climbing gear company he'd founded back in the 1980s. Accardo lived in the suburbs of Chicago and had become an accountant. Cook had gotten into snowboarding and created his own line of snowboards.

It did Mitch good to see his friends so happy on this side of life. "Who … would think… dir…dirt… b-bags would… do … so well."

Megs offered to give them a tour of The Cave.

"Why do you call it The Cave?" Accardo asked.

Megs grabbed her parka. "It's basically an old firehouse with a bay for our rescue vehicles. Lots of gear and high ceilings."

They walked down to Team headquarters to find all of the Team's members present, gathered, no doubt, to meet some true legends of climbing.

Megs made the introductions. "This is Gabe Rossiter, one of our tenured members. Rossiter, I don't have to tell you who these guys are."

Rossiter, who'd kept climbing after losing a leg in a terrible fall, shook their hands, a broad smile on his face. "I've watched all of the Lords of Stone videos. I probably have them somewhere."

Sasha, who had been the most excited about meeting the dirtbags, beamed when Accardo told her they all knew who she was.

"It's good to know there's a new generation kicking ass out there," he said.

The dirtbags all knew about Conrad and his exploits, of course.

"The Triple Crown, man." Cook shook his hand. "You must have balls of steel."

When they learned that Conrad, Taylor, Hawke, O'Brien, Moretti, and Belcourt had helped rescue Mitch, Gridwall shook each man's hand. "You saved my brother. Thank you."

They mingled in the operations room for a time, smiles on everyone's faces. Then Megs gave Kurt, Jennifer, and the dirtbags a tour, explaining how the operation worked, how they maintained the quality of the equipment and the discipline necessary to take on high-risk rescues day or night anywhere in the state at any time of year.

"Holy shit!" Gridwall stared at the walls around him, pointing. "You've got a fortune in gear hanging in here. That's some of my company's stuff. This must have cost hundreds of thousands of bucks. Check that out. What's that?"

"It's a special belay device created by Belcourt. He's a mechanical engineer."

"I'm going to have to talk with him. Where do you get the money for all of this?"

Mitch answered this time. "Dona… donations."

"Donations? From the *public*?" Accardo looked like he couldn't quite grasp that.

"No," Megs quipped. "From the Gear Fairy."

Cook picked up a first aid kit. "This was because of Dean's death, wasn't it?"

"Yes." The smile left Megs' face, her gaze fixing on Kurt. "Your father died in part because there was no one prepared to undertake a rescue in bad weather. No one had the staff or the technical expertise. We decided we needed to fill that gap. It was the best way we could think of to honor his memory. We got donations wherever we could, bought this old firehouse, and began searching for volunteers."

She spoke the words without emotion, but Mitch knew how hard it was for her to discuss Dean's death. The way he'd died had haunted both of them.

"Volunteers?" Gridwall seemed confused. "They don't get paid?"

Around him, Team members laughed, amused by his reaction.

"No one gets paid—not me, not Mitch, and not our volunteers. Every penny we receive goes directly into equipment, training, and operational expenses. We're a nonprofit if you want to write us a fat check."

More laughter.

"How do you survive?" Accardo asked.

Leave it to the accountant to ask that question.

"We live frugally off capital gains on our retirement accounts."

Kurt had listened quietly, standing off to the side with Jennifer. "How quickly are you able to reach people?"

Conrad answered this time. "That depends on a variety of factors—time of day, weather, where they are, whether it's a simple trail rescue or a technical rescue. Our average response time is under two hours. We got to Mitch a little more than two hours after he was injured, and he was on the Western Slope."

In that moment, it hit Mitch in a way it hadn't before. The rescue team he'd worked with Megs to create, equip, and train had saved his life.

As they left The Cave in groups of twos and threes, everyone talking, Kurt and Jennifer made their way over to him and Megs.

"Mitch, I want to thank you for keeping your journal. I

hope it was okay with you that Megs read some pages to me—entries that involved my father."

Mitch smiled. "Fine… with me."

Kurt's next words hit Mitch square in the chest. "If it's not too much to ask, I really want to know whatever you can tell me about how my father died."

Chapter 23

WITH THEIR GUESTS settled in the living room, Megs walked to the bedroom to retrieve Mitch's journal, a knot in her stomach. Dean's death was the greatest regret of her life, a subject she rarely mentioned. Now she was going to read about it in detail to Dean's adult son and the dirtbags, who had also been Dean's friends.

She wasn't sure she was up for this, but they all deserved the truth.

Mitch walked in behind her, shut the bedroom door, his eyes full of concern. "You d-on't have to … do this. Just an… answer quest… quest… questions. Or cop…copy it."

He had more trouble speaking when he was upset.

Megs tried to explain. "I owe Dean this much. *We* owe him. His son should know exactly why his father wasn't there for him when he was growing up."

Mitch rested his hands on her shoulders. "H-hard for… *you*. I never …saw you so… broke… broken… as then."

It had been one of the few times in her adult life that Megs had curled up in a fetal position and sobbed. She'd barely been able to function for weeks afterward. It was only the idea of free climbing The Nose that had gotten her back into the world. But that had been twenty-eight years ago.

"I'll be okay." Then it hit her that Mitch might not want to share his journal entry with anyone, that this might feel too personal. "Are you okay with my reading this aloud to everyone?"

He nodded, resignation on his face. "My job is… take care of… *you.*"

"I know, and I'm grateful. It didn't kill me then. It won't kill me now."

She walked back to the living room, journal in hand, Mitch behind her. "Does anyone need anything to drink before we start?"

Heads shook, the room silent.

While Megs searched for the entry, she gave them all the background. "Dean and Beth were living in Ridgeway on the Western Slope. We hadn't seen them for a while, so when he invited us to visit, we were happy to make the trip. We were still living in California at the time. We'd been at their place for three days when he proposed we climb El Diente, one of the fourteeners in the San Miguel range. It was late August, so we left the house prepared for possible rain. We had planned to be back at Dean and Beth's place by dinnertime. But that's not how it went."

Megs found the right page, skimmed over it, and decided to skip straight to the three of them on El Diente's summit. Then she steeled herself and began to read.

—

August 17, 1992

MITCH STOOD on the summit of El Diente with Megs and Dean at a little after two in the afternoon, the three of them posing for Dean's compact Olympus, doing their best to recreate their photo from the summit of Mt. Everest.

Dean set the delay timer on his camera. "Everyone look cold, hypoxic, and exhausted."

Mitch and Megs laughed, Dean hurrying to join them. *Click.*

They signed the summit registry, admiring the view and reminiscing about their days climbing together in Yosemite and the Himalayas.

Mitch ripped the wrapper off a granola bar. "The scenery makes me miss Scarlet Springs."

"That's where you grew up, right?" Dean didn't wait for an answer. "I've been through there. It's beautiful country. Have you thought of settling there?"

Megs answered without hesitation. "No! Don't give him ideas."

Mitch laughed. "I've thought about it."

Mindful of the dark clouds that heralded an approaching storm, they didn't stay too long, taking time for hydration and a snack before they started down.

Dean went first. "Watch the loose rock."

"This is one hell of a mountain." Mitch followed, taking care where he placed his feet before he stepped. "It might be less than half as high as Everest, but it's no walk-up."

There was no clear trail to the summit, and some of the terrain was deadly, with unstable rock, cliffs, and exposed ridges. There were snowfields and stretches of ice, too. A slip or a sudden gust of wind could result in a fall of hundreds of feet. The stretch near the summit was class four scramble, reminding Mitch of the Hillary Step but without the snow, ice, or extreme altitude.

Megs went last, reaching down carefully with her feet and testing each rock before putting her full weight on it. "Does this remind either of you of the Hillary Step?"

"Yes," Mitch and Dean answered almost in unison.

They were still up high and picking their way through boulders and talus, when the wind picked up, those storm clouds blowing closer, the temps dropping rapidly. They stopped to put on rain gear, then shouldered their packs once again and moved on.

Dean glanced up at the sky. "I think this storm is going to hit before we get back to the vehicles."

He took a step, and the large block of talus beneath his foot flipped backward onto his shin, knocking him to the ground, making him cry out. Groaning, he pushed the rock aside and grasped his leg, a grimace on his face.

Mitch and Megs reached him as quickly as they could.

He spoke through gritted teeth. "I think... it's broken."

Megs slid her hands over his leg on the outside of his jeans, her gaze meeting Mitch's. "His tibia is definitely displaced. It could be a tib-fib fracture."

Dean was sucking in big breaths, fighting with pain. "Fuck."

The danger wasn't the broken bone itself. There were arteries in the leg that could be severed by displaced bone, causing a person to bleed out. A talus field at fourteen thousand feet was no place for triage. Dean needed a hospital—fast.

Mitch ripped into his backpack. "I think we've got Advil in the first aid kit. We can probably rig some kind of splint once we reach timberline."

"I'll hike ahead and come back up with something we can use." Megs set off, moving a bit too fast for Mitch's tastes.

"Be careful!" he shouted after her.

"Apart from the leg, how do you feel?"

"I'm okay."

If he'd severed an artery, he would probably have collapsed by now. Instead, he seemed like himself—coherent, focused, normal respiration. If he had severed an artery up here, there was likely nothing they could have done for him anyway. It was several hours to the nearest town.

By the time Megs returned carrying two thick sticks of about the same size, a freezing rain had begun to fall. "This is the best I could do."

Working carefully, she and Mitch rigged a splint, tying the two pieces of wood together on opposite sides of Dean's lower leg with fabric they'd torn from a sling in the first aid kit.

"We'll head down with you between us." Megs looked down at the path below them. "It's going to be a long, slow descent. We'll take a step, and you hop on your good leg. We'll rest when we can, but we need to get out of this weather."

Grim-faced, Dean nodded. "Right."

They helped him to his feet, Mitch slipping his arm beneath Dean's, Megs wrapping hers around his waist.

"Okay, we step and you hop. Step." She and Mitch took a step. "Hop."

Dean hopped, the movement clearly causing him pain.

"Great." Megs tried to encourage him. "A few thousand more times, and we'll be at the vehicles."

Step. Hop. Step. Hop. Step. Hop.

Rain pelted them, making the talus slick and hitting exposed skin like icy daggers.

Step. Hop. Step. Hop. Step. Hop.

Mitch could see that Dean was suffering. "You're doing

it, man. It's not easy, but nothing you've done has been easy. You can do this."

Step. Hop. Step. Hop. Step. Hop.

On and on they went, their progress slow, each step grueling for Dean.

Then the talus slope beneath their feet shifted in a mini-avalanche of stone, dropping them all to their asses and knocking the air from Mitch's lungs.

Dean cried out, his face twisted in agony, his injured leg bent.

"Jesus, Dean!" Megs scrambled to help him.

Mitch got onto his hands and knees and crawled over to him. "Hang on, buddy."

They got him to his feet, but an hour later, they'd gone only a couple hundred yards, rain turning to snow as they reached a more technical bit of climbing.

Mitch and Megs stopped and settled Dean under an overhang out of the wind and rain as they worked out how to get him safely down a steep and narrow stretch of class three scramble. If they'd had rope and harnesses, this would be a lot easier.

Megs climbed the chute to get a feel for it. "I'll carry his legs down, drape them over my shoulders like backpack straps, and you support his upper body. Or we could scoot on our asses and—"

"No. Just go. Head down before it gets dark. Get help." Dean's face was lined with pain. He fished his keys out of his pocket, held them out for Mitch. "Just leave me some food and water, maybe the first aid kit and an emergency blanket, too."

Megs climbed back up to him. "I'm not leaving you here alone."

"I'll go." Mitch took off his pack, grabbed the keys. "You can stay—"

"No! Both of you should go. I mean it. Go. What happens if you get hurt, Mitch? Megs and I will be stuck here all night not knowing what happened to you, and no one will know we're here. It's getting slick, turning to snow. Go—both of you—before this gets more dangerous than it already is."

In the end, Mitch and Megs decided to do it his way, leaving him with their food and most of their water, as well as the first aid kit and the emergency blanket from Mitch's pack.

Megs hugged him. "We'll be back as soon as we can be."

"You're a good friend, Megs, and one hell of a climber. You can do this. Tell Beth not to worry. Tell her I love her and the kids and that I'll be okay."

"Will do."

Mitch took his hand. "Stay warm and dry and hydrated, okay?"

"Got it. You're a good man, Mitch. You stay safe and take care of our Megs."

"I will."

Then Megs and Mitch set off down the mountain.

━━

IT WAS dark by the time they reached the parking area near the trailhead. Up on the summit, it was snowing hard. Down here, it was raining.

They climbed into Dean's SUV and drove to the nearest gas station, where Mitch used the payphone to call 911.

He explained what had happened. "It's snowing hard up there, and he has a broken leg. We need to mobilize a rescue and bring him down."

Dispatch put him on hold for several minutes.

"What's happening?" Megs asked.

"I think she's patching me through to the Dolores County Sheriff's Department."

But when he had dispatch on the line again, the woman told him they would have to wait for any rescue until morning.

"There are blizzard conditions up there now with zero visibility. No pilot is going to fly a helicopter among those peaks in this storm."

"Then we need a team of climbers to head up there with some kind of litter."

"Sir, I'm sorry, but we don't have officers available. We have reports of flooding in campgrounds along the Dolores River. I'm sorry, but no one is going up the mountain in this storm at night."

Mitch had to fight not to shout. "Our friend is in pain! His life is in danger! He's got a wife and kids. We need—"

"Our deputies have wives and children, too. The sheriff was firm on this. No one is heading up the peak until morning after the storm clears. If you'd like to help guide them to your friend, be at the trailhead by six tomorrow morning."

Six in the morning? That was twelve hours from now.

"They'd damned well better show up then. We'll be waiting." Mitch slammed down the receiver. "That got us nowhere."

"They aren't sending a rescue team?" Megs gaped at him in disbelief.

"I don't think they have one. It's just the sheriff's deputies."

"Oh, for fuck's sake!"

Then Mitch called Beth to tell her the news. "We're doing everything we can. Unfortunately, they won't mount

257

a rescue until tomorrow morning. We left him with everything we could. He told us to tell you that he loves you and that he'll be okay."

Mitch hung up again. "To hell with this. Let's buy a thermos, fill it with coffee, and head back up to him. We can ride the storm out with him."

"Shit." Megs walked up to the counter. "We need a fresh pot of coffee. Do you sell hand warmers?"

"In the summer, ma'am? No, we do not. I'll thank you to watch your language."

Megs glared at him. "Our friend is in dire straits, and you worry about profanity."

They bought the thermos, coffee, beef jerky, cheese, crackers, and plastic garbage bags to help keep them dry, and then drove back to the trailhead. They made holes in the garbage bags for their head and arms to keep the rain from drenching them and started back up the mountain, climbing with the light of their headlamps. But after about an hour, their headlamps began to fail because of the rain, leaving them in the dark.

"Megs, we have to turn back!" Mitch shouted to be heard above the storm. "If we can't see where we're going, we might walk off a cliff or miss the route and end up on another part of the mountain!"

"Damn it! We should never have left him!"

Defeated and demoralized, they struggled to find their way back to the parking lot, where they once again took shelter in Dean's vehicle, shivering and wet to the skin despite their best efforts to stay dry.

"Jesus." Megs stared up through the windshield toward a summit that wasn't visible from here. "He's up there with a broken leg."

Mitch turned on the engine, started the heater, while he and Megs stripped out of the plastic bags and their soaked parkas. "The sheriff will be here in the morning. At least we set that in motion. Have some coffee. You're shaking."

Megs sipped from the lid of the thermos. "Imagine how cold *he* is."

Neither of them slept, the night seeming to last forever, rain falling off and on, the wind relentless. Finally, around four in the morning, the sky cleared to reveal stars. They climbed out of the vehicle at dawn, looked up at El Diente, saw that its summit was blanketed in white. As tempted as they were to head up, they were only a handful of minutes away from the sheriff's arrival. Someone would need to lead rescuers to Dean.

The sheriff, an older man with a sun-browned face, asked a few questions as other deputies and a few volunteers rolled in. "There's no place to land a chopper up there. We'll need to get him down to a safer location before we can call for a bird."

And so Mitch and Megs started up the mountain again, followed by the sheriff, a deputy who was also a paramedic, a firefighter who had volunteered to help, and a couple of EMTs, one of whom carried a folding stretcher. More than once, Mitch and Megs were forced to stop so the others could catch up.

It was almost one in the afternoon when the overhang where they'd left Dean came into view. A flash of silver from the emergency blanket. The blue of his parka.

Megs waved, called for him.

He didn't answer.

Was he asleep?

Mitch and Megs set off at a faster pace, the talus buried in snow and treacherous. They had just reached the top of that chute where Dean had stopped them yesterday when they saw him.

Mitch's heart hit his breast bone, his stomach seeming to drop. "*Jesus.*"

"No!" Megs scrambled over the snowy talus on her hands and feet. "No! Dean!"

Almost buried in snow, he was slumped over, eyes open, skin blue, snow covering his hair and lashes, the emergency blanket peeking out from behind him.

Megs dropped to her knees in front of him, tried to dig him out with her bare hands. "Help me! We need to start chest compressions! You remember CPR, right?"

Mitch caught her, drew her back against his chest, held her. "He's gone, Megs."

"No!" She screamed the word into Mitch's parka, pounded him with clenched fists, fought to turn back to Dean. "Maybe they can revive him."

The note of desperate hope in her voice crushed Mitch, left his heart broken.

"Megs, he's dead. He's gone." Mitch wasn't sure how he found the words, his brain seeming to move in slow motion. "He unzipped his parka. See? He wasn't wrapped in the blanket. He was probably hypothermic and couldn't feel the cold."

Megs pulled away from Mitch, held Dean's head against her shoulder, and broke down sobbing. "I'm sorry. I'm so, so sorry."

Tears stung Mitch's eyes.

His best friend was dead. Dean was dead.

It didn't seem real or even possible. Dean Calder, an elite climber, had survived war in Vietnam and made it to the top of the world's highest mountains only to die on El Diente Peak, forty miles from his home.

How were they going to tell Beth and his two little kids?

The firefighter reached them first, assessed the situation at a glance and spoke into his radio. "We have a deceased climber. This is no longer a rescue. This is now a body recovery."

Beneath the overhang, Megs was still holding Dean and sobbing.

———

MEGS HATED crying in front of people, but she couldn't help the tears that spilled down her cheeks, the pain of Dean's death as raw as it had been so long ago. Mitch came to stand behind her, placed his hands on her shoulders, offering her the only comfort he could. Gridwall had tears on his face, too.

"The coroner said he'd died of hypothermia sometime around four in the morning, around the time the storm stopped and the stars came out. God, what a lonely way to die." She willed herself to meet Kurt's gaze, saw the tears on his cheeks. "I'm sorry, Kurt. I'm so sorry. If we had stayed…"

Kurt stood and walked over to kneel before her, Dean's eyes seeming to look up at her. "If you had stayed, you probably all would have died together."

Megs sniffed. "I won't lie. There are times I would have preferred that."

"I'm sure. Survivor guilt is tough." Kurt managed a sad smile. "My dad was an expert climber. He knew what he was doing. Now that I've heard the whole story, I believe he sent you to get help, not because he expected you to get back to him in time, but to spare your lives. He didn't want you to die up there with him. That's why he insisted that you *both* go for help. I'm sure of it. Those last words he said to you, his message to my mother and to us—they were his way of saying goodbye."

Megs had never thought of that, and it brought a fresh rush of tears.

Megs fought for composure. "Your father was the first person who took me seriously as a climber. His approval made other climbers respect me. He was my first friend—and one of my best friends. I loved him. We all did."

"I know. He loved you, too." Kurt took her hands. "I don't blame you for my father's death, so please quit carrying that weight on your conscience. You created the Team so no one would die like that again. How many lives do you think you've saved through the years? Dozens?"

"Hundreds." She didn't want him to think she was exaggerating. "It's in a spreadsheet somewhere."

For some reason, that made everyone laugh.

"Because of my father's death, you went on to form what has become the premier mountain rescue team in the country, maybe the world, and you have saved hundreds of lives. You two have given his death meaning. He couldn't ask for a more profound legacy. You turned tragedy into a chance for life for so many."

Megs tried to accept the absolution Kurt was offering, but after years of blaming herself, it wasn't easy. "Thank you for saying that."

Kurt stood and went to sit next to Jennifer, who was wiping her eyes. "I didn't just say it. I mean it."

"I know."

Gridwall handed Megs a tissue. "The kid is right. You probably would have died with Dean. We all wondered how the hell this could have happened, but now that I've heard the details… I don't see what else you could have done. The terrain was slick and steep, and he couldn't walk."

Megs wiped her eyes, still fighting to pull herself

together. "Dean was only the first to go. Six months later, Baker was dead."

He'd fallen five hundred feet while free soloing in Utah.

"The following spring, Yoder got caught in a slab avalanche on Annapurna."

He was still up there, buried in a grave of ice and snow, the mountain as his monument.

"François died when his charter plane crashed above Telluride." That had hit Megs hard, too.

Mitch squeezed her shoulders. "W-we … are all… th… that's left."

"That's a reason for a drink, if you ask me." Gridwall glanced around, as if searching for something.

Megs put her hand over Mitch's. "The booze is in the kitchen."

"Come." Mitch motioned for Gridwall to follow him.

"Thank you for reading that." Kurt took his wife's hand. "I know it wasn't easy, but it gave me closure—and a sense of peace."

"In that case, it was worth it. We owe it to Dean to keep his story alive."

"You've done that."

A moment later, Gridwall returned, holding a bottle of their best scotch and a few glasses, Mitch behind him carrying several more glasses. Gridwall poured and handed everyone a tumbler. "Drink hearty, mates."

He raised his glass, his voice tight when he spoke. "To the dirtbags. May they live in legend forever."

"To the dirtbags!"

Megs tossed back her drink. As she looked at the faces around her, the weight she'd been carrying since Dean's death seemed to lift from her shoulders.

Chapter 24

MITCH SLIPPED into his parka and double-checked his pocket, ready for the walk to Knockers, butterflies in his stomach. Tonight was his big night, and he wasn't sure he was ready. He had practiced what he wanted to say with his speech pathologist, but words still didn't come easy. "Ready?"

At least he was rid of that damned cervical collar.

Megs seemed to have recovered from reading about Dean's death, her sharp wit and sharper tongue back in action, a smile on her face. Kurt's words seemed to have reached her, and Mitch hoped she would finally be able to find peace.

She grabbed her jacket. "By the way, consider that shot of whisky a pact, a kind of nondisclosure agreement. You never saw me cry. Got it?"

Gridwall snorted. "Don't worry. Your secret is safe with us. Our Meggie is crispy on the outside and sweet and gooey on the inside."

Accardo chuckled. "I didn't realize that was a secret."

"Are you kidding?" Cook grabbed his parka. "Our Megs would rather eat nails than let anyone see that she's human."

"Go ahead. Dig your graves deeper, guys." Megs' voice was stern, but there was a smile on her lips.

Not bothering to lock the door, Mitch followed Megs toward their SUV.

Gridwall stopped the two of them, motioning toward the Lamborghini. "Tonight, Ahearn, you and your lady ride in style."

While the others rode down with Kurt and Jennifer, Megs got into the back seat while Mitch folded his legs into the front passenger seat.

"Not very roomy, is it?" Megs said.

Gridwall started the engine, revved it a few times, a big grin on his face. "Listen to those horses! We got it up to two hundred miles per hour on the interstate."

Mitch glanced back at Megs, saw that she, too, was amused by this.

"I have to ask." Megs leaned forward until her head was between them. "Does going fast in the fancy car work better than Viagra or…?"

Gridwall laughed. "She's still a smartass, isn't she?"

Mitch did his best deadpan voice. "You ha-have no… idea."

Motor purring, they made their way down the mountain through town to Knockers, where the parking lot was already overflowing. Joe and Rain had set up a heated party tent on the side of the building just in case everyone in town showed up, light making it glow from the inside.

Gridwall cruised through the parking lot, heads turning as people stared at the car. "You must be popular, Ahearn. Go figure."

Megs pointed. "They saved us a parking spot toward the front."

"I see it. VIP, huh?" Gridwall teased. "And all you had to do was get bonked on the head by a big-ass rock."

Mitch held the door for Megs, the place bursting into spontaneous cheers and applause when they stepped inside. The entire town *had* turned out, familiar faces everywhere, everyone smiling.

Megs took his hand, squeezed. "They love you."

Rain hugged them both. "We've got your usual table ready."

Joe always set aside a table for Team members back near the climbing wall. It was his way of thanking them for their service.

They walked toward the back, Mitch shaking hands with friends and neighbors along the way, managing to get out the words "Thank you" a few dozen times without too much struggle.

The Team table had been replaced by several tables with enough seats for the Team members, their spouses and kids, the dirtbags, and Kurt and Jennifer. Most of the Team was already there, though Nicole, Sasha, Creed Herrera, and Moretti were climbing and not in their seats.

"A climbing wall in a pub?" Gridwall's face lit up, and he dropped his jacket over the back of his seat. "Booze and big jugs. Mama, I'm home."

Rain set menus on the table. "We told our route-setter who was coming tonight, and she put extra effort into creating some tough routes for you. Oh, hey, it looks like the rest of your gang is here. Welcome to Knockers. I'm Rain Moffat."

After they had given Cheyenne their drink orders, they hit the wall, Megs and Mitch only too happy to join them. Gridwall and Cook flashed the hardest route on the wall—

a 5.14. Accardo slipped once, but otherwise nailed it. Then it was Megs' turn, her first climb since the accident.

God, it felt good.

Soon, almost everyone in the restaurant had come to watch, the area around the climbing wall crowded.

"Do you know who these guys are?" Joe said to someone. "They're climbing royalty. They basically invented this sport. Don't let the gray hair fool you. They're the best of the best."

Sasha lowered Megs to the floor. "Do you want to go next, Mitch?"

Mitch's pulse spiked. "I d-don't know if…"

Megs didn't want to push him. "I'll belay if you want to try. You don't have to prove anything to anyone. You can start out with the 5.9 route."

"Okay." With Megs' help, he got into the harness and moved to the bottom of the easiest route on the wall. "On belay."

"Belay on."

"Cl…climbing."

"Climb on, love."

After a moment of sheer panic, Mitch began to climb, the room falling still. It was both more complicated and simpler than Mitch had imagined. Because of his neck injury, it was hard to look up, and the area near his healed clavicle hurt every time he used that arm. But his muscle memory was still there, the moves almost instinctive. Before he realized it, he was nearly there. When he topped out, the room exploded into cheers.

From below, he heard Megs' voice. "That's my man."

⸺

MEGS' heart was full. Kurt's words about Dean's death. Climbing with the dirtbags again. Seeing the town rally around the man she loved. Watching Mitch climb again. Tonight, life was good.

She sat beside Mitch, their fingers entwined as they watched Gridwall coach Kurt to the top of the 5.9 route. "If Dean could see Kurt, he'd be so proud of his boy."

"How do you ... kn-know ... he doesn't see?"

"I hope he does. I truly hope he does."

Marcia brought another round of brews. "I'm so glad you're doing better, Mitch. We were so worried about you."

Mitch gave her that gorgeous smile of his. "Thanks, M-marcia."

They cheered for Kurt when he topped out, Gridwall slapping Kurt on the back. "You're a natural, just like your old man."

Megs could tell from Kurt's expression that those words meant something to him.

Then Joe got on the stage, tapped the mic. "Can you all hear me?"

"Yes!" the crowd shouted in near unison.

Megs leaned close to Mitch. "Here we go."

"We are all here tonight to welcome back a favorite son. Mitch Ahearn grew up in Scarlet and learned to climb and ski here. Though his family moved to California, he came back when he had the chance, and he brought the love of his life with him, our own Megs Hill. Together, they founded the Rocky Mountain Search and Rescue Team, putting Scarlet Springs on the map."

Cheers.

"That's sweet." Megs wasn't kidding. Joe's words truly did touch her.

"It's been almost two months since a falling rock almost

killed Mitch, leaving him in a coma in ICU for eight days." Joe paused as if gathering his thoughts. "I've never seen this town come together the way it did to help him and Megs. You all raised more than a hundred fifty-thousand dollars to help pay for his medical expenses and rehab."

"Scarlet flipping rocks!" Sasha shouted.

Laughter.

"We are thrilled to officially welcome Mitch home tonight." Joe waited for the applause to die down. "We also want to welcome Jim Gridwall, Rick Accardo, and Ron Cook, who, along with Mitch and Megs, are climbing legends. Scarlet Springs is proud to welcome the legendary Lords of Stone—the original dirtbags of Yosemite."

Cheers.

Mitch squeezed Megs' hand, motioned her toward the stage with his head. She nodded, and the two of them stood. This was their chance to thank Joe and Rain and everyone else who'd been there for them over the past two months.

Joe went on. "In other business, Vicki would like me to remind you that there are a few copies of the Scarlet FD firefighter calendar left. You can buy them at the bar."

Laughter and wolf whistles.

Then Joe saw them. "Please welcome Mitch and Megs. I think Mitch has a few things he'd like to say tonight.

Mitch walked with Megs across the dance floor to the stage.

Megs leaned close, whispered, "You don't have to do anything that makes you uncomfortable. I can thank everyone for both of us."

Mitch smiled down at her. "You go… first. Then I w-will talk."

"You got it."

They climbed the stairs to the stage, where Joe stepped

aside, the Timberline Mudbugs waiting off to the side for their set, everyone cheering for Mitch.

Megs accepted Joe's help adjusting the mic for her height. "Mitch and I want to thank everyone for your prayers and your incredible generosity. Without your help, this might have turned out very differently."

Cheers.

"We're especially grateful to Joe and Rain for their help immediately after the accident. Without the helicopter you sent, Mitch probably wouldn't be here. We also want to thank Eric Hawke, Harrison Conrad, Austin Taylor, Chaska Belcourt, and Jesse Moretti. They climbed into that chopper and flew out to rescue us. You saved Mitch's life. Thank you."

Not very eloquent, but at least she'd gotten through it without getting emotional.

Then it was Mitch's turn.

He adjusted the microphone, and Megs couldn't help but be nervous for him. "Th-thank you all for your …help. I can't imag… imagine …living in any… other town. I am so… grate…ful."

Applause.

"I want to th-thank Megs. She never … left my side. Her …voice w-was my light… in the dark of … c-coma."

Megs could see that Rain had tears in her eyes. Well, fine, but *no way* was Megs going to cry in front of the whole damned town.

Then Mitch got down onto one knee, a little velvet box in his hand.

The crowd exploded—cheers, whistles, applause, people jumping to their feet.

It took Megs a moment. "What the hell are you doing?"

Laughter.

He opened the box to reveal a diamond solitaire engagement ring. "Megs, will you ... please m-marry me?"

The blood rushed from Megs' head, and for a moment, she stood there, open-mouthed, gaping at him. "We've been together for forty-eight years. We're probably already married, according to Colorado common law. Why do this now?"

"Life is ... short. I d-don't want to be your part-ner ... any longer. I want to spend wh-whatever ... time we have left ... as your ... husband."

His words and the look in his eyes made her heart melt.

"Oh!" Her vision blurred. "Yes! I'll marry you."

While the crowd cheered for them, he stood and slid the ring onto her finger, then drew her into his arms and kissed her. "I love you."

"I love you, too."

The Timberline Mudbugs took the stage—and the mic.

"Congratulations to our happy couple. Megs, Mitch requested this number especially for you tonight. Clear the floor, folks. This first dance is for them."

Overcome with emotion, Megs let Mitch lead her off the stage and into the middle of the dance floor, just as the Mudbugs broke into a version of *Baby, I Love Your Way*.

With the whole town watching, she slipped into his arms, and they began to move around the floor, Mitch singing along, getting every sweet word right.

━━

MITCH AND MEGS spent the rest of the weekend hanging with the dirtbags. It felt like old times—except for the ring on Megs' finger. Mitch had seen her staring at it more than once, the diamond glittering in the light. He supposed it would take her a while to get used to it and what it represented.

After forty-eight years as his partner, she was now his fiancée.

On Saturday, they had a late breakfast and drove the dirtbags to Rocky Mountain National Park, then spent the evening looking at old photos and magazine articles and reminiscing about old times. They also watched the PSA they'd made together, which had begun running on major networks and online as of yesterday.

Mitch was touched. "Thanks for d-doing that."

Accardo gave him a gentle slug in the shoulder. "For you, man? Anything."

On Sunday morning, they went out with the Team, watching Conrad supervise the rescue of a climber who'd lost his nerve and gotten stuck high on a wall in Eldorado Canyon State Park.

Gridwall stared up at the rockface as they lowered the climber safely to the ground once more. "You two have done good. Uncle Jim is so proud of you."

But then it was time for the dirtbags to head back to Las Vegas to turn in the car and catch their flights home.

Gridwall hugged Mitch tight, slapped his back. "I'm sorry I was such a dick in the early days. You're the best of us. Megs was right to pick you. I'm so damned glad you got through this. My world wouldn't be the same without you, brother."

"Thank you… Jim. You are … family to us."

While Gridwall said goodbye to Megs, Mitch helped Accardo and Cook load up the Lamborghini, which had a surprisingly small trunk. "Not... much room."

Cook turned to Accardo, a grin on his face. "Speaking of no room, it's *your* turn to sit in the back."

"Great." Accardo turned to Mitch. "You take care, man."

"You, too." Mitch hugged him and then Cook. "Good to … see you."

Mitch stood with Megs on their front steps and watched their friends climb into the vehicle and drive away, engine roaring.

"And there go the crazy relatives."

"Makes me … sad… to see them… go."

Megs leaned into him, her fingers twined with his. "Me, too."

Snow began to fall, a cold wind blowing from the northwest.

After such a busy weekend with so many guests, the house seemed quiet. While Mitch built a fire in the wood-stove, Megs reheated their leftovers from Knockers. After supper, they snuggled on the sofa in front of the fire.

"This town, your friends, me—so many people love you."

He chuckled. "You didn't w-want to m-move here."

"I didn't, but, to be fair, Scarlet Springs isn't what it was back in the early Nineties. There was a grocery store, a gas station, the inn, that awful pizza joint—and not much else. It was like a ghost town waiting for someone to shut off the lights."

"Hold on." Mitch got to his feet, walked to his office, and returned with the journal, which he had opened to a specific entry. "Read this. Then we can … p-put the … j-jour…journal away … for now."

Megs took the journal from him, skimmed the page, and laughed. "I remember this. We had decided to create a rescue team, and you wanted us to settle here. As I recall, you had to work hard to sell it."

A smile on her face, Megs began to read.

———

September 3, 1993

MITCH WALKED hand-in-hand with Megs down Main Street, trying to remember Scarlet Springs as it had been when he was growing up. "The Seventies were hard on this town. High gas prices and a few bad ski seasons really hurt it economically. So many families, like mine, moved away."

Megs spoke in a sarcastic voice. "I can't imagine why they would do that."

Mitch knew she wasn't impressed, and he couldn't blame her. There were empty houses with For Sale signs that had faded in the sun. The town's only restaurant sold shitty pizza and featured extra protein in the form of dead flies on the unwashed tables. But the Forest Creek Inn was still standing, along with Rose's New Age Emporium across the street. The schools were exactly the way he remembered them.

There were signs of new life, too. The town had recently built a new firehouse. A shop selling geodes and semi-precious stones had just opened on Main Street.

Mitch pointed this out. "It's coming back to life."

"Speaking of new life, there's a place next to the pretty rock store where they cryogenically freeze your severed head after you die on the off chance that science will find a way to bring you back from the dead."

Mitch laughed. "Okay, Scarlet Springs is strange, but that's what I've always loved about it. It's not a town of middle-class conformists and perfectly manicured lawns. It's *weird*. I'm a Yosemite dirtbag, for God's sake. Normal is overrated."

"Okay, you have a point. I *hate* small towns. You know that."

"Not all small towns are the same. There are *good* people here. This is nothing like the town where you grew up. I promise."

"What's his story?"

Mitch followed the direction of her gaze and smiled. "Bear! It's good to see him."

"Bear?"

"No one knows his real name. He started showing up in town a long time back. He's a gentle giant with the mind of a child. Something happened to him, but no one knows what or where he came from. He lives somewhere in the mountains west of Scarlet. He's got the Bible memorized, chapter and verse, and stands in the roundabout and preaches. Once he knows you, he never forgets your name."

The curiosity on Megs' face became compassion. "Poor guy."

"I don't think he believes he's poor." Mitch waved to him. "Hey, Bear! Good to see you again."

Bear walked over, studied Mitch's face—and stared. "Mitch Ahearn."

"That's right." Mitch clapped Bear on the shoulder. "It's been almost twenty-five years since I last saw you. How are you?"

"A joyful heart is good medicine." Bear grinned, looked at Megs.

"This is my partner, Megs Hill. She's a climber like I am."

"Megs Hill," Bear repeated.

Megs held out her hand. "It's good to meet you, Bear."

Bear carefully shook her hand then turned back to Mitch. "Are you home now?"

Mitch couldn't help it. Those words tugged at his

heart. "That's what we're trying to decide. I'm introducing Megs to the town."

"Scarlet Springs is home," Bear said.

Megs nodded. "I see that."

They talked for a few minutes. Then Megs gave him money for a meal, and they moved on. They had an appointment with Caribou Joe, or Joe Moffat.

Joe owned some real estate they were considering for the headquarters of the rescue team they hoped to launch. They had already filed the papers for nonprofit status, but they needed a home base.

"Why do you call him Caribou Joe? Does he have antlers?"

Mitch explained the history. "This is an old mining town. Back in the day, his great-great-great grandfather operated the Caribou Silver Mine above town. Most of our ancestors worked for his ancestors—to their great regret. The Moffats didn't care much for the town or the people who lived here. They were always just about the money."

"So, you're telling me that this guy will screw us over if we make an offer on the old firehouse?"

"I don't know. I've never met him. They say he's a bit of a hermit, but I don't want to misjudge him just because his forbears were dicks."

"Fair point."

Joe was waiting for them outside the old firehouse, long hair pulled back in a ponytail, a neatly trimmed beard on his face. He held out his hand. "Mitch Ahearn and Megs Hill. I recognize you both."

Mitch shook his hand. "My parents moved us away from Scarlet around the time you were born."

"That's what I hear. Now you're thinking about moving back. That's great. That's what this town needs."

Mitch caught the look on Megs' face. "We're thinking about it."

"What do you want to do with the old firehouse?"

Mitch explained that a friend of theirs had recently died because there was no rescue team capable of bringing him to safety. He told Joe that he and Megs hoped to create a top-notch rock and alpine rescue unit so that nothing like that would happen again.

"We need a place big enough to house rescue vehicles and all of the technical gear necessary to run an operation like that."

Joe listened, one hand thoughtfully stroking his beard. "What a great idea. Let's look at the property and see if you think it meets your needs."

He unlocked the door, and Mitch and Megs gave themselves a tour. The firehouse had two big bay doors that opened onto a cavernous space that had once held firetrucks.

Megs glanced around. "It's certainly big enough for a couple of rescue vehicles. The quarters upstairs could be converted to storage."

"There's a kitchen and an operations center through here." Joe led them out of the vehicle bay and into a vacant conference room with a small kitchen off to the side. "Everything works."

He studied them for a moment. "If you like it, it's yours for one dollar."

They gaped at him, mouths hanging open.

"*One dollar?*" Megs repeated.

"I acquired the property in a trade deal. The land where the new firehouse sits used to belong to me. I traded it for this, but I have no need for this property. If you can use it for the community's benefit, then I'm ready to sell it on the cheap."

Mitch and Megs walked a short distance away to discuss the offer.

"We'd be crazy not to accept. We could use the money we've raised so far to remodel the place and buy gear rather than spending it on real estate. We'd get up and running faster."

Megs didn't look convinced. "What's in it for him?"

"Ask him."

So Megs did.

Joe grinned. "Scarlet used to be a thriving town of more than three thousand, and my father and grandfathers bled it dry. I want to give back what was taken and bring the town back to life."

Megs stared at him for a minute. "I think I like you."

He threw his head back and laughed. "I *know* I like you. Let me show you what else I'm doing."

Joe drove them toward the center of town to a construction site not far from Food Mart. "This is going to be a brewpub. I named it Knockers after the tommy-knockers that the old Cornish miners believed lived in the mines."

He gave them each a hard hat and led them through the site. "I want the place to be known for good food and excellent homebrews. Over there, we'll have a stage and a dance floor. The kitchens will be toward the back. We'll have pool tables, too. I want it to be a hub for the town, a place for locals and tourists alike. I don't care if it ever makes a profit. If I break even in the first decade, I'll be more than happy."

Megs glanced around them. "If you want it to be a destination, you ought to put in a climbing wall."

Joe stared at her, clearly confused. "A *climbing* wall?"

"Yes, a climbing wall. Make your place a destination

278

for the outdoorsy crowd that passes through on the way to the mountains."

Mitch nodded. "Not a bad idea."

Joe seemed taken by the concept. "I like that."

One of the construction workers motioned for him, so Joe left them to find out what the man needed.

Megs waited until he was gone. "I can tell you really want to move here, that it means a lot to you."

"We can be a part of bringing Scarlet back to life. We're up in the mountains, close to the busiest climbing areas where people will need our help. We already know some of the folks who live here."

Megs drew a breath, kicked at a rock in the dirt. "Okay, love. We'll settle in your crazy little hometown and give it a go."

Mitch drew her into his arms. "Thanks, love. I'll make sure you don't regret it."

———

MEGS CLOSED THE JOURNAL, smiling at the memories. "I completely forgot that the climbing wall was *my* idea. It worked out well, if I do say so myself."

"It did." Mitch took the journal, set it on the coffee table, and drew her close. "Thank you ... for trust... trusting me, for being w-will... willing to try."

"I love you, Mitch. I wanted you to be happy. I still do." But there was something she needed to say. "All these years, I'm the one who's been in the spotlight. I've gotten most of the attention and acclaim."

"That's ... okay with me."

It wasn't okay with Megs. "There isn't a thing I've accomplished that didn't involve you. You have belayed me through life."

She knew he would get the metaphor, but she spelled it out anyway. "You've been the one who lifted me up, who believed in me, who gave me the confidence to keep going. You've been my confidant, my safe place. When I've fallen, you've caught me. Without you, there's no Megs Hill, climbing legend. You've taken me higher than I would ever have gone without you."

He looked like he wanted to say something, but she pressed her fingers to his lips.

"Just listen for a minute. When you were hurt, I was terrified that I was going to lose you. The hours went by so slowly. For days, I was afraid that every heartbeat would be your last. You want to know who got me through that?"

"Who?"

"*You* did." Her vision blurred, the emotional toll of the past two months welling up inside her. She blinked the tears away. "Your journal did. I started reading entries because Dr. Schwartz said it might help you. But when I read your entries, you were there with me, beside me. Like everything else in my life, *you* got me through that."

"I'm glad." He drew her close, rested her head against his chest. "When I die... you will still... have the journ... journals."

"What if I die first?" She'd thought about this. "I haven't written anything down—nothing. I kept your notes and letters, but that's it. You won't have anything."

Mitch laughed—not what she'd expected. "Oh, Megs, my ...ang... angel. "There's nothing... in my life th-that isn't you—the Team... our home, every mem-memory since you ... showed up in Yosemite. Those journ... journals... You are on ... every page... in every word. You are the breath and the ... l-light... between *every* line."

Megs saw the love in his eyes, and her heart seemed to melt. She straddled his lap, cupped his face between her palms. "Then I guess it's a good thing I'm going to marry you after all these years and make an honest man of you."

He chuckled, flipped her onto her back in one smooth motion, his brown eyes going dark. "Let's forn… fornicate … while we still can."

Megs' blood went hot. "I love the way you think."

Epilogue

May 28

RAIN AND SASHA pinned the wreath of pink roses, pine, and baby's breath in Megs' hair, Megs standing with her back to the mirror.

Rain took the last bobby pin from her mouth. "Are you nervous?"

"Not really." Okay, maybe she was a little nervous. She didn't want to screw up her vows in front of everyone. "Mitch and I have been together for forty-nine years today, so it's not like I have to worry about what our life will look like."

Rain laughed, adjusted the wreath. "I guess not."

"It's your anniversary?" Sasha leaned around from behind Megs, bobby pins between her fingers, a bright smile on her face. "That's so cool!"

"I arrived in Yosemite Valley on this day forty-nine years ago." Thanks to the journal, Megs' memories were as fresh as if it had happened yesterday. "Gridwall tried to hit on me, and though I handled it myself, Mitch came down on him."

Sasha put the extra bobby pins back in their case. "I wish I'd been there in those days. It must have been the best time ever."

Megs couldn't help seeing herself in Sasha. They'd both been sports climbing world champions, after all. "You would have owned the Valley."

Rain stepped back. "Okay. You're all done."

A knock.

Rose poked her head inside. "I just wanted to see the bride. Oh. That's what you're wearing to your wedding? I saw that on the rack at Target."

Megs couldn't help but laugh at Rose's disappointment. "You don't approve?"

Megs had refused to spend money on some ridiculous wedding dress that she would never wear again, opting instead for a pretty white sundress with spaghetti straps and white sandals. Given that she rarely wore anything but jeans, this was going all out.

"Well…" For a moment, Rose was unusually bereft of words. "It *is* you."

"It is." Megs was pretty sure that was an insult, but to be truthful, she really didn't care how she looked or what people thought of her. She wasn't a shopper, and she'd never understood the fuss some women made over the superficial stuff—clothes, makeup, handbags, shoes, jewelry. It meant nothing to her.

Climbing gear, on the other hand…

Yeah, okay. Maybe she *was* a shopper.

Sasha kissed her cheek. "I think you look hot."

Rain handed her the bouquet. "You look beautiful, and the dress is perfect."

"Yes, of course, she's beautiful," Rose agreed. "All brides are beautiful."

"Thanks." Megs turned to face the mirror.

In a blink, her life seemed to rush across her reflection. She saw the sixteen-year-old who'd fallen in love with Mitch, the young woman who'd finally taken him as her lover, the climber who'd touched the top of the world.

She saw Mitch, too—young and strong, fighting his attraction to her, making love to her, seizing all of the adventure he could with her, carrying her through life.

The vision, if that's what it was, lasted only a moment, memories seeming to slide across the glass, making her throat go tight. Now she was about to marry Mitch, all of their shared experiences coming together in a special celebration.

The vision faded, leaving her shaken in the best possible way. She cleared her throat. "Well, let's get on with it."

Rain and Sasha laughed.

"You are the least fussy bride ever." Rain reached for her handbag. "For a while, I thought you weren't going to let me talk you into flowers."

"I know you said no gifts, but I wanted to offer you two a couple's tarot reading for free anytime. I've always thought Mitch had such Charioteer energy—so in control of his physical and emotional drives. And you Megs, maybe Star energy—a light in the darkness, offering hope to others, though you're pretty bossy. It would be fun to see what the cards say."

"That's a very generous gift, Rose. Thank you." Megs knew Rose meant well. "Thanks, too, for helping to raise money for Mitch with your … craft."

Rose's face lit up. "It was the least I could do. See you up there."

Megs, Sasha, and Rain left the house and climbed into Rain's SUV for the trip up to Caribou, white ribbons and flowers tied to the vehicle's grill. Once the site of a mining camp, Caribou was now a wide-open meadow that was ablaze with wildflowers each spring. With the white-capped Indian Peaks in the background, it was one of the most scenic spots around Scarlet and was featured on a lot of postcards.

The drive didn't take long—ten minutes tops. Cars were parked along the dirt road, chairs set out in neat rows for their guests, the center aisle leading to a low stage with a sound system and two enormous standing rose bouquets. Mitch stood beside Kurt, Gridwall, and Accardo near the stage, dressed in a nice pair of khakis with a white shirt and a tan waistcoat.

Damn, he was hot.

He saw the SUV and walked over to help Megs out, his gaze raking over her, his expression telling her he wasn't disappointed. "I think I like you in dresses."

He kissed her cheek.

"No kissing yet!" Sasha admonished them.

Mitch chuckled. "I suppose she's right."

While guests took their seats, the two of them stood back by the vehicles, waiting for the cue to start down the aisle. They'd decided to do what a lot of couples did in Europe and walk down the aisle together. It was *their* wedding, after all. They could do whatever the hell they liked.

Mitch took her hand, looked at her engagement ring. "Why didn't I propose forty years ago?"

"Probably because you knew I'd say no."

They laughed because they both knew it was true. It wasn't that Megs hadn't loved him or wanted to spend the rest of her life with him, but at that point, she'd viewed marriage as a silly social convention and weddings as a waste of money.

His brown eyes looked into hers. "What changed?"

"I did."

It was hard to fathom that eight months ago, he'd been in a coma. His speech was more or less normal now. He still got terrible headaches once in a while, and he had some residual short-term memory problems. But he had worked hard to reach this point.

Gridwall ran up to them. "They're almost ready. God, I'm nervous."

"Why are *you* nervous?" Megs had to ask.

"I've never been a bridesman before."

Gridwall was standing with Megs as her bridesman, while Accardo was Mitch's groomsman. The two were charged with carrying the rings—and making sure neither of them forgot their vows. Unfortunately, Cook hadn't been able to come, as the date had conflicted with his oldest grandson's high school graduation.

Music began to play.

Gridwall kissed Megs and Mitch on the cheeks. "See you two at the altar."

Mitch took Megs' arm. "Are you ready?"

"After forty-nine years?" She laughed. "I'm more than ready."

⸻

MITCH WALKED UP THE AISLE, proud to have Megs on his arm, blue sky above them, wildflowers at their feet. Bach's *Air on a G String* drifted over the speakers as their friends stood, smiles on their faces. Most of Scarlet Springs had gathered to celebrate with them, some folks in chairs, the rest on blankets, everyone smiling.

Mitch's heart swelled, a part of him blown away to think that this brave and beautiful woman he'd loved for so long was finally going to become his wife. If it weren't for Megs' love, skilled doctors, and the people of this town, he might never have seen this day. He was the luckiest son of a bitch alive.

They reached the dais, Mitch stepping carefully so as not to lose his balance. Accardo gave him a nod and patted the pocket of his waistcoat, letting him know that Megs' wedding band was safe. Then the music stopped, and Kurt, who was officiating, began the ceremony, mic clipped to his clerical robes.

"Good people of Scarlet Springs, today we are gathered to join Mitch Ahearn and Megs Hill as they celebrate a long and happy life together by at last becoming husband and wife."

Mitch glanced at Megs to see if his words made her cringe, but she only smiled.

Kurt went on. "Usually, when I officiate a wedding, some part of me wonders about the couple's future. Will they be faithful to each other? Will they work together to overcome life's challenges? Will their marriage last beyond the honeymoon? This time, I don't have to worry about any of that. Mitch and Megs have proven their love for one another and for their community over and over again."

Laughter and cheers.

"My father, Dean Calder, was their best friend. He often talked about the two of them and their climbing exploits. He also told me about their integrity and the support they gave other climbers. 'They're not just great climbers,' he said. 'They're great people.' After my father's death, Mitch and Megs showed the world who they truly were by turning tragedy into hope and creating the Rocky Mountain Search and Rescue Team. Their selfless decision to leave professional climbing and focus on rescue work has saved hundreds of lives."

Cheers and applause.

"But today is a celebration of their love for one another—a love I witnessed in the ICU as Mitch clung to life last fall. Megs responded with a strength that is only borne of deep love. It was Mitch's love for Megs that helped him hang on through his coma and through months of challenging rehab. Megs and Mitch, to officiate your wedding as Dean's son is a great honor."

That hit Mitch in the chest, putting a lump in his throat—which was super inconvenient because it was about time for their vows.

"Mitch and Megs have written vows they'd like to recite to one another. If the two of you would please join hands…"

Megs handed her bouquet to Gridwall, which made people laugh, and she and Mitch held hands.

Mitch swallowed—hard—and looked into Megs' beautiful eyes. "Megs, you came into my life like a sunrise, and everything changed. Because of you, I have touched the sky. You've been my muse, my North Star, and my greatest joy. Today, I take you as my wife, to love and to cherish, to comfort and to protect until my last breath."

Tears welled in Megs' eyes, but her smile was all happiness.

Now it was her turn.

"Mitch, you and I have shared a thousand adventures, but the greatest adventure of my life has been living by your side. You've taught me everything I know about love, selflessness, and devotion. You gave me wings and helped me fly. Today, I take you as my husband, to love and to cherish, to comfort and to protect until my last breath."

Then Kurt spoke. "The two of you have chosen to

exchange rings as symbols of your love for one another and to seal the vows you've made today."

Mitch turned to Accardo, who handed him Megs' wedding band, gold glinting in the sunshine. He slid the ring onto her finger. "With this ring, I offer you all that I am and all that I ever will be. Accept it as my gift and a symbol of my undying love."

Megs looked at the rings on her finger—the engagement solitaire and the gold band—then met Mitch's gaze, her eyes bright with tears. She turned to Gridwall, who had to search a couple of pockets before finding Mitch's wedding band, making everyone laugh once again, lightening the mood.

Megs took the ring, slid it onto Mitch's finger, and repeated the vow, her voice strong and clear. "With this ring, I offer you all that I am and all that I ever will be. Accept it as my gift and a token of my undying love."

Kurt opened his Bible, took out a piece of paper. "Mitch and Megs have asked me to read this poem, which holds great significance for them.

"Love has no other desire but to fulfil itself. But if you love and must needs have desires, let these be your desires: To melt and be like a running brook that sings its melody to the night. To know the pain of too much tenderness. To be wounded by your own understanding of love; And to bleed willingly and joyfully. To wake at dawn with a winged heart and give thanks for another day of loving…"

As Kurt finished the Kahlil Gibran poem that Mitch had read to Megs the night they'd first had sex, Mitch's heart *was* winged. Because of her, Mitch finally understood the meaning of Gibran's profound words.

When Kurt had finished, he concluded the ceremony by pronouncing them husband and wife. "You may kiss the bride."

To cheers and applause, Mitch drew Megs into his arms and kissed her.

Then Gridwall swept the two of them into an unscripted hug, tears spilling down his grizzled cheeks, bridal bouquet still in hand. "I love you, man!"

———

MEGS SAT beside Mitch at the Team table, both of them buzzed on champagne, the two of them watching as Sasha and Gridwall took turns belaying each other on the climbing wall. "Sasha is enjoying herself."

Mitch squeezed Megs' hand. "So is Gridwall. He told me that Sasha reminds him of you when you were that age."

"No. She's a lot more cheerful than I ever was, and she's a better climber." Megs didn't mind admitting it. She'd left her ego behind a long time ago.

Mitch looked down at her, a frown on his face. "Hey, Sasha stands on *your* shoulders. Before she and the rest of these youngsters came along, you were up there, figuring out how it works. You did things that people said were impossible. It takes guts to be the first."

She laughed. "Says the guy who was up there with me."

They'd accepted Joe and Rain's invitation to hold their reception at Knockers with the strict understanding that no one was to bring gifts—except for tax-deductible donations to the Team, of course. The Mudbugs had already played a couple of sets, and Megs and Mitch had done the obligatory first dance. The only thing left to do was to toss the bouquet and head home. But Megs wasn't in a hurry.

At the other end of the table, Kurt was having an animated discussion about something with Accardo,

Hawke, Taylor, and Lexi, little Kit now six months old. Joe and Marcia worked the bar, while Rain helped Sam, Cheyenne, and Lark wait tables. Bear sat at his favorite table, enjoying a plate of fried chicken with a tall glass of milk. Vicki had popped out of the kitchen a few times to talk with Hawke, who was holding Mollie, their toddler. Caden, now in preschool, sat beside his father in a booster seat, making a grand mess with French fries and ketchup.

Meanwhile, Jason Chiago and Winona made their way back from the dance floor, hand in hand, their baby boy on Win's back. Naomi and Chaska Belcourt and Ellie and Jesse Moretti supervised their little ones on the beginner's end of the climbing wall.

"Do you regret not having kids?" Megs asked Mitch.

"No." He kissed her hair. "Where did that come from?"

"The town is going through a baby boom—or hadn't you noticed?"

"Oh, I noticed." He chuckled. "You and I had other things we wanted to do with our lives. I'm content with that decision. How about you?"

"Every once in a while, I wonder what it might have been like to see a little Mitch running around. Then I see Lexi looking so uncomfortable at nine months pregnant or watch little Mr. Ketchup creating dirty laundry over there, and I'm good."

Mitch laughed. "I hear that."

Rain approached. "How are you two doing? More champagne?"

"I think I'm past my limit. How about you, Mitch?"

"No, thank you, Rain." He had to watch his alcohol intake because of anti-seizure medication. "I think we'll be heading home soon."

"At the end of this set, I can invite all the single women to the dance floor so you can toss your bouquet."

As far as Megs was concerned, it was a bizarre tradition, but she'd gone this far. She might as well go all the way. "That sounds good. Thanks."

Rain smiled, touched a hand to Megs' shoulder. "Thank *you*! It's a fun party."

Kurt stood and walked over to them, a small package in his hand that was wrapped in silver paper and topped by a pretty bow. "How are the newlyweds?"

Megs raised an eyebrow. "Is that a gift?"

"I know you said you didn't want any presents, but I'm pretty sure you'll want this." He handed them the gift and a card. "Open the card first."

Megs and Mitch did as he asked. It was a wedding card, full of sweet wishes. But the words Kurt had written hit home.

```
Getting to know you has brought so much of
my father back for me. I am blessed to have
spent time with you. Thank you for sharing
your journal with me. I've shared the copied
pages with my mother, who sends her love and
her apologies for not staying in touch.
Congratulations on your marriage, and
thanks for allowing me to play a part
in it.
Warmly,
Kurt
```

Megs held it so that Mitch could see. "Thank you, Kurt. Having you in our lives has helped heal a lot of wounds. We are so grateful to you."

Then they opened the gift.

It was a picture frame.

Megs turned it over to see the picture—and the breath left her lungs in a rush. "Oh, my God. Mitch!"

Mitch cleared his throat. "It's the three of us on the summit of Everest."

In the photograph, they stood close together, exhausted, cold, and jubilant, the light of a Himalayan dawn on their faces, so young and truly on top of the world.

"My mother has a lot of old photos of you three, including the last ones from the summit of El Diente. She would love to get together sometime and share. She thought you might have some of my dad."

Megs nodded. "We do. That would be wonderful."

She stood, hugged Kurt. "Thanks for everything. I've said it before, but I'll say it again. Your father would be so proud of you."

"Thanks. Given how well you knew him and how much he respected the two of you, that means a lot."

Mitch hugged him, too. "You and Jennifer are welcome at our home anytime, as are your mother and sister. Please give them both our love."

"I will. I'll be in touch soon." Then he turned and walked away.

Megs held up the framed photograph. "It's almost like it was yesterday."

Then the music died out, and Rain took the mic. "All you single ladies make your way to the dance floor. The bride is about to toss her bouquet."

This was followed by squeals and a rush of young women.

Megs and Mitch got to their feet and threaded their

way to the dance floor and up the stairs onto the stage. "How do I do this?"

Rain demonstrated. "Turn your back to the crowd and toss the flowers over your shoulder. No peeking."

"Easy enough." Megs turned her back to the women—and let the bouquet fly.

Cheers.

She turned to find Sasha, who was standing off to the side and not on the dance floor, holding the flowers, a stunned look on her face. "I don't even have a boyfriend."

Laughter.

Megs and Mitch thanked Joe and Rain and their friends, wished everyone a good night, and then gathered their belongings. The entire pub seemed to follow them outside, where Gridwall was waiting by their SUV.

"Your chariot awaits." He motioned toward the vehicle, its rear bumper festooned with white streamers.

Then Megs and Mitch saw the rear windshield and laughed.

Written in white were the words, *"Finally Married."*

CONTINUE READING for a personal word from the author.

Author's Note

I grew up in the foothills of Boulder, Co., the daughter of a semi-professional climber. Most of our weekends were spent in the mountains, hiking, camping, and climbing. When other kids were playing on their swing sets, we were learning to rappel. My father was part of the 1970s climbing scene in Boulder and even put up some first ascents of routes in the area, including Cadaver Crack in Boulder Canyon.

I never became the climber that my father and my younger brother Robert were. Both have climbed all of Colorado's 14ers, as well as Mt. Rainier, Mt. Hood, Mt. Baker, and, in my brother's case, Aconcagua, the highest peak in the Western Hemisphere. Watching Robert rock climb a 5.11 at the rock gym is inspiring.

Unfortunately, my contribution to our family's climbing legacy isn't about climbing. It's about falling.

My father and I set off on a five-day backpacking trip, when we came to an unexpected wall of ice off the summit of Mt. Ida in the backcountry of Rocky Mountain National Park. My father, who has done ice climbing and participated at the Ouray Ice Fest, kicked in some footholds and climbed down the ice like Spiderman. I tried to do what he'd done, but slipped on the ice and fell.

By the time I came to a stop, I'd fallen forty feet—twenty vertical feet and twenty feet of bouncing over talus and boulders. I blacked out for just a moment and then found myself facing down the steep slope, my right leg wrapped around a large rock. I heard my father shout for me as he made his way over to where I was. He asked me to say something, but I couldn't. I could hear him. I could understand him, but I couldn't say a word. I couldn't even lift my gaze to look at him. I had zero control.

To make a long story shorter, I'll skip the part where I came back to myself and spent the next two hours painfully creeping down the mountainside to a tent. Instead, we'll go straight to the helicopter ride to the trauma center, where they found I had a ruptured quadriceps, a torn Achilles tendon, a broken tibia, broken ribs, and too many bruises and contusions to count. The ruptured quad got the most attention, and, indeed, it took forever to heal. It still aches twenty-seven years later.

But the most complicated injury was the complex concussion and the post-concussive syndrome that followed. Because I had bounced over rock, my brain had gotten injured by slamming around inside my skull.

In the aftermath, I suffered from migraines almost daily. I also had short-term memory loss. The memory loss was so severe that my young sons had to remind me—and keep reminding me—where we were going any time we got into the car. They turned it into a game, and my older son especially found it quite funny.

"Mom, do you know where we're going?"

"Um…no."

"The grocery store."

And again, two minutes later.

"Mom, do you know where we're going?"

"Tell me again."

"The grocery store."

I would say good morning to people at work repeatedly without knowing it. Some coworkers were patient. Others weren't. One even shouted in my face that I'd said hello five times already.

When my sons and I saw *Finding Nemo*, the boys pointed to the screen and shouted, "Mom, you're Dory! You're Dory!"

I had to laugh. They weren't wrong.

Now, so many years later, my short-term memory is better but not as good as before. Thankfully, migraines are rare. Instead, I have difficulty concentrating for long periods. I suppose I'll have problems for the rest of my life.

It's really no wonder that I decided to write the Colorado High Country series. With my family's climbing background and my personal experience being rescued, it felt like a great way to share bits and pieces of the Colorado I know and love in all of its craziness and beauty. This book was particularly emotional for me because it includes a special period in the history of rock climbing, a history in which my father participated.

But it also shows the deep and lasting love that Megs and Mitch have for one another, a love that goes far beyond youth and sexiness to the deepest part of the human heart. I hope you've enjoyed their story as much as I have.

Thank You

Thanks for reading *Take Me Higher.* I hope you enjoyed Megs and Mitch's story. Follow me on Facebook or on Twitter @Pamela_Clare. Join my reader's group on Facebook to be a part of a never-ending conversation with other Pamela Clare fans and get inside information about my books and about life in Colorado's mountains. You can also sign up to my mailing list at my website to keep current with all my releases and to be a part of special newsletter giveaways.

Also by Pamela Clare

Contemporary Romance:

Colorado High Country Series

Romantic Suspense:

I-Team Series

About the Author

USA Today best-selling author Pamela Clare began her writing career as a columnist and investigative reporter and eventually became the first woman editor-in-chief of two different newspapers. Along the way, she and her team won numerous state and national honors, including the National Journalism Award for Public Service. In 2011, Clare was awarded the Keeper of the Flame Lifetime Achievement Award for her body of work. A single mother with two sons, she writes historical romance and contemporary romantic suspense at the foot of the beautiful Rocky Mountains. Visit her website and join her mailing list to never miss a new release!

www.pamelaclare.com

Made in the USA
Las Vegas, NV
21 September 2021

30770943R00182